Colorado
GOLD

Colorado
GOLD

Roberta E. Lonsdale

Sterling House
PUBLISHER
Pittsburgh, PA

ISBN 1-156315-105-7

Mass Market Paperback
© Copyright 1998 Roberta E. Lonsdale
All rights reserved
First Printing—1998

Request for information should be addressed to:

Sterling House Publisher
The Sterling Building
440 Friday Road
Department T-101
Pittsburgh, PA 15209

Cover design & Typesetting: Drawing Board Studios

This is a work of fiction.
An resemblance to any real persons, living or dead is coincidental.

Library Of Congress Number
97-062411

Printed in the United States of America

For Tom, who makes many things possible.

Chapter One

Jen noticed the scent of pine needles and the fresh fall air of early September as a light breeze shifted the curtains in the kitchen nook window where she sat puzzling over her checkbook, wondering how she would make her co-payments to The Children's Hospital. Jen sighed, closed the cover, and picked up her Sunday newspaper.

"Are you in the paper today, Mama?" Sarah asked as she dipped her finger into her cereal bowl to treat her cat to a drop of milk. The cat jumped to the only vacant seat remaining at the table and looked at Sarah in anticipation of a second treat.

Jen scanned the paper for the first installment of her series of articles on AMAC mining operations.

"Yes, sweetie," she said, holding the paper for her daughter to see.

Sarah peered through her thick glasses and said with excitement, "I see your name."

Jen smiled at her youngster's reaction to seeing her mother's by line. Her five-year old only knew her mother as an environmental reporter for *The Front Range Journal*, one of Denver's two daily papers, and never as the gold exploration geologist she once was.

Jen read the piece dealing with AMAC's history. She wanted to see how the editor had handled those technical geology and mining words she was fond of using in her stories. It had become something of a game— she would put them into the pieces and he would take them out. Fortunately, he was very good and the essence of each story was preserved.

As a student in the 1980's, Jen had come from Chicago to study geology in Colorado. She used to joke that Denver was her favorite cow town, but she realized that the city of the 90s was no longer really small. Almost the perfect place to live, if it just hadn't been for all the heartbreak.

As Jen read, she heard Kaari walk down the hall and into the kitchen.

"Hi, young lady," Kaari said to Sarah in her light Swedish accent as she patted the child's blond curls.

Sarah smiled as she looked up into her nanny's face. "Pet Moppet,

1

too," Sarah said as Kaari reached for the cat, stroking the purring animal's long gray fur.

The tall young woman poured coffee for herself and refilled Jen cup before shooing Moppet off the kitchen chair. She sat down and pulled her thick blond hair behind her head, letting it fall to her waist. Except for her height, Kaari could have passed for Jen's sister. Jen, of course, didn't have either Kaari's incredibly long hair or her accent, but they shared enough similarity to seem as family. People who didn't know the threesome often mistook Sarah for Kaari's daughter.

Kaari was a good-natured young woman with a winning smile. She had been a life-saver during Sarah's infancy and had become Jen's friend. Without her loving care and attention toward Sarah, Jen was sure that she wouldn't have survived the changes in her life since her daughter's birth.

Kaari had wanted to study in the United States and had advertised for a nanny's position in several newspapers in the Chicago area. Jen's mother had forwarded the ads to Jen before Sarah was born, thinking that her daughter might need some help. Because of Jen's uncertain financial situation at that time, Jen's mother had offered to pay for Kaari's expenses and salary for the first year. Jen had gladly accepted, not only because her employer had declared bankruptcy and laid off the staff during her seventh month of pregnancy, but also because she was uncertain of Sarah's father's commitment to herself and the unborn baby.

Jen asked Kaari how her Saturday night had been and what she thought her plans were for the day. Because Jen worked six days out of the week for the newspaper, Sunday was her nanny's only day off. Jen wished that she could give Kaari more time off, but Sunday was the best she could do.

"I'm done, Mama," Sarah said as the telephone rang.

"I will take her into family room," Kaari said lifting the child from her chair as Jen answered the phone.

Jen was delighted to hear from Aunt Norma. Through her pleasure, however, she could hear from Norma's tone that something was wrong.

"I've been out of town," Norma said, "and I'm coming into Denver tonight. I wanted to stop by and see you and Sarah before heading home to Colorado Springs."

"We'd love to see you," Jen said. "What time?"

"My flight arrives at 7:15, so I should be in Morrison by about 8:30. Is that too late for Sarah?"

"Oh, no. She can stay up a bit later to see you." Jen paused and asked, "Is something wrong?"

"Yes, dear," Norma said with sadness in her voice, "but I'd rather tell you about it in person."

Jen was alarmed and felt a touch of fear. She called Norma her aunt, but they had no formal relationship. Norma was the widowed aunt of Sarah's father, Greg Myerhoff, who had left Jen nearly five years ago, shortly after the baby was born.

Aunt Norma had no children of her own and loved Sarah like a grandchild. She had been supportive to Jen after the baby was born and horrified at Greg's desertion. Even though Greg had acted like his move to South America was the professional opportunity of a lifetime, Norma knew better, and gave him hell for his decision and lack of responsibility. As a consequence, Norma was always ready to atone for Greg's sins and supported Jen with letters, phone calls, and visits through the years. She was a true friend to Jen.

"What is it?" Jen asked, feeling anxious that the bad news might concern Greg.

"Let's just save it for this evening," Aunt Norma said, adding, "It doesn't have to do with Greg."

She must be reading my mind.

They finished their conversation quickly and Jen returned to her coffee and newspaper.

❅   ❅   ❅

After Sarah's evening bath, Jen carried her daughter into the child's bedroom. She smelled the scent of the baby shampoo in her daughter's damp hair as she helped Sarah change into her favorite Disney pajamas.

"Look, Mama," Sarah said, "Moppet's getting ready for bed, too."

Jen and her daughter sat together on the bed, watching the cat nose her way into a sweatshirt that Jen had dropped onto the seat of Sarah's wheelchair.

"Maybe she wants to wear jammies tonight," Sarah said with a giggle as the cat disappeared inside the sweatshirt. Jen smiled as they watched the cat peering out at them through the shirt's collar.

Moppet's favorite sleeping spot was the seat of Sarah's wheelchair—

when Sarah wasn't using it (and sometimes even when she was). The cat slept next to Sarah's bed in the wheelchair every night. Cats prefer the most comfortable spot available for sleeping, Jen had often thought. She hadn't understood why the cat chose the wheelchair until she noticed that it was usually parked over the heating vent in Sarah's room.

Jen hugged her daughter, thinking how much her child enriched her life and how, at the same time, she had brought so many changes. There had been difficulties from the moment of her birth, and different surgeries over the past five years to repair the spina bifida. Sarah couldn't walk unaided yet, but Kaari took her to therapy three times a week, and her legs were gaining strength. Jen had hope, and so did Sarah. Only a matter of time. Jen recognized that most parents don't know what it's like to have a physically handicapped child, but she felt that all the love she'd given to her daughter had forged the strong bond she shared with Sarah.

Sarah and Jen had moved into the kitchen of their ranch-style house and were sharing popcorn in the kitchen nook when the doorbell rang. Jen picked Sarah up and carried her into the front room. When she opened the door, Norma smiled and held out her arms for Sarah.

"Aunt Norma!" Sarah squealed with delight, wrapping her arms around her great aunt's neck as Norma took the small child into her arms.

"Honey, I'm so glad to see you. You're my favorite girl." Jen stepped aside to let Norma in and put her arms around them both, kissing Norma's cheek.

"Come in and sit down," Jen said. Norma sat Sarah on the sofa next to her before taking off the light jacket she wore over a black sweater embroidered with fall leaves.

Jen went into the kitchen for two cups of coffee and popcorn for Sarah. As she returned from the kitchen, she watched Moppet stroll royally into the front room and jump up on Jen's intended seat.

Sarah finished her popcorn as she chatted happily with Norma and objected when Jen suggested that it was bed time. Jen carried her daughter into her bedroom. Tucking her in, she kissed Sarah's forehead as she heard Moppet jump up on the wheelchair and settle down. She turned off the light and closed the door quietly, leaving the room illuminated by a dim night light.

Jen returned to the front room feeling anxious about Norma's news. She had seen the strain around Norma's eyes when she had entered the house.

"You've been out of town?" Jen asked as she sat next to Norma on the sofa.

"Yes, I've been to my sister's in Indiana to help them bury Steve," she said quietly. Jen saw the tears form in Norma's eyes and was moved by her grief.

"Oh, no," Jen said. "What happened?"

"Well, they said he had a climbing accident in Monarch County."

Jen was shocked. She had been friends with Steve, Greg's brother, for years. In fact, Steve had introduced her to Greg when she and Steve were graduate students together at the Colorado School of Mines in the early 1980s. At the same time that she felt the loss of a friend, Jen was relieved that the death wasn't Greg's. She was angry with herself for her relief and felt guilty.

Although Jen desperately wanted to know if Greg had attended his brother's funeral, she said, "Oh Norma, I'm so sorry. I know how much you loved Steve."

"Steve was always my favorite nephew—more like a son," Norma said as she searched her jacket pocket for a tissue.

"Do you know what happened?" Jen asked.

"Well, he was rock climbing by himself sometime during the week before Labor Day and fell. He died of head injuries. It was an isolated place on private land and nobody found him for a while. Some other climbers were there during Labor Day weekend and reported it to the Monarch County sheriff's department."

Jen absorbed this news, feeling grim disbelief. She was upset, thinking of Steve and how much she had enjoyed his company. He had been sharp, if a bit of a curmudgeon. Steve was the best in the class when it came to mineral identification and had always been willing to share what he knew. The School of Mines had been a challenge for Jen, and she thought about how much she had struggled to finish her master's degree in geology. For Steve, it had seemed like a breeze; he had always had time for other activities.

Although they had had many interests in common, such as skiing, camping and hiking, they had never dated, but had remained close until her tumultuous relationship with his brother. They had drifted in different directions and lost touch, although Norma occasionally gave her an update on his adventures.

Jen remembered Steve as having an athletic build, muscular frame, ice blue eyes, wild dark brown hair, and a bushy beard, a real contrast to his tall, slender, fair-haired brother. Steve's bushy beard was her favorite feature. *What a character he had been. What a wonderful rock climbing partner. Crusty, tactless, but with a great sense of humor and undeniable skill.* She wondered what he would be like now at 38. She sighed. *Now I'll never know.*

"But Steve was an expert rock climber. How did this happen?" Jen asked. "He was always so careful. It's strange."

Jen and Steve had gone climbing and rappelling in the Flat Irons around Boulder many times, and she remembered that Steve was attentive to his equipment and wouldn't allow anyone he was climbing with to use faulty equipment or to climb under hazardous conditions. He was very good at teaching climbing. Steve had been an advisor to a co-ed Boy Scout High Adventure Explorer Post and had taught 14- to 19-year olds to climb and rappel. Jen had gone with him on many climbs with the Explorers, and she knew his technique.

"I don't know, honey. I'm still in a state of shock," Norma said.

"Do you have any more information?" Jen asked.

"That's all I know."

Jen was thoughtful for a moment. "My boss just assigned me to do the annual assessment of casinos in Monarch County. I can look into it when I'm there investigating the casinos."

"Oh, would you?" Aunt Norma asked. "It would mean a lot to the family, and to me."

"And to me, too."

Norma dried her eyes and said, "Guess I'd better head for the Springs—it'll take a hour to drive home."

"Norma, I'm really glad that you stopped here to tell me this news. I appreciate you letting me know. I understand how you must feel about losing Steve, especially to an accident. I feel really sad about it."

They rose from the sofa and embraced before Norma departed.

❋   ❋   ❋

Enduring the blinding sunshine along with thousands of other eastbound commuters, Jen made good time on Monday morning as she drove downtown to her office. She tolerated the drive because she preferred Morrison and its charming foothills location to Denver and its flat-land suburbs.

Jen arrived at her favorite discount parking lot in 30 minutes. *What a pain in the neck parking has become.* Jen rebelled, refusing to pay premium prices for covered parking. She fantasized that one day her employer would provide free covered parking as a benefit to employees; thus far, all her suggestions to that effect had been ignored.

In her office cubicle, Jen briefly scanned the morning edition of the *Journal* and sipped her coffee, enjoying the aroma. She set her cup down amidst the clutter of her work area and absently pulled her telephone book from its sacred spot under her desk as she turned the pages of the newspaper. Her small cubicle allowed no room for a bookshelf, so she kept the telephone book and any other references in the only available spot. Jen opened to the blue pages and found the number for the Monarch County sheriff's department listed with a half-dozen other municipal numbers for the town of Dawson, the county seat.

Jen dialed the sheriff's number and, as she waited for an answer, thought about the town of Dawson. Not too long ago, it was just a small, quaint tourist town with a little bit of gold panning, an old saloon, and an historic gold mine tour. The ruins from mining operations conducted during the last century were reminders of the town's earlier history. Now that the town had legalized gambling, she'd heard that the atmosphere had changed. Jen shied away from the commercialization of such places and had not been there since the casinos had opened. She didn't want to go on principle, and preferred to remember Dawson as it was in the pre-gambling days.

A man answered the telephone, "Sheriff's department, Deputy Manydeeds speaking."

Manydeeds? What an unusual name. Perhaps it's Native American. "Good morning," she said. "My name is Jennifer Slater and I'm a reporter with *The Front Range Journal.*" She paused to see what response she would receive. Sometimes, law enforcement agencies felt that reporters were a nuisance and tended to brush them off. She needed to hear how Deputy Manydeeds would react to her introduction.

"Good morning, Ms. Slater," Manydeeds said. "You write for the *Journal?*" He paused. "I think I've read some of your work. Did you just do a piece on the history of AMAC mining operations?"

His friendly voice put Jen at ease. "Yes," she said. "It was published yesterday in the Sunday edition."

"That was a nice story," he said.

"Thank you," she responded, pleased that someone had noticed her work and remembered her name.

"How can I help you?" Manydeeds asked.

Jen explained that she was assigned by the journal to conduct the annual assessment of casino operations in Monarch County. Manydeeds said that the sheriff's department was available to help, as needed, and told her that the Colorado Division of Gaming had an office in Dawson.

Jen felt comfortable asking Deputy Manydeeds for information on Steve's death. "I just heard that a friend of mine, Steve Myerhoff, died in the county in a rock-climbing accident before Labor Day. Do you know anything about that accident?" Jen asked.

"Not much. I don't recall the details and was out of town when the body was recovered. Would you like to speak with one of the deputies who was on duty that day?"

"Oh, no. That's okay," Jen said. "I'm just curious about the accident. It's actually more of a personal interest. I knew Steve when we were students together at the School of Mines and was shocked to hear about him. I was wondering if I could get more information?"

"Sure," Manydeeds said. "I can pull out the sheriff's and coroner's reports and read them to you, if you'd like. I'll see if I can find the files. Hang on a minute."

"That's great," Jen said as she heard the phone clank down on a hard surface, thinking that Deputy Manydeeds had a nice voice.

She pulled her shoulder-length hair behind her free ear, intrigued by this flicker of interest in the opposite sex. *It's been a long time since I've found a male voice attractive.* Such feelings had been a rarity since Greg's departure. Of course the depression had drained her dry. Therapy and anti-depressants had helped to turn her around, and she had been doing well enough that she only needed to see her therapist once every two months. That was a significant improvement over twice a week. Greg had left her quite a legacy.

At the time Steve introduced them in 1981, Greg had been married, a botanist with the Colorado Museum of Natural History, and an adjunct professor at the University of Colorado. His specialty was tropical flora. She had been volunteering at the museum on Saturday mornings when they met again, by chance, five years later.

As they became reacquainted, Jen learned that Greg was now divorced. They began dating and their relationship flourished for two years until Jen accidentally became pregnant. Greg hadn't wanted the child, but Jen had.

After Sarah was born with so many problems their relationship deteriorated over the following six months, ending when Greg found a "temporary" position with the Ministry of Forests in Colombia, South America.

He'd called the job the opportunity of a lifetime, and he'd assumed that Jen would understand.

Jen recalled their bitter argument over his departure. She was most shocked by his attitude towards their daughter and his revelation that he couldn't deal with a disabled child that he hadn't wanted in the first place.

He departed in January, promising he would return to her and the baby when the assignment was finished. He'd also promised to send money for support, especially since Jen was just starting a new career as a reporter. Greg had disappeared from their lives, and she still wasn't sure where he was.

Sarah was the joy of her life, and Jen couldn't understand how Greg could leave someone as precious as their child. She convinced herself that if Greg could just see Sarah now, that he'd love the child as much as she did. Jen often imagined their reunion—the many ways it might occur. Jen knew that she was too stubborn to accept Greg as an irresponsible partner and parent. Instead, she thought of him as a person with a major character defect. It didn't help much, because she was continually strapped for money. At least she didn't have to live at home with her mother in Chicago. She suspected that her mother didn't want that either, and that was why she'd continued to help Jen pay Kaari's expenses.

Jen's reflections were interrupted when the deputy asked, "Are you still there?"

"Yes," she responded, slightly flustered. "Find anything?"

Manydeeds read her the file contents and Jen concentrated on taking notes.

❋ ❋ ❋

That evening, after Sarah and Moppet were in bed and Kaari had gone to class, Jen had time to study her notes more thoroughly. She pulled her geologic atlas of the Front Range from the shelf in the family room, carried it to the kitchen table, and opened the book to Monarch County to locate the site of the accident.

With her notes and maps spread out on the table, Jen called Norma.

They chatted for a moment before Jen said, "I've found out more about Steve's death. The deputy read the sheriff's and coroner's reports to me and I've been thinking about the accident."

Norma was interested. "What did you find out, honey?" she asked.

"I've tried to reconstruct the circumstances. You might know some of this already, but I'm still sorting it out."

"That's okay," Norma said. "You just tell me what you've learned."

Jen settled into a worn kitchen chair and picked up her notes. "I guess Steve had gone rock climbing by himself on the Saturday before Labor Day. He went to a remote site on private land. The place he went isn't popular; I've never heard of it before. You need the landowner's permission to climb at the site. There're much better places to climb than those red sandstone cliffs—in the granite along the foothills and in the canyons, for instance.

"The sheriff thinks that Steve slipped during his climb, fell, and lost his helmet when he hit the ground. The coroner determined that he died right away from head injuries because his head wasn't protected."

Jen paused at Norma's deep sigh. "Go on, honey," she reassured Jen.

"On Labor Day weekend, other climbers went to the site. They found Steve's truck first and then his body. The climbers reported it to the sheriff's department and they contacted the landowner. According to the landowner, Steve hadn't gotten their permission to climb at the site. That seems out of character to me. Steve was always respectful of people's property." Norma agreed.

"I know that there're lots of climbing accidents in Colorado each year," Jen said, "but most involve inexperienced climbers. Or people who don't have the right equipment or training. Steve was an expert. Too many things are wrong with this. It's not like Steve."

"Tell me what's wrong. Maybe we can sort some of this out," Norma said.

"Knowing Steve, I guess I have trouble accepting that he had a fatal fall. All of the equipment he needed for a safe climb—like ropes, pitons, carbiners, harnesses, and a rock climbing helmet—were at the site. But the sheriff's report says that his helmet had a 'broken strap.' Why would Steve use a helmet with a broken strap? I know how meticulous he was with his equipment."

"You're right," Norma agreed.

Jen took a breath and continued. "Another thing is that you should never climb without a rope and safety harness. That's a standard safety precaution designed to catch you if you fall and to keep you from hitting the ground. A harness and rope were at the scene, but hadn't been in use at the time of Steve's accident. Why wasn't Steve wearing his safety equipment?

"Also, it's safer to climb with a partner. Steve must have been by himself, because no one reported the accident. His body was there for a week.

Why'd Steve gone climbing by himself? Or why didn't he let someone else know his plans, just in case there was a problem? He was gone for a week and nobody missed him?"

"These are important question, honey," Norma said. "I wonder if we can ever find answers for them." They both paused in thought.

"Maybe I'll go to Dawson on Saturday and find out if there's more to the story than I see here. I have to go anyway for my job."

"That's a good idea. Maybe being there will help you see things a different way. Let me know what you find out," Norma said sadly, "though nothing can bring back Steve."

They consoled each other about their mutual loss, remembering Steve and feeling his absence. Their conversation left Jen even more determined to make sense of Steve's death.

Chapter Two

On Saturday morning, Jen woke early and stretched as she lay underneath her white comforter decorated with North American wildflowers. After breakfast and a shower, she dressed in an old pair of belted jeans and a striped, long-sleeve shirt over a matching blue tee shirt. She carried her thick white socks and her gray hiking boots into the family room and put them on.

Jen found Sarah and Kaari having breakfast in the kitchen nook. "I'm driving up to Dawson," Jen said to Kaari as she hugged Sarah. "I should be back in about three hours. I have the cell phone if you need anything."

Jen took a light weight jacket and a white baseball cap from the coat rack beside the kitchen door and slipped the cell phone into her jacket pocket. She liked baseball caps because they kept the sun out of her eyes and she preferred them to sunglasses. She knew this habit was a hold over from her days as a geologist, where sunglasses were generally discouraged when working in the field. They distorted the natural colors of the rocks, making their field descriptions inaccurate.

Jen left by the kitchen door and entered the detached garage where her elderly dented white Ford Bronco, with its pitted windshield, was parked. She dropped the jacket and hat onto a passenger seat that had been much repaired with duct tape that almost matched.

Although there hadn't been any repairs for the last five months, she called her Bronco "Wild Bill" as a reminder that problems could develop at any time. Jen told herself that it was just about time for something else to break—*I can't become complacent.*

The morning was calm with a clear blue sky and bright sunshine as Jen drove north on Foothills Road. She passed through the valley formed between the hogbacks on the east—those discontinuous ridges of sedimentary rocks pushed up by the mountains and literally standing on end—and the granitic foothills of the Front Range on the west. The sun hadn't risen above the tops of the hogbacks yet and Jen drove in and out of the shadows they cast. Where the road rose higher, she caught glimpses of the city between breaks in the hogbacks. She drove past Red Rocks

Amphitheater, where outdoor concerts were held seasonally, through the underpass at the intersection with Interstate 70, and into Golden, a town made famous by the Colorado School of Mines and Coors beer.

Jen turned west onto Darkhorse Canyon Road from Foothills Road. A highway sign read "Darkhorse 12 Mi." and "Dawson 18 Mi." A second sign read "Entering Monarch County." The two-lane paved highway and shoulders soon narrowed as she entered the canyon. On the north side of the roadway rose gray granite walls of pre-Cambrian-aged rocks. These ancient rocks were shot full of fractures and white veins of quartz. The fractures were of interest to the area's rock climbing community, providing excellent hand- and foot-holds for climbers. It was a popular rock climbing location, and one that Jen had used years ago. She saw several groups of people in the process of climbing as she drove through the canyon. The quartz veins were of interest to miners, too; many contained gold, making the area famous during the last century. When the gold played out, the towns had diminished in size and economic importance and, until gambling, they had survived on tourism as quaint symbols of a bygone era.

On the south, between the road and the far canyon wall, Darkhorse Creek rushed eastward over gray stream-rounded boulders and cobbles. There was nothing natural about the stream—the entire bed had been disturbed in the quest for placer gold over the last 150 years. The stream was artificially channeled between mounds of boulders and cobbles rearranged during historic mining operations to recover the gold. Early miners had dredged most of the gold from the stream years ago, but gold flakes and "dust" were still there. Today one or two small commercial operators worked the stream bed with dredges, and, during the warm months, people using gold pans and small homemade sluice boxes still worked the sediments; Jen saw several in operation as she drove up the canyon.

As Jen approached the town of Darkhorse, the canyon widened as the Darkhorse Creek flood plain, dotted with a few small cabins, broadened. Jen slowed as she entered the town. Darkhorse didn't have legalized gambling, so it had retained its historic appearance. The first major gold strike in the Colorado territory was made here in 1857 and had sparked a boom that lasted 30 years. When the town had burned to the ground in 1875, the wood-framed structures and false-front buildings had been completely destroyed. Once rebuilt, the town had the Victorian flavor typical of the 1870s. These new structures provided a wonderful continuity that preserved a different time, hence the town's classification as a national historic district. Jen, along with tourists from all over the world, felt the town's charm.

The main street and narrow sidewalks through town were cramped, with a single lane of traffic moving in each direction and parallel parking permitted on both sides of the street. To Jen, Wild Bill felt large and awkward moving slowly along the main street. Many of the narrow brick buildings facing the street had flat roofs sloping to the rear of each building. Each two-story building had three or four rectangular or arched windows on its upper floor, while the large ground-floor windows revealed shops, restaurants, or arcades. The upper floors were used for storage, apartments, or offices.

Names were neatly painted in ornate Victorian-style letters on the shop windows and above the single or double-door entrances. Several of the taller buildings had enormous faded signs painted on their sides, advertising products from years ago. A number of the painted and natural brick buildings were decorated with elaborate brickwork or wood trim in contrasting colors. Although the buildings were narrow, 30 to 40 feet wide, they stretched back into the mountain side up to 100 feet.

From the street, Jen could see the evidence of former mining operations, now long abandoned. She lowered her window and breathed in the cold, fresh, mountain air that was tainted with a slight acidic odor from the yellow and orange tailings. Devoid of gold, tailings had been dumped from the mine entrances by early miners and still prominently scarred the mountain sides. An unfortunate feature resulting from underground mining, tailings were made up of waste rock that had been removed to reach the gold-bearing quartz veins. Miners blasted underground, loaded the waste rock into ore carts, rolled them out of the mine along narrow-gauge rail lines, and dumped the loads outside of the mine entrance. The deeper the miners blasted their way into the mountain, the larger the tailings grew. Some tailings were large enough to cover acres and had narrow-gauge rail lines extending across their surfaces so that the miners could reach the front of the slope to empty the ore carts. In the modern world, reclamation was required, but in this historic district, most of the original mining operations had been left undisturbed.

Dilapidated buildings and mills, built more than 100 years ago, were weathered dark brown and in a state of collapse. Battered ore cars with missing wheels, nine-man cages used to lower miners underground, and scattered rusted equipment lay about the abandoned mines and mills.

Old railroad grades and road beds were still visible, slashing across the face of the mountains in parallel strokes. Trees removed from the mining areas had struggled to return when mining operations ceased. Of course, nothing grew on the tailings.

Exciting, Jen thought, to think that these ruins were once viable, lucrative, mining operations. Tourists loved them too, and that had its problems. The ruins and mines were dangerous and closed to entry, although the tourists were able to view them from established observation points along the road and from the town of Darkhorse. Acid water drained from the mine openings, especially during spring runoff, and entered the area waterways causing harmful increases in pH. Corrective actions taken over the last five years by the Colorado Department of Health had controlled acid mine drainage to some extent, allowing the streams to slowly recover after years of sterility.

The traffic was light as Jen drove out of Darkhorse and westward into the Roosevelt National Forest. She had been climbing steadily and had gained 2,000 feet in elevation since leaving her home. She passed a sign for the Darkhorse Picnic Grounds, located near the confluence of Darkhorse Creek and a smaller stream. Now that she was in the forest and away from the effects of the mining operations, trees covered the mountain sides and the acidic odor was gone from the air, replaced with a clean pine scent.

Summer was always a relatively short season in the high country and leaves turned in early- to mid-September and fell to the ground by early October. Jen realized with pleasure that she was in the mountains at the right time to catch the short season of autumnal change. Unlike trees in New England, Colorado's high country had a single color change during autumn. There were no oak or maple trees here, unless they had been transplanted by some hopeful homeowner. In the fall sunshine, the golden aspen leaves and white-barked trunks and branches were brilliant, creating a beautiful contrast to the dark green lodgepole pines and blue spruce native to the Front Range.

Jen was approaching Dawson. The town was set in a valley between the high forested mountains which made up the Roosevelt National Forest. She had climbed another 1,000 feet in elevation, to over 9,000 feet, and she felt Wild Bill strain against the incline and the thinner air. *No speeding today*.

The two-lane highway was freshly repaved and widened. Jen slowed the Bronco as she came to the edge of town. Gravel parking lots were squeezed into every available flat area and had hand-written signs saying, "Park All Day $8.00" or "Parking $1.00 per hour, $10.00 maximum." *Outrageous, you can park in some downtown Denver lots for 75 cents a day. I hope the sheriff's department has a parking lot.* The make-shift parking areas were not yet full, but she suspected that they would be filled during the day by sightseers, gamblers, and people with show tickets.

New buildings had been constructed along the narrow main street since limited gaming had been legislated in 1991. They hadn't wasted any time in tearing down the older commercial buildings and constructing new ones. Jen remembered that Dawson had been a larger version of Darkhorse just a few years ago. The atmosphere in the town was no longer either charming or Victorian.

Why, Jen thought, along with other Colorado residents, hadn't the officials used better judgment in developing the zoning regulations for Dawson? Why hadn't they developed architectural standards consistent with the look and feel of the old mining towns? Historically, gambling had been a significant part of these towns, and modern gambling could have been done just as easily in newly constructed casinos retaining the essence of the original town. *Oh, well, it's too late now.* This area used to be called the richest square mile in the world. The riches are here, all right, Jen mused, but have changed from gold nuggets to casino tokens. More money has come back into this town through gambling than ever went out from gold mining.

Dawson was larger than Darkhorse because the valley was wider, allowing room for several streets parallel to the main street, called Grand Street. The two other streets, paralleling Grand Street, were North and South Streets. North Street ran for the full six blocks through town. South Street, adjacent to Darkhorse Creek, extended four blocks before terminating against tailings on the west end of town. Cross streets were numbered. First Street was located at the eastern entrance to Dawson with Sixth Street at the western end of town. Dawson was compact, and the town and vicinity were home to fewer than 300 permanent residents. Housing was scarce and Jen assumed that many of the casino employees were forced to live in neighboring towns or in mountain cabins.

Darkhorse Creek flowed between mounds of gravel and yellow tailings littered with the debris of earlier mining operations. Nothing grew there. Collapsing bridges and trestle railroads crossed the stream, joining South Street to the railroad grade that cut into the steeply rising mountain side.

Although test pits and smaller tailings were found on the north side of town, the main mining activities had been to the south at the Cory Lane Mine, which now operated commercial mine tours. North of Dawson, unpaved roads leading into the national forest extended from First and Fourth Streets. These two roads, winding their way into the mountains, were dotted with cabins and small homes.

Jen entered Dawson on a narrow two-lane road similar to that of Darkhorse. However, parallel parking on Grand Street was prohibited to prevent pedestrian accidents and congestion. She wondered why they didn't close Grand Street to vehicular traffic and re-route the traffic to North and South Streets. It could be better organized, Jen found herself thinking, but she realized that the town was still adjusting to the huge influx of gamblers.

Seeing a blue sign that read, "Municipal Buildings Next Right," Jen turned north onto First Street and saw the combined City Hall and County Court House located in the original red brick building. On the north side of City Hall, sat a small yellow clapboard building with a pitched roof over the second story. Black Victorian-style letters arching across the large store-front glass window said "Monarch County Sheriff's Department." There were four parking spaces in front of the building. Two were occupied by official vehicles, one was reserved for the handicapped, and the fourth said "Visitor." Jen, delighted, pulled in.

The building was typical of many older, wood-frame structures still in commercial use in small Colorado towns. It was constructed on a slope and the narrow concrete sidewalk in front of the station angled down to her left toward Darkhorse Creek, and up to her right toward the mountains. As Jen climbed out of the Bronco, she shivered against the chill mountain air. She stepped across the sidewalk, opened the glass door of the station, and entered the building, noticing that when she opened the door half of the narrow sidewalk was blocked. *Probably forces unwary pedestrians into the gutter.*

A buzzer sounded as she entered the small waiting room that extended the width of the old converted store front. Jen caught the combined scent of fresh coffee, printer ink, and old wood floors. The waiting room was furnished with metal chairs, apparently long in use. The worn wood floors creaked as she stepped up to the counter. On her right, the counter abutted the plaster wall. On her left was a swinging gate leading to the rear of the counter and into an office area. The walls were covered with maps, bulletin boards containing signs and notices, a clock with a large face and hands, official posters, and a calendar with wildlife scenes from the Front Range Arsenal.

Behind the counter, four desks were crowded into the small office area. Every square foot of available floor space held filing cabinets, bookshelves, or tables cluttered with fax machines, telephones, radios, and other electronic equipment Jen didn't recognize. *Crowded but cozy—I'd feel right at home here.*

Beyond the office area was an open doorway leading into the rear of the building where a small refrigerator, coffee pot, and photocopy machine were visible. Jen heard voices at the rear of the station and footsteps coming her way. A tall man entered the office area and approached the counter, deftly maneuvering around the desks and other obstacles. He was dressed in his uniform and carried a cup of steaming coffee.

"Morning," he said, "Can I help you?"

"I hope so," Jen said. "My name is Jen Slater and I'm a reporter with *The Front Range Journal*. I just wanted the sheriff to know that I'll be investigating casino operations in Monarch County for the newspaper."

"I'm Charlie Manydeeds. We talked earlier," the deputy said, "but I'm afraid you won't find the Division of Gaming open today."

"True. It's Saturday," she replied. "This is sort of a preliminary trip for me. I haven't been to Dawson since gambling started and I wanted to see the place."

"Did you find the information on your friend's death useful?" he asked.

"I did," she answered, "and I appreciate your help. I actually have a few more questions about the death."

"Sure. Would you like some coffee first?" Jen nodded and the deputy said, "I'll get it for you. How do you like your coffee, Ms. Slater?"

"Oh. Please call me Jen. Black coffee is fine, thanks."

As he wound his way back toward the rear room, Jen thought that he was as attractive and friendly as his voice, although his face was impassive when he spoke. He was tall, about six feet. His straight black hair reached to his collar and was parted on the left. His eyes were light brown under dark eyebrows. His clean-shaven, squarish face was tanned from work outdoors during the summer. His lips were full and his nose was straight.

"Here you are. Call me Charlie, everyone does. Even the locals I arrest on a regular basis." He set the cup on the counter. Jen noticed that his hands were large, with blunt rounded fingers and trimmed nails. He wore no wedding band. Jen flushed when she realized that she had looked for a wedding band, as though she hoped that he was available. She was surprised at herself and secretly pleased that he wore only a watch.

"Thanks," she said. "Looks like quite a trek through the obstacle course to reach coffee. Your office is packed."

"Actually, we just moved into this building three months ago. Before, we were located with the Dawson town police in City Hall, next door. With the town's growth, the hall was too small for everybody, although lockup is still over there. This building isn't much better."

"No new building, complements of gambling revenues?" Jen asked.

"The county was supposed to build a new station, but the price of property skyrocketed, so it's on hold. We could use some more space. We grew from four to six full-time deputies in the past two years. Big time." Although he didn't smile, Jen saw a twinkle in his eyes. She smiled in response.

"I haven't been to Dawson since gambling started. The town has changed so much. I saw parking lots squeezed in everywhere along the road when I drove into town. It looks like a nightmare," Jen said, sipping her steaming coffee.

"Yeah. Parking has been a serious problem," Charlie said, nodding. "The mayor would like to build a municipal parking lot, but the cost of land is unreasonable. Cars are parked all the way up onto the unpaved portions of First and Fourth Streets during the weekends, blocking driveways and creating a nuisance. I've even seen four-wheel drive vehicles trying to park for free on the tailings out at the Cory Lane Mine. We ticket those."

Jen smiled and said, "Glad I didn't park there. Although 'free' sounds like my kind of price. I saw a sign that charged $8.00 for a full day," she said shaking her head in disbelief. "I can park for less in Denver."

"The casinos have really brought in a flood of folks," Charlie said, finishing his coffee. "Sometimes Darkhorse Canyon Road is backed up for miles. It's a problem when we need emergency vehicles in here. Accidents have to be air-lifted by helicopter to Front Range Hospital in Jefferson County. It's the quickest way to get injured people out. I guess you can always come to Dawson by helicopter," he suggested with a hint of irony.

"I'll try putting that on my expense account," she said, smiling and thinking of her boss' face. "Where do the pilots land?" Jen asked, as she knew there was no airport in Dawson.

"The Golden Nugget Casino has a helipad on the roof to accommodate the high rollers who don't want to wait in traffic," he said. "The county commissioners agreed to allow the helipad, but only if the pad was also available for emergency air lift."

"The casino has a helipad? It must be big," Jen said.

"The Golden Nugget is enormous by Dawson standards. It takes up a full town block. It's six stories tall and has a penthouse apartment at the top for the manager. Looks nothing like the buildings that used to make up this town. More like…Las Vegas. It's quite a piece of work. You should stop in and see it while you're here. They have free breakfast."

"I'm sure I will be seeing it as part of my investigation," Jen said. She pause and asked, "So, which are you? A new deputy or one of the four old ones?" She was not used to making casual conversation with an attractive man, but was intrigued enough by her interest to ask the question anyway. At the same time, she hoped that he wouldn't think she was flirting.

Charlie, easy going and good-natured, seemed as though he didn't mind her question."Old. Ten years with the sheriff's department and an expert on search and rescue. Before that? Too many years in the marines." Twinkling eyes again. "And before that, years growing up on the Blackfeet Reservation."

"Oh," Jen said, "I thought Manydeeds might be a Native American name."

He nodded once in acknowledgment, rotating his coffee cup between his hands.

Jen sipped her coffee too, and ventured, "Search and rescue is something I'm interested in. I have experience in rock climbing and rappelling."

Another deputy entered the room, sat at a desk next to the counter, and began to search through files. Jen, feeling uncomfortable engaging an on-duty deputy in a casual conversation, decided it was time to pursue her professional queries.

Hoping her transition wasn't too abrupt, she asked, "What can you tell me about the scene of Steve Myerhoff's death?"

Charlie paused before answering. "The accident occurred on private land owned by the Elbert family. They ask climbers to let them know when they want to climb. The family has information posted at the site. All it takes is a phone call."

"Can I go there?"

"Sure. Probably the easiest way would be to walk down to the Miner's Tavern on the west side of the Golden Nugget and ask for Allison Henry. She knows the family and can arrange a visit for you."

"Okay. I'll do that. Thanks for your help, Charlie," Jen said turning away from the counter, "Oh," she turned back, "should I move my Bronco? I'm parked in the only visitor's spot." She flinched at the thought of moving to a pricey lot and hoped the thought didn't show in her face. However, she realized that her professional relationship with the sheriff's department might be important to her investigation and she couldn't afford to be a nuisance.

"Yeah, better move it. You can take it around back through the alley and park behind the fire station."

"Okay. Great. Thanks again," Jen smiled in relief.

Jen left the building and walked to Wild Bill. *Too bad I can't be on a case with him, but I'm sure he wouldn't be interested anyway.* She sighed as she climbed into the Bronco. *So now I'm a size 14. My shoulders are narrower and my hips broader than I would like. I have thighs like tree trunks. I have too much famine guard and I need to be in better shape. Why can't I seem to find the time to work out?*

Famine guard was the way Jen jokingly thought of those extra pounds that had gathered over the last five years. The joke was her coping mechanism for dealing with a less than perfect figure. The pounds just seemed to stick around, even when she was under treatment for depression. Most people lost weight on anti-depressants, but not Jen.

Oh, well, at least my hair isn't gray yet and I don't look my age. My skin is clear with few wrinkles and only tiny crow's feet around my eyes when I smile. All that sun block over the years has kept away the aging caused by too much sun. Good genetics, too. Mom still doesn't look sixty. And I have nice teeth, paid for by my parents.

Charlie's thoughts about Jen were quite different. As they had talked in the station, he had noticed her small, delicate hands with trimmed, unpolished nails. Her face was round and broad, probably from Scandinavian stock, he thought. Her nose was turned up slightly, a bit large for her face, but shapely and attractive. Jen didn't wear make up and Charlie had noticed that, too. Her skin was fresh, with a natural blush to her cheeks which gave her a wholesome look. Jen's blue eyes sparkled when she was amused or smiling. Her shapely light brown eyebrows complemented her hair. Occasionally while they talked, Jen drew her hair away from her face behind her right ear. She wore no jewelry.

As she left the station door, Charlie saw that she was not tall. He noticed the gold in her hair, highlighted by the morning sun. *She's as nice as her voice, and old enough to be mature.* There had already been too many young women in Charlie's life, and at 36, he was tired of the lack of maturity exhibited by so many of them.

Jen climbed into the Bronco and saw Charlie standing behind the counter looking out at her. She smiled and waved from behind the steering wheel and he nodded his head once, raising the fingers of his right hand slightly with his palm still resting on the counter. He turned away as Jen started the engine.

Chapter Three

Jen parked Wild Bill behind the fire station. She slipped her jacket and baseball cap on and climbed out. Jen walked to Second Street in front of the fire station, and south to Grand Street, where she turned west.

Few of the original narrow brick buildings remained along the main street. Most had been replaced with large, modern multi-story casinos or hotels built in a variety of styles. They had bright neon lights and flashy exterior decor that contrasted sharply with the small number of old Victorian buildings still standing. She saw the bright, flashing lights of modern electronic roulette wheels and slot machines through the windows. Even the older buildings were a disappointment, as most of them had added slot machines in an effort to remain competitive with the larger casinos. *No more local flavor. Gaudy. It is just like a mini-Las Vegas.*

Jen approached the corner of Third and Grand Streets. She saw the Golden Nugget's white stucco exterior, which she thought was appropriate for the southwest but mis-matched with Dawson's Victorian setting. The building filled the entire block between Third and Fourth Streets. The main entrance, facing Grand Street, had an enormous recessed entryway with a red, white, and gold striped awning stretching from the building to the curb. Large, stylish letters on the side of the awning said "Golden Nugget Casino." Jen looked at the awning. *Just wait until the winter wind and summer hail hit that impractical thing.*

Jen stopped at the corner. She saw the large windows on the ground floor opening into an room packed with rows of electronic gaming equipment. The other stories had smaller windows, although she couldn't see inside from the street. Peering through the ground floor windows, she saw a dark interior, lit mainly by the machines themselves. She looked up Third Street to her right and saw the entrance to the coffee shop where the window advertisement said "Free Breakfast All Day."

She skipped the free meal and walked on to the main entrance, where she was politely greeted by the doorman dressed in black pants, white shirt, gold tie, and red jacket to match the awning. The doorman held the door for her and, overcome by curiosity, as she went inside. Jen noticed immediately the odor of tobacco smoke and wondered why smoking wasn't banned inside the casino.

Jen stepped onto a dark red carpet with a fleur-de-lis pattern. The red, gold, and white interior, decorated with a pseudo-Victorian flourish, including red and gold striped wallpaper above walnut wainscoting, clashed with the southwestern stucco exterior. There were large dusky mirrors, reflecting the gaming machines and giving the illusion of a much larger room. Crystal chandeliers hung from the ceilings, adding some light to the dim interior.

Jen, hearing the coins clinking in the slots and the quiet whir of the machines, knew that die-hard early morning gamblers were already installed in front of "their" machines. The old style mechanical one-armed bandit slot machines were gone, replaced by push-button electronic machines.

She walked between two rows of slot machines, side-stepping dark red, vinyl covered stools with gold-tone metal legs. *How thoughtful. Now weary gamblers can sit comfortably until their money is gone.* Jen brushed her hand over a cold, impersonal, vinyl stool cover and decided that the place was a fright, completely lacking in charm and grace.

Jen returned to Grand Street and walked the rest of the block to Fourth Street, where she saw an old one-story saloon sitting in the shadow of the Golden Nugget Casino. The building was narrow and long, typical of historical buildings in towns like Dawson. Above the covered porch of the clapboard building was a quaint painted Victorian-style sign saying "The Miner's Tavern, est. 1867, Allison Henry Prop."

Jen studied the old building, contrasting the saloon with the garish casino. The building's exterior was painted dark brown and had a pitched roof of black shingles. A covered porch contained a swing on the right and benches on the left. On either side of the double front door were two narrow sashed windows with eight panes each, trimmed with cornflower blue shutters. Through the windows, matching blue and white checked curtains were tied back to let in the natural light. Wood planters were attached below the windows, holding pink and red geraniums that had survived the early fall frost.

Although a sign in the window said "Closed," the main doors covering the double-swinging saloon doors were open, and Jen decided to go inside. She gently pushed her way through the swinging doors and stepped into an authentic saloon, complete with a polished walnut bar on her left running nearly the full length of the deep room. *Wow, it must be an original.* The bar was about chest high to Jen and had polished brass foot rails and walnut bar stools with leather seats. Behind the bar were mirrors with glass shelves holding many different bottles. Those on the upper shelves were antiques, while those on the lower shelves appeared to be in use. Noticing the scent of lemon oil, wood and leather, Jen reflected on the contrast between the tavern's charm and the glaring casino.

The wall opposite the bar was white plaster and held six tall, narrow windows with blue and white checked curtains, like those at the front of the building. A booth of old polished walnut, scratched and nicked through the years, was placed below each window. Dusty stuffed heads of North American mammals, some ferocious and others grimacing, hung between the windows. Looking up, Jen saw the woolly head of an American bison hanging over the entrance.

The white plaster ceiling was vaulted and supported by dark wood beams. Several fans with light fixtures extended down from the ceiling and were revolving slowly, stirring the air. Above the bar, in opposite corners of the room, hung two large electric space heaters used to warm the room in winter. Jen imagined that early on the room had been heated by a pot-bellied stove.

On the wall at the far end of the room, next to a hallway leading to the restrooms and the rear of the building, hung a large framed print of Native Americans riding their brown and white painted ponies through the snow, red rocks, and aspens. The wood floor, polished by years of use, was well cared for, although scratched where the bar stools had scraped over the surface. The room was beautiful and simple, retaining its original Victorian atmosphere.

A stocky young man with blond hair and full beard came into the barroom from the kitchen and walked behind the bar toward Jen. He was dressed in a gray and black flannel shirt, black cloth vest, bolo tie, and jeans.

He said pleasantly, "Hi. We aren't open for another hour yet. Can I help you?"

"I hope so," Jen said. "I was just down at the sheriff's department and they thought Allison Henry might be able to help me. Is she here this morning?"

"Yes, she just came in. I'll get her for you."

He walked down the hallway at the rear of the room and knocked on a door. Jen heard voices, a chair moving across the wood floor, and footsteps. A woman in her early thirties entered the barroom. *She's at least four inches taller than me and twenty pounds lighter,* Jen judged wryly, hoping that her envy didn't show in her face. She was wearing a cowgirl outfit, including a red and white checked shirt, brown leather vest decorated with silver buttons, a full calf-length denim skirt, and cowgirl boots. Her rich naturally wavy brown hair was tied back into a long pony-tail with a white bow.

As she moved into the room, Jen stepped forward and introduced herself. "Good morning. My name is Jen Slater and I'm a reporter with *The Front Range Journal.*" She extended her hand.

The woman shook her hand warmly and smiled. She said, "Pleased to meet you. I'm Allison Henry. Would you like to sit down? How about some coffee?"

Jen nodded, saying, "Yes, thanks."

"We can sit here," Allison said, as she walked toward the last booth near the back wall. Although she had a long stride, she was graceful and her movements were fluid, even in cowgirl boots.

"This is my 'reserved' booth," Allison said with a smile. The table was cluttered with newspapers and glasses, as though Allison wanted to let the tourists know that the booth was taken.

As Jen slid into the booth, she felt the comfortable leather seat beneath her hand and appreciated the warmth, compared to the cold feel of vinyl.

"Rick," Allison called out to the bartender, "two coffees, please." To Jen she said, as they settled themselves, "Like anything else to go with your coffee?"

"Oh, no thanks," Jen said.

"How can I help you?" Allison asked, sitting back in the booth and folding her hands in front of her on the table.

"Deputy Manydeeds at the sheriff's department suggested that I see you, and that you may be able to help me. I'm not on an official assignment this morning, it's more of a personal quest." Allison nodded for Jen to continue. "I knew Steve Myerhoff when we were graduate students in the early 80s. I'd like to know more about his death. The deputy said that you may be able to help me arrange a visit to the scene of his accident."

Allison's pleasant face saddened at the mention of Steve's name, and Jen noticed a change in her eyes. She wondered how well they had known each other. *Maybe they were lovers.* Rick arrived with coffee, creamer, and sugar and they spent a moment attending to their spoons and cups.

Jen studied Allison as she casually stirred her coffee and collected her thoughts, noticing the other woman's striking gray eyes. They were large, round, and friendly—the kind of eyes that invited confidence in others and made her approachable. Her mouth turned down ever so slightly, but it didn't detract from her well-proportioned, attractive features. Creases around her mouth suggested to Jen that she usually smiled a lot. But she wasn't smiling now—the subject appeared to be too painful.

"The place where Steve died is located on private property owned by the Elberts. You need permission to enter if you want to climb there. I don't climb, and I've never been there."

Jen sensed that Allison was reluctant to talk about the accident. She decided to share some of her experiences with Steve, hoping to encourage Allison.

"When Steve and I were grad students, we spent a lot of time together. We both enjoyed rock climbing and rappelling. I sort of lost track of him, but we were great friends." She paused before asking, "Did you know Steve well?"

"Yes, I did," Allison sipped her coffee before continuing. "I inherited this tavern from my mother's brother, my Uncle Ralph, when he died of a heart attack in August of 1992. I came home from St. Louis to my uncle's funeral and that's where I met Steve. He was a friend of my uncle's and a regular visitor at the tavern between prospecting trips. After I took over, Steve continued to come in.

"Steve and Uncle Ralph were two of a kind—both were crusty and rough around the edges." Allison smiled slightly at her recollection of the two men. "Uncle Ralph was quite a character. Inherited his eccentricities from his grandfather, who was an early prospector in Monarch County. Poor old Great Granddad. He spent years here in this county prospecting for gold and never made a strike. Of course, by the time he arrived in Dawson, all the best claims were taken. His choices were to either work underground for someone else as a miner or find a grub stake and prospect on his own. He decided to go it alone. Great Granddad eventually gave up and opened the Miner's Tavern in 1867. He never got rich, but he did have a steady income from all those thirsty miners."

Jen wondered if she had opened a flood-gate of family and local gossip, but simply nodded for Allison to continue her story.

"Anyway, after I took over, I eventually waded through the papers

Uncle Ralph had left behind and found some that were related to mines and mining claims. I didn't know if they were worth anything, so I asked Steve to look them over. He sorted through them and discovered that Uncle Ralph had a pre-existing claim on the tavern's property and on the property where the Golden Nugget Casino now stands. Uncle Ralph had owned the Golden Nugget's property, but had sold it to the present owners in May of 1991 so they could build the casino. It turns out that Uncle Ralph had sold the surface property to the casino owners, but not the subsurface mineral rights. As someone who went to Mines with Steve, you can probably guess how much that intrigued him—subsurface mineral rights below that eyesore."

"How did that happen?" Jen asked, knowing that surface property and subsurface mineral rights were generally transferred together.

"Their lawyers weren't on the ball, I guess, because if I'd been the buyer, I would have wanted the subsurface rights, too, along with the surface property. I can't imagine why they let that one slip by." Allison paused to sip coffee. "How's your coffee? Ready for a refill?" she asked Jen.

Jen shook her head and asked, "Do you know if your uncle had maintained the claims and filed annual assessments on the mineral rights?"

"Yes," Allison responded. "Steve said that Uncle Ralph's paperwork was all in order until the time of his death. Steve and I brought it up to current status and the claims are valid. Steve told me that, according to the old assays from the 1890s, the claims were not economically viable, but he was interested in checking them out. Steve's specialty was reassessing abandoned claims for their economic value in today's gold market."

Jen nodded, thinking it sounded just like something Steve would have enjoyed doing for a living.

"Steve went down to see Barbara Knowles at the county clerk's office to look for additional information on the two properties. It's too bad that county clerk isn't an elected office, because I sure would love to vote her out. She's a most unhelpful person and Steve's hated trying to work with her. They'd been butting heads for years because she's in charge of all the maps from the old mining claims in the county. Actually, a lot of people hate her."

Jen, fearing that Allison was straying from the story she was interested in, asked, "What did Steve find?"

"Oh yes, Steve found an old drawing showing the entrance to an abandoned shaft on the tavern's property. I didn't even know it was there and I've hung around this place much of my life. I grew up here. My family has lived in Monarch County for over 120 years, and this tavern has been in the family since it was built. Uncle Ralph never discussed the shaft. Of course, there are shafts all over the place in Dawson, so that's nothing unusual. Still, he maintained the claims for all those years."

Allison paused for coffee before continuing.

"This seems like a small piece of property," Jen said. "Was the entrance to the shaft hidden?" she asked.

"Yes," Allison answered, "the entrance is in the northwest corner of the tavern's parking lot next to the fence, behind the dumpster. It was covered over with blacktop years ago when the lot was paved. Apparently, before that, it was just covered with a grill and rubble to keep people out. Anyway, that's what we found when Steve opened the shaft."

Jen's interest in the story continued to increase and she thought, what did Steve find in the shaft? Gold? She leaned closer to Allison to encourage her to continue.

"Even though the old assays showed the gold content to be too low to be of economic interest, Steve wanted to reopen the shaft and go down and have a look. Take some samples for a new assay. So, I said it would be okay. Steve got the permits he needed to reopen the shaft. He cut away the blacktop and removed the grill and rubble over the shaft entrance. He put on all of his rappelling and rock climbing equipment, rigged up a rope, and went down. He entered the shaft four, maybe five times in all. He said that at the bottom of the shaft was a tunnel. What did he call it?" She paused.

"It's called an 'adit' if it goes straight like a tunnel," Jen said, "or a 'drift' if it follows an ore vein."

"Right," Allison said. "An adit. Steve collected samples that he sent out for assay and made maps of the adits. He showed them to me, but I couldn't tell what they meant." She smiled slightly, as though to excuse herself for not having a full understanding.

Jen was thoughtful. She asked, "There was more than one adit? Do you still have the maps?" She was curious to see Steve's work, knowing how thorough he was.

"Yes, there were several adits; and no, Steve kept the maps at his cabin so he could study them. I suppose they're still there. I should go get them before some family member shows up and clears everything out."

Jen nodded in agreement and asked, "What about the assays? Did you see those data?" Jen was ever curious and always wanted the details.

Allison raised her eyebrows and said, "Steve was excited by the results and tried to explain them to me. He showed me the old data and the new data for comparison, but I don't remember the numbers." She paused. "I do remember what Steve said about it, though—he said that the old data showed that there wasn't enough gold worth mining."

Allison leaned toward Jen in a confidential manner. "I haven't told anyone about this, but the new data showed that the old data was way off. He said 'by an order of magnitude,' and that there was enough gold down there to make the 'whole town rich again, without gambling.'"

Jen sensed Allison's excitement as she related the information.

"Steve was ready to tear down all the casinos right away and start mining," Allison said with amusement. "He was like that when he became enthusiastic about something. He hated the casinos because they spoiled the flavor of Dawson."

"I can appreciate his attitude about that," Jen said.

Allison leaned back in her seat and sipped her coffee before continuing.

"The Golden Nugget's manager, Tony Delano, was always over here asking what was going on in my parking lot; and what Steve was doing down in the old mine shaft. Tony is such a snoop. When he found out that Steve was prospecting under his casino, he was livid. I think they may have had words, but Steve didn't want to discuss it. That was three weeks ago. Now Steve is dead and I wonder…"

Jen and Allison both paused to reflect, looking each other in the eye.

Jen said, "I have wondered that, too… I was upset to hear that he died during a climbing 'accident.' I know he was a cautious climber and cared for his equipment. I just can't believe that he died from a climbing accident and that he wasn't wearing his safety harness. Or that he didn't get the owner's permission. Or that he went climbing by himself. Too many things seem wrong. I want to know more."

Jen watched Allison's face and decided now was the time to ask for help with access to the property.

"Maybe if I visit the site I might see the accident in another way," Jen said. "Can you arrange a visit to the scene for me? I'd really like to go."

"Sure," Allison said, "Actually, I'd like to go, too. Are you free next Sunday morning?" Jen nodded. "How about 9:00 a.m., here at the tavern?"

"Okay," Jen said, feeling pleased that Allison was interested in going along. *Maybe I can learn more about Dawson from Allison… and about the deputy.* She felt herself flush slightly and hoped that it didn't show in her face. *Why am I thinking about that? I sound like a teenager with a crush.*

"Maybe if we have time, we can visit the cabin and retrieve my maps and papers," Allison suggested. "I haven't been up there for a while and it's a nice location. This is the right time of year for a visit." Jen agreed.

They rose from the table and walked toward the front door.

Jen said, "It seems funny that your uncle didn't tell Steve about the shaft, if they were such good friends and he knew that Steve was a gold prospector."

"Who knows," Allison said facing Jen. "Uncle Ralph was secretive sometimes. Maybe they never got drunk together." She paused. "That seems doubtful." They both smiled.

After exchanging telephone numbers, Jen thanked Allison as she left. Jen looked back at the tavern as she stepped onto the sidewalk and saw Allison at the front window reversing the "Closed" sign to read "Open."

Chapter Four

By 8:00 the following Sunday morning, Jen was dressed in jeans and a plain blue button-down shirt over a white tee shirt. She had dressed Sarah in similar attire. After pulling on her hiking boots, she went into the kitchen and picked up her jacket, hat, and cell phone and retrieved their lunches and bottled water from the refrigerator. Moppet twined around her feet, looking up expectantly into Jen's face with her large golden eyes.

Jen stroked the gray head and said, "Mama already fed you."

She took her keys from their accustomed hook by the door and said to Sarah, "Sweetie, I'll get you and your blankets and wheelchair second, okay?" The child nodded in sleepy acknowledgment.

On their way out of Morrison, Jen stopped at the McDonald's drive-through window for their breakfasts. They ate in the car parked in the restaurant's parking lot. For Jen, it was easier than unloading Sarah and her wheelchair and Sarah didn't mind.

It was sunny along the foothills and all the way into Dawson. Another perfect fall morning. Jen arrived early and they sat in the empty parking lot of the Miner's Tavern waiting for Allison to arrive. It was chilly in the shadow of the Golden Nugget Casino, and Jen left Wild Bill's engine running and the heater on, to little effect.

Jen unbuckled her seat belt and leaned over the seat. "Are you warm enough?" she asked Sarah as she reached for a blanket to tuck around her daughter's thin legs. Sarah was small enough to use a child's car seat, and preferred it so that she could see out the windows. Jen snuggled the blanket around Sarah and they smiled at each other.

At 9:10, Allison pulled her four-wheel-drive pickup into the parking lot, and waved to Jen. Her full-sized truck was a burnt orange and had the inevitable cracked windshield. She pulled along side Jen's Bronco and rolled down the driver's side window. Jen did the same.

"Morning, Jen," Allison said. "Sorry I'm a bit late."

"No problem," Jen responded. "Shall I drive and you navigate?" she asked.

"Sure. I'll just park, and then we can go."

Allison parked and stepped down from her truck. Jen noticed that she was wearing a different cowgirl outfit and carrying several maps, a thermos, cups, and a lunch in a brown paper sack. Allison climbed into the Bronco and settled her armload of belongings on the seat between them.

"Who do we have here?" Allison asked as she smiled at Sarah.

Sarah returned her smile and said, "I'm Sarah Slater."

Allison introduced herself and they chatted for a moment about Sarah's age and favorite cartoon characters.

Allison turned her attention to Jen and she pulled out a map, spreading it across the dashboard.

"Here's Dawson. We'll go back toward Golden and then north to the Elbert's property."

Allison traced the route with her finger, east on Darkhorse Canyon Road, north on Foothills Road, and then west on an unmarked jeep trail.

"The climbing location is about four miles from the Foothills Road turnoff. When we're done there, we'll drive to Steve's cabin on Master's Creek. It's about twelve miles west of Dawson in the national forest. It's hard to find, but I know how to get there. We'll be back in the afternoon."

"That's fine," Jen said as she put Wild Bill in gear and drove through the parking lot to Grand Street. They passed through the town and east on Darkhorse Canyon Road.

"Coffee?" Allison asked. Jen nodded. Allison poured and they sipped in silence for several miles.

"So, the Miner's Tavern was built in 1867?" Jen asked, "and it's the original building?"

"Yeah, and it was the only clapboard structure in Dawson when it was built," Allison said with pride. "Original structures along Grand Street were false-front buildings with clapboard fronts and log-cabin sides and backs. Until the brick buildings were constructed in the 1880s, it was the best-looking place in town," Allison said.

"Your family's taken good care of the tavern. It looks so authentic. You grew up here?" Jen asked, as she drove carefully along the narrow road.

"Yeah, and when I was a kid, I was always hanging around the place. I guess I was my uncle's favorite. Since Mom had died, and I have no siblings, and Uncle Ralph was a bachelor, he left the place to me. I came back for his funeral, and decided to stay." Allison poured more coffee.

"I left Dawson after high school and went to Washington University for two years. I was married briefly and realized it wasn't for me, not with Jack, anyway. Then I trained as a paralegal and took a job with a large St. Louis law firm.

"How did you like working with attorneys?" Jen asked, sensing that Allison's personality might have conflicted with lawyer types.

"I worked with those SOBs for 10 years. Believe me, I would much rather be running a tavern in Dawson than spending another hour taking abuse from those people. They are all so egotistical. I didn't meet one that was a decent human being when it came to dealing with support personnel. An experienced paralegal always knows more than a lawyer fresh out of law school, but they have the piece of paper so they are right, no matter how wrong they are. I guess my personality isn't equipped for a life-time of that type of treatment. I'm glad to be back."

They reached the intersection between Darkhorse Canyon and Foothills Roads and turned north.

"How about you? How did you get into the news business when you're a graduate from the School of Mines?" Allison asked.

"It was a circuitous route," Jen answered, thinking briefly of her past life as a geologist and how, over the years, her desire to practice geology had not diminished much. "After the School of Mines, I worked for a mining company and explored for gold in North America. The company folded and I was unemployed for a while. I just happened to be in the right place at the right time and got a job with *The Front Range Journal* through my contacts with the Colorado Museum of Natural History. It's different, but it almost pays the bills." Jen sighed.

"Is Sarah your only child?" Allison asked.

"Yes," Jen said, adding, "I'm a single parent."

Jen didn't want to elaborate on her personal situation and hoped that Allison wouldn't press her with questions. Allison seemed to understand and they rode in silence.

"In about half a mile, we'll see the turnoff for the Elbert's property," Allison said. Jen slowed the Bronco.

"There it is, on the left," Allison said. "Turn onto the road and I'll jump out and open the gate."

Jen pulled onto the road and through the opened gate. Allison closed the gate behind the Bronco and climbed back in. Jen saw the large sign to her left that provided notice warning climbers that permission was required from the land owner. The sign gave the Elbert's telephone number. *Not the kind of sign Steve would miss.*

They slowly drove down the rutted trail and were soon surrounded by red rocks and pine trees exuding a fresh scent in the morning sun. The trail turned north and climbed in elevation. The red sandstone cliffs rose around them as they entered a dry canyon. Jen knew these rocks as the Morrison formation, characterized by distinctive red sandstone and famous for their dinosaur bones.

Through her passion for paleontology, Jen knew that Jurassic dinosaur skeletons had been recovered from the Morrison formation between 1876 and 1878, bringing worldwide fame to Colorado. Complete skeletons had been pulled from these rocks, including remains of the so-called "brontosaurus," the largest dinosaur known at that time. The spectacular discoveries had ignited a westward rush by large museums in the east to collect these fantastic fossils. The competition between eastern museums for prime fossil collecting sites had been fierce and had included shoot-outs and "claim jumping."

After almost four miles, Allison looked around at the canyon walls and instructed Jen to pull over and stop. "According to the information I got from the Elberts, we're almost there. Let's walk the rest of the way."

Jen parked and they got out. Allison moved away from the Bronco and lit a cigarette. Jen took one of Sarah's blankets and placed it in a sunny spot. She unbuckled Sarah's safety seat and lifted her daughter out of the Bronco, seating her on the blanket.

"I'll get your other blanket in case you are cold," Jen said as she returned to the Bronco to retrieve a second blanket. She draped the blanket around Sarah's shoulders and patted her back.

"I have some work to do. Can you stay here with Allison for a little bit?"

"Okay," Sarah said. "Will I see you?"

"Yes. I'm going to be working around the cliff. You can see me."

The cliff walls were about 50 feet high and looked good for climbing, but compared to other more accessible sites, this was not a prime climbing locale.

Allison sat on a large rock near Sarah. As Jen moved away, from Sarah, she heard her daughter say innocently to Allison, "Smoking is bad for you." Jen cringed until she heard Allison laugh in good humor and agree. Jen smiled to herself. She had told Sarah numerous times not to mention this to smokers, but the child persisted anyway.

Jen examined the site at the base of the western canyon wall. She went back to the Bronco and picked up a clipboard from the back seat that held her notes from the sheriff's and coroner's reports. The sheriff's report indicated where the body had been found and provided the distance from three fixed points. Jen located the points and paced off the distance from each to determine the place where the body had been. The location was among boulders that had fallen from the cliff and collected at the base.

It hadn't rained since the death, and the tracks of the rescuers and the tire marks from the rescue vehicles were still evident. Jen examined each of the boulders but couldn't decide which had been the one to crush Steve's skull. *Maybe he hadn't bled much after he'd died.*

Jen looked up the face of the cliff. She turned and walked over to Sarah and Allison. "I think I'll climb up and have a look around," she said. "When I reach the top, Sarah, you can see me. I'll wave."

"Okay."

Jen walked southward to where the cliff was shorter and was soon out of sight of Sarah and Allison. She found a spot along the cliff face that was about 20 feet high with good hand- and foot-holds. Jen started her climb. *Here I am climbing without my equipment.* She reached the top and pulled herself up onto the red rocks. She sat with her feet dangling over the cliff edge thinking, I need to spend more time at the rock climbing gym. I'm too old for this, and too out of shape. I would never have made it up the 50-foot cliff.

Jen walked the quarter mile back along the cliff edge to where she could see Sarah and Allison. Now they were sitting together on the blanket, chatting. They waved to each other. Jen saw pine trees on her left and a few bits of dried grass jutting from cracks in the red rocks. The air had begun to warm and the sun was bright. Jen looked over the edge to see the rocks where Steve had landed. She turned around and looked at the stunted trees growing in the poor soil 30 feet away from the cliff edge. She walked back to the trees and noticed the faint trace of a jeep trail winding between the trunks. *This trail isn't marked on Allison's map.*

Near the trunk of one of the pine trees, and partially hidden in the dried brown grass, she saw something rounded and gray. She walked over to it, squatted, and parted the grass. Jen saw a stream-rounded granite cobble typical of those found in Darkhorse Creek. It was about the size of a large grapefruit. *What's this doing here? A stream-rounded gray granite cobble on top of a red sandstone cliff? Someone must have brought this here, because it would never appear here naturally.*

She picked it up and turned it over. On the opposite side of the cobble, she spotted brown stains on the surface. She looked more closely, and then nearly dropped the rock. The brown stains looked like dried blood, and sticking to the stains she'd found several dark hairs. Jen's heart beat faster. *What if this is blood? and hair?*

Jen decided to save the rock. She unbuttoned the top of her long-sleeved shirt and slid the rock gently inside between her outer shirt and tee shirt to rest above her belt. She retraced her steps to the point where she had climbed up and began her descent. As Jen neared the bottom, she lost her footing and slipped the last five feet, landing on her right side. Fortunately, there were no boulders here, and she landed on dried grass and leaves. The cobble, however, had slid around and bruised her ribs when she landed. It hurt. *I wonder if I broke my ribs. Steve would say it serves me right for climbing without proper equipment.* She deciding to check for the suspicious bruises of a broken rib later. She shifted the rock to the front of her shirt and hurried back toward the Bronco, wincing with each breath.

Allison stood up and waved as Jen approached the Bronco. "Find anything?" she asked Jen.

"Maybe," Jen answered. She and Allison converged at the Bronco leaving Sarah sitting on her blanket in the sun. Jen unbuttoned her shirt and pulled the rock out.

"A rock?" Allison said with amusement.

"Yes. I found it at the top of the cliff."

"I see rocks like this every day in Darkhorse Creek," Allison said. "It's common."

"Common for Darkhorse Creek, but totally out of place on top of a red sandstone cliff."

"Well, somebody must have carried it up there."

"I think so, too. And look at these brown stains," Jen said as she turned the rock over in the sunlight. "I wonder if they're blood. And there are hairs," she said as she looked closely, frowning. "Well, there *were* hairs."

"I see the brown stains, but no hairs."

"Ohh…" Jen groaned with disappointment. "I guess they rubbed off when I climbed down the cliff." She didn't mention her fall.

"Maybe they are still inside my shirt," Jen suggest as she carefully unbuttoned her outer shirt.

Sarah sat watching Jen slowing removing her shirt and asked with a mix of curiosity and alarm, "Mama, what are you doing?"

"It's okay, sweetie," Jen answered reassuringly. "We're just looking for something lost in my shirt."

Together, Jen and Allison inspected the tee shirt and outer shirt for signs of the hair, but found nothing.

"Let's keep the rock, anyway," Allison said. "Maybe we can show it to the sheriff, or something. We can save it in my lunch sack."

Allison emptied the contents of the sack onto the car seat and Jen placed the rock inside the paper bag. She slid it under the front seat. Jen was disappointed—she was sure that she'd seen hairs stuck on the brown stains.

"Well," she said, "it'll have to do. At least we found something that may be helpful."

Jen drove back toward Dawson and they stopped in the picnic ground just west of Darkhorse. They sat at a picnic table eating their lunches and drinking water.

When they had finished eating, Jen carried Sarah around the grounds, helping her collect pine cones and bird feathers from camp-robber jays for her nature collection. Jen thought the picnic ground was beautiful this time of year, with the aspens still in their prime and the evergreens surrounding the picnic tables.

They drove through Dawson and west into the Roosevelt National Forest. The paved road gave way to a gravel road and eventually a one-lane jeep trail. They made so many turns that Jen doubted she could find her way out alone—or that anyone else could find their way in—but others obviously had. As they approached Steve's home, they saw the yellow plastic tape around the cabin that said "Police Line" in black letters.

"Looks like the sheriff's been here," Allison said as they climbed out of the Bronco. "They must be waiting for Steve's next of kin to come and clear the place out." She stooped to pass under the tape.

"Think we should cross the police line and go inside?" Jen asked, waiting by the Bronco.

"Sure. Anyway, I have a key."

Jen told Sarah she'd be back in a minute and followed Allison to the door where she stood looking through her set of keys. The old log cabin was small and had a stone chimney on one wall standing high above the pitched roof. She doubted that the cabin had more than one or two rooms. The small windows were shuttered, and there were no electric lines running to the cabin. There was an old outhouse downslope and to the rear. Upslope from the cabin was a well house and a hand pump.

Hmm, primitive, but inexpensive. Looks just like the kind of place I would expect for Steve.

"It'll be dark in here, Jen. Can you go around the cabin and open the shutters, please?" Allison asked, as she found and inserted the correct key.

Jen found herself wondering about Allisons and Steve's friendship again. *Why does she have a key? And why ask me to open the shutters? Perhaps Allison wants a moment alone in the cabin.*

Jen chastised herself for her curiosity and her unusually romantic thoughts as she found and opened the shutters covering five small windows. At the rear of the cabin, she discovered an attached lean-to that was not visible from the front.

When Jen came back around, the door was open and Allison was inside. Jen slipped under the police-line tape and stepped through the door into a homey cabin. Everything was neat in Steve's small home. The dishes were washed and sitting in the dish rack by the sink, the cupboards were closed, the chairs under the table, and the books standing neatly on the shelves. The rugs and wood floors were swept clean and the ash was removed from the fireplace.

"Looks like a tidy home," Jen observed.

"Yes, Steve liked it tidy. He lived here three seasons out of the year. In the winter, the snow was too much for him to drive. Sometimes he would come in on snowshoes, but usually he stayed with friends during the winter."

"What's in the back?" Jen asked as she moved toward the curtain covering the entrance to the lean-to area of the cabin.

"Steve had his cot and desk in there."

Jen pulled back the curtain and saw a neatly made cot, a night table with a coal oil lamp, and a desk cluttered with papers, maps, and cross sections.

Looking over Jen's shoulder, Allison said, "Oh, here are my uncle's papers."

They stepped into the room and Jen asked, "May I have a look?"

"Sure."

Jen sat at the desk and started to examine the maps and cross section Steve had drawn of the properties. She saw his sampling locations marked on the maps and looked through the papers on the desk until she found the assay results. *With results like these, no wonder Steve was excited.*

"I don't suppose we can take them, can we?" she asked Allison.

"I think it would be okay to take Uncle Ralph's historical papers," Allison said, adding thoughtfully, "but maybe we'd better leave Steve's stuff here. I probably need the family's permission before I take anything else. Besides, I don't know if the sheriff's department made a detailed inventory or not. We don't want them to suspect that someone crossed their precious police line without their okay."

"Well, I would like to study this material in a little more detail. I have one of Sarah's disposable cameras out in the Bronco. Do you mind if I photograph these papers?"

"No. Let me help you."

"Great. Why don't you put your uncle's papers into the Bronco and we'll take the rest of the stuff outside for better lighting. I don't have a flash on the camera."

They gathered the remaining papers, maps, cross sections, assay reports, and other related documents, including Steve's field notebook, and laid everything out flat on the drive. With her permission, Jen used Sarah's small camera to photograph the documents. She couldn't photograph every page of Steve's field notebook, so she selected several pages that seemed pertinent. They returned the documents to the cabin and laid them back on the desk as they'd found them.

On the drive back to Dawson, Jen checked on Sarah in the rear view mirror and saw that she was asleep. She asked Allison, "Do you think Steve's death was really an accident?"

"Seems hard to believe, don't you think?" Allison said.

"Yes. You said that he had trouble with the casino owner? What do you know about him?"

Allison grimaced. "He's a slimeball from Chicago. The current rumor is that he's Mafia. Although why the Mafia would be interested in limited stakes gambling in Dawson, Colorado, is beyond me. Maybe they expect to expand into other related 'businesses,' or maybe they need a cover to launder money."

"What's his name again?"

"Tony Delano. He's about 40, 42. Somewhere in there. Unmarried. Average height. On the heavy side—maybe 200 pounds. Tony wears black suits and shiny, patent leather shoes, to match his hair, I guess. I thought that look went out with the 1950s. He dresses as though the arrival of the Godfather is imminent. He has brown eyes, a round face, and must need to shave three times a day. He takes himself seriously and expects everyone else to do the same." Jen smiled as she imagined such a comical figure strutting around Dawson.

"You'd spot him a mile away—he really stands out. He hates mountain sports and drives his enormous black limo around town, which is silly because you can walk everywhere. Maybe he wants to impress the gamblers, or something. The locals don't like him and make fun of him when he isn't looking. Everyone except Barbara Knowles, that is. She can hardly wait to march Tony down the aisle. Fat chance. He can't stand her, but he's charming enough to her face. I guess he recognizes the advantages of connections with government officials, even small-time county clerks."

"How come you know so much about Tony?" Jen asked.

"It's a small town," Allison said, "you find out all the dirt when you don't like someone. Anyway, he comes into the tavern to chat. He's definitely an extrovert. Tony thinks I'm interesting—a virtual urbanite because I at least lived in St. Louis for 10 years. In his view, everyone else in town is hopelessly unsophisticated. He also wants to buy the tavern, tear it down, and put in a high-rise parking garage. I'm holding out, but he still makes the offer from time to time."

"How would you sum him up?" Jen asked.

"Smooth. Persistent. Good manager. Ruthless. I expect him to knock me off and buy the tavern at an estate sale," she joked. "I know that his goal is to have the most lucrative gambling business possible, so that he can be promoted to Las Vegas ASAP. He thinks his assignment to Dawson is banishment from mainstream operations. He's anxious to make things look good."

Jen thought for a while as she drove down from Steve's isolated cabin. They were already to a gravel road and would soon be on pavement and into town.

"Do you think that Steve and Tony might have had an argument over the gold prospects underlying your properties?" Jen asked.

"Seems like a good possibility. If Steve's death wasn't an accident, I'd bet Tony had something to do with it. Especially since we found a blood-stained rock at the climbing site. Maybe the 'accident' was planned."

Jen said, "Let's not jump to conclusions." She was quiet. "I need to think for a few minutes."

They drove in silence until Jen asked, "From what you know of Tony personally, do you think he is capable of murder?"

"Yes. He's Mafia, isn't he?" Allison asked.

"That's a rumor," Jen replied.

"Well, his name sounds Italian to me."

"That's circumstantial," Jen replied.

"Okay. What do we really know that would link him with Steve's death?" Allison asked. "Only that he was upset over the thought of tearing down the casino for a gold mining operation. Would that make you want to kill someone?"

"Maybe, if I was ruthless and thought it would ruin my career if I didn't," Jen replied.

Jen pulled into the tavern's parking lot.

"What do we do next?" Allison asked. "What about the bloody rock?"

"I need to think it over before I call the sheriff. Are you interested in pursuing an investigation?" Jen asked.

"Definitely. Steve was my friend and I think the circumstances of his death are suspicious. Of course, I also want to save the tavern from mutating into a parking structure. In fact, I'd love to turn the tables on Tony and tear down the casino to open a gold mine."

"Okay," Jen said. "I need to think on it a bit. How about if I call you tomorrow? I have your number."

Allison agreed, and Jen thanked her again for her help. As she drove home, she mulled over what she had learned and considered the next possible steps.

❀   ❀   ❀

Sunday evening, after Sarah was in bed, Jen called Allison at the tavern. "Hi," she said when Allison answered the phone, "it's Jen." They chatted for a minute and Jen asked, "Can you talk now? I have some thoughts I want to share with you."

Allison said, "Sure, I'm in my office, and I have some thoughts for you, too. You first."

"What would you think about helping me look into Tony Delano's business dealings and personal life? I think I can conduct an investigation of his business activities from Denver as part of my job assignment."

"And I can certainly find out more about him on a personal level," Allison added.

"You wouldn't mind? It could be dangerous, especially if he really is Mafia. I wouldn't want to involve you if you're not comfortable with the idea."

"Not at all. I owe it to Steve. Besides, I'd welcome any opportunity that might lead to the demolition of the casino. It'll be easy for me to find out about Tony's personal life. All I have to do is encourage his interest in me a little bit and mention that I want to discuss the parking garage idea."

"Okay," said Jen, "but just be careful. We had better find another meeting place. If he's so snoopy, he's sure to find out that I've been there and that I'm a reporter. Why don't we meet in Darkhorse from now on?"

"Good idea," Allison said. "There's a cafe on the main street that should be convenient. Or somewhere in Golden. We can call each other later in the week. What did you decide to do with that rock you found on the Elbert's property? Are you going to give it to the sheriff's department? Do you think they'll take it seriously as a potential murder weapon?"

Jen sighed, "I don't know what they'll think. I'll see how things go during my investigation this week. I can always call Deputy Manydeeds. He seemed helpful."

"He's a good man. I'll talk to you later."

Jen agreed and hung up, thinking that it would be nice to have another reason to call Charlie.

Chapter Five

On Monday morning, after arriving at her office, Jen sketched out a plan for her investigation. She decided to contact the Colorado Division of Gaming to learn what she could about the casinos operating in Monarch County, with an emphasis on the Golden Nugget and manager Tony Delano. Jen reached for her telephone book, found the number, and dialed. She asked for the person in charge of Monarch County casinos.

"Mr. Fred Gray speaking," greeted her. She could hear his pompous tone from four spoken words and wondered how helpful he would be.

Jen explained who she was and what she wanted. Mr. Gray agreed to meet with her on Tuesday at 11:30 a.m. at his office on Colfax and Lincoln. After she hung up she realized that she should have insisted on a different time. She suspected that Mr. Gray would spend about 30 minutes with her and plead a pressing luncheon engagement, asking her to return on another day. She suspected she would leave his office with her questions unanswered.

Knowing that parking around the state capital would be a challenge, Jen decided to walk to her Tuesday morning appointment with Mr. Gray. She entered the dreary state offices and rode the elevator to the seventh floor. Jen entered the offices of the Colorado Division of Gaming and asked the receptionist for Mr. Gray. She waited in the reception area for 10 minutes before Mr. Gray entered to greet her. He offered his hand without smiling and shook in a curt manner dropping Jen's hand abruptly.

Jen followed Mr. Gray to his office. He was tall and muscular with brown hair and blue eyes. He walked quickly, as though each minute were valuable.

"Please, have a chair," he said to Jen as they entered his office and he seated himself behind the desk.

Instead of sitting right away, Jen walked to the wall opposite his desk to admire a series of photographs showing Mr. Gray with Beechcraft[a] and Piper Cub[a] airplanes. Other photographs showed him skydiving.

"Nice aircraft," Jen commented, hoping to thaw Mr. Gray. "Are they yours?"

"Yes. How can I help you?" he asked.

Jen, seeing that Mr. Gray would be all business, sat across the desk from him and explained again the nature of her assignment to investigate Monarch County casinos, with a particular interest in the Golden Nugget.

Mr. Gray frowned briefly.

"Do you know Tony Delano?" Jen asked.

"Delano? Hmmm…" Gray rubbed his chin and narrowed his eyes slightly. "Yes," he said.

"The division issues licenses, doesn't it?" Jen asked.

"Yes."

Jen paused waiting for an explanation of the types of licenses. She realized he would offer as little as possible and she would have to ask direct questions.

"Can you tell me about the types of licenses?"

Mr. Gray pulled a state publication from his orderly bookshelf.

"It's all explained in this book," he said dropping the document on the desk as he sat back in his chair.

Jen looked him in the eye, smiled, and reached across the desk to pick up the book. *I won't let him intimidate me.*

"Thank you. I'll be sure to study this. Which licenses have been issued to the Golden Nugget?"

Mr. Gray stared out of his window. Sighing at Jen's persistence, he reached his file drawer and lifted a manila folder onto his desk.

"The state has issued two licenses to Mr. Delano," Mr. Gray said as he quickly located the documents. "The first is a Retail License that permits him to conduct limited gaming on the premises. The second is called a Key Employee License, which is issued to a person responsible for making management or policy decisions in a gaming establishment."

"I see," Jen said. "Do you monitor the recipient after the license is issued?"

"Yes."

"What do you monitor the recipient for?" Jen asked patiently.

"For such problems as hidden ownership interests and organized crime involvement. Everything's in order. So far, Mr. Delano is clean," he said as he shuffled through the file contents. Jen saw records such as investigations, licenses, and monitoring reports flash by as Mr. Gray rearranged the material in the file without offering her any of the documents to examine.

"Does the division conduct a background investigation before issuing a license?" Jen asked.

"Yes."

"Who did the investigation for Delano?"

"I did."

"How did you go about the investigation?"

Mr. Gray sighed again. "I scrutinized his personal and financial history and the sources of money for investment in the casino. I was able to certify that Mr. Delano has no record of having committed such crimes as felonies, fraud, and gambling-related offenses; and that he has no known ties to organized crime."

"May I have copies of your records?" Jen asked.

"Of course. They're public records. You'll have to see my secretary for the details on requesting public records." Gray checked his watch and said, "I'm sure she's gone to lunch and won't return before 1:00."

Jen knew that he could provide photocopies now if he wanted to, and suggested, "Since she's gone, maybe you could help me out by making copies for me while I'm here." She smiled again.

Gray checked his watch and said, "I'm sorry, I won't have time today. In fact, I'm late for a luncheon meeting." He rose and reached for his jacket, saying, "Thanks for coming by, Ms., ah…?"

"Slater," Jen finished his sentence for him and rose from her chair, thanking him for his time as he ushered her out the door and into the hall by the elevator. *I'm not ready to leave just yet. Why am I letting this guy herd me out of the building.*

"Thanks again," she said. "Can you tell me where the restroom is?"

"Down the hall on the left," he answered as the elevator door opened and he stepped inside.

Jen started down the hall toward the restroom and reversed course as soon at the elevator door closed. She walked back into the reception area, smiled to the receptionist, and introduced herself to the young woman seated at the desk.

"Can you tell me if there's a gaming division office in Monarch County?"

"Yes," the receptionist said. "There's an office in Dawson to monitor gambling operations for the state."

"Is it a big office?" Jen asked.

The receptionist nodded, saying, "They have a staff of 10 investigators, auditors, accountants, administrators, and support people."

"I was just in to see Mr. Gray," Jen said. "How long has he been with the gaming division?"

"Since it opened in 1991," she said.

"Do you know what he did before that?" Jen asked.

"I think he was a pilot for law enforcement with the state, or something like that. I don't really know," she said with a smile.

Jen leaned against the counter and said, "I was hoping to get copies of records for the Golden Nugget Casino and other gambling operations in Monarch County. How do I make that request?"

"Well, you just ask me," she answered pleasantly. "When do you need them?"

"Would you be able to send them over this afternoon?" Jen asked hopefully, sweeping her loose hair behind her ear.

"I think so," she said smiling, "seeing as how *The Front Range Journal* is my favorite newspaper."

"Great," Jen said with a smile. She handed her business card to the receptionist and gave her instructions for sending the information via courier. "You've been helpful."

Jen walked back to her office, thinking about her conversation with Mr. Gray. She wondered absently how a state employee could afford to own and maintain two small aircraft on a state salary. *Well, maybe he has a rich spouse or companion.*

While Jen waited for the information to arrive from the gaming division, she called the Dawson mayor's office and the Monarch County sheriff's department to see if there was any interest in re-opening the investigation into Steve's death. She received negative replies from both offices.

Later that afternoon, a thick package of documents arrived from the gaming division, as promised. She began to study the information and learned a great deal about the distribution of gambling revenues.

✳   ✳   ✳

On Wednesday morning, Jen called Allison to tell her that, according to the gaming division investigation, Tony was unaffiliated with organized crime.

"You're sure about the Mafia business?" Allison asked. "I can't believe that Tony isn't Mafia. Maybe someone at the division is covering for him," Allison said with interest.

"It's possible, but we don't have any supporting evidence at this point," Jen said. "I also touched base with the mayor's office."

"Did you talk to him about investigating Steve's death?" Allison asked.

"Yes. I mentioned it and he blew me off. He isn't the least bit interested in Steve's case. As far as he's concerned, the case is closed, and he can't be bothered because he has too many other obligations to manage." Jen felt a touch of frustration. "He told me to contact the sheriff's department."

"I imagine he has more than he can handle, considering how fast Dawson has grown in the last two years," Allison offered.

"I think he must appreciate the growth in revenues generated by gambling," Jen said arranging her notes. "Listen to this—after operating expenses are paid for the gaming division, part of the money left in the Limited Gaming Fund is distributed to the county and town. In 1993, Monarch County received $2.7 million and Dawson received $1.1 million."

"Sounds like a cash cow to me. I can see why the town officials have an interest in supporting the casinos."

"Yes, but considering the gross revenues, the town isn't making that much. Here's another one for you—gross revenues generated by Dawson's casinos on a monthly basis started at $8 million during the first month of operation in 1991. By August of 1993, the amount was over $25 million. It's a cash cow for Tony and his 'investors,' too."

"I bet he'll protect his precious cash cow, come hell or high water," Allison said, and added, "or an enthusiastic prospector. So what did the sheriff say about investigating Steve's death?"

Jen placed her notes in a manila folder. "Sheriff Beamer was curt and basically said the same thing—case closed. He has no reason to suspect foul play and is badly understaffed. His priority is managing parking in town. He stopped short of telling me to mind my own business." Jen had felt that he had been rather curt with her on the phone and wondered why.

"That sounds like Beamer," Allison said with a sigh. "Did you tell the sheriff about the bloody rock?"

"No. He didn't seem very receptive. I'll call Deputy Manydeeds later to see if he might be interested. How 'bout you? Have a chance to talk with Tony yet?"

"He was over at the tavern for his usual Tuesday night beer, sitting at his favorite intimate bar stool, and dressed in his goofy black suit. You know, he would fit in much better if he'd wear jeans and cowboy boots."

"What a charmer," Jen said in a teasing tone.

"Oh, he is, let me tell you. I suggested that we sit somewhere more comfortable, meaning my favorite booth, and his response was, 'My place or yours?' Slimeball. He told me that he misses Chicago but says he can't go back—the only way out of our 'little hick town in the sticks' is a transfer to Las Vegas."

Or maybe via the morgue.

"What if he got into trouble in Chicago and they sent him to the Golden Nugget to redeem himself," Jen suggested. "I suppose that he has an incentive to succeed with the casino. That might motivate him to preserve the building. Maybe that's why he doesn't like the thought of mining on the property."

"Could be. I told him that I sometimes thought of leaving. You should have seen the avarice light up in his eyes," Allison said with amusement. "Suddenly, he was no longer interested in me, but wanted to know what would happen to the tavern."

"What'd you say?" Jen asked with curiosity.

"Oh, I was non-committal and said I was still in the 'thinking' stage. Well, he invited me to think about it over dinner, so we have a dinner date for Thursday night."

"I bet you can hardly wait," Jen said.

"Considering how many times he's asked me out for dinner, I think he was shocked when I accepted. He's so macho," Allison complained, "he just tells me that he'll pick me up at 6:00 at my place and to dress formally. I didn't have any choice in the matter!"

"Think of it as an exercise in the search for truth," Jen said teasingly. "Besides, think of Steve," she said more seriously. "Anything we learn has the potential for helping us determine what happened. Even information that seems unrelated might be important."

"True," Allison agreed. "Anyway, if you want, we can meet on Friday afternoon and I can give you the gory details of my date."

"Okay," Jen agreed. "Where?"

"How about the Mexican restaurant in Golden on 6ᵗʰ Avenue before you get to the School of Mines? Then you won't have to drive so far to get home." Jen agreed to meet Allison at 5:00 and, with the arrangements complete, they finished their conversation.

❋ ❋ ❋

On Friday afternoon, Jen left her office about 4:15 and drove to Golden. Allison was waiting for her inside the restaurant.

"I see you survived your date," Jen said as she sat down in the booth across from Allison. A basket of chips and freshly made salsa sat on the red linoleum table top.

"Yeah," Allison said. "I was out late, though."

A waiter took their orders for coffee.

"Did you find formal attire that met Tony's expectations?" Jen asked as she took her jacket off and laid it on the seat beside her.

"Oh, yes. When I worked with the law firm, I always needed formal wear. I kept my dresses as souvenirs. I even have a mink coat, given to me by my ex-husband. I doubt Tony expected a black sequined cocktail dress and a full-length mink." Allison smiled as she recollected the look on Tony's face.

"I'm sure he was impressed," Jen said lightly as their coffee arrived.

After the waiter left, Allison leaned toward Jen and said, "You should have seen him stare. I thought his eyes were going to pop out. At least he showed up with a dozen red roses—long-stemmed and boxed."

"That was thoughtful," Jen said, reaching for a chip.

"I accepted them with grace, of course, and asked him to sit on the sofa while I went to the kitchen to put them in water. He gave my sofa a real look of disdain and followed my into the kitchen. He's so obnoxious. And guess what he wore?" she asked Jen.

"Hmm, black suit, white shirt, patent leather shoes, and matching hair?" Jen answered.

"Right, but he changed from a red to a maroon tie, to match his car."

"I thought he had a black limo?" Jen said.

"Surprise! He has a second car," Allison said sipping her coffee. "I live on the north side of Dawson at the edge of the national forest. The road and driveway are unpaved. I wondered how he would maneuver that monster limo up there. However, he came in a more modest-size car—a Porsche." Allison smiled at Jen's surprise.

"That's smaller, all right," Jen agreed, enjoying Allison's story.

"He really loves his car. Pampers it. I said I hadn't seen it before and he told me that he had it brought down from Chicago last month. He parks it in an underground parking garage at the casino. I didn't even know that they had underground parking there."

"I wonder what else they have we don't know about," Jen commented taking several more chips.

"He told me that he has a private, enclosed parking area he reaches through the delivery ramp on the north side of the building. That must be where the limo parks when he isn't congesting the streets with it," Allison said, amused. "Actually, I've never seen the limo parked on the street.

"Tony also told me that he has a nice set up. He said, 'I can drive down the ramp and open my garage door, park, and take a private elevator right to my office and living quarters on the top floor. Nobody sees me or my guests.' Then he offered to show it to me after dinner in a suggestive sort of way."

"Did you accept?" Jen asked, wondering if Allison really had a secret interest in Tony.

"I suggested some other time and then distracted him, asking about his Porsche. You should have seen him swell with pride. He spent the rest of the trip to Denver bragging about his car, how much it cost to own and operate, its prowess. He even revealed the history of all the fine automobiles he'd owned over the years."

"Where'd you go for dinner?" Jen asked, thinking of food.

"We went to the Colorado Country Club."

"Sounds expensive. Is he a member?" Jen asked.

"Apparently, so. He drove right up to the colonnaded entrance and greeted the valet by name."

"How did he come by a membership there? That place has a waiting list a mile long, outrageous fees, and a grueling approval procedure," Jen said as she sipped her coffee and tried to ignore the basket of chips.

"I don't know," Allison said, "but there we were."

Jen thought Allison sounded more impressed with the experience than she really wanted to be.

"What was it like?" Jen asked, curious. She'd driven past the wrought iron gates and flower beds many times, but had never been inside the grounds or buildings.

"Fabulous. The dining room overlooks the golf course and we were seated by the maitre d', who kept calling Tony, 'Monsieur Delano.' 'Right this way, Monsieur Delano,'" she mimicked in a snotty French accent, "'I have the seat you requested tonight, Monsieur Delano.'" Jen and Allison laughed.

"Actually, the dining room was very romantic. The only disappointment was the company," Allison said with a sigh. "There was soft piano music coming from the bar. The room was lit by chandeliers. The tables were formally set, with fancy gold-tone flatware, fresh flowers, and candles."

"How was the food?" Jen asked, wishing she could have been there for a sample, but settling for more chips instead.

"Terrific, even though Tony's macho act required that he order everything. He didn't even let me see the menu. He said he already knew what was the best and he wanted 'nothing but the best' for me. The food and wine were so good, though, that I almost forgave his annoying behavior."

"What did he order?" Jen asked.

"We had cocktails, hors d 'oeuvres, wine, veal piccata, dessert, and gourmet coffee. When I complimented Tony on his choices, he was visibly pleased and proceeded to talk extensively about his commitment to fine dining and excellent wines. What a bore."

Jen, trying not to imagine the meal's rich aroma, said, "You must have been there for hours. What time did you leave?"

"We left after 9:00, but not until Tony talked more about himself and his family."

"Did he say anything interesting?" Jen asked with curiosity.

"His father is now in his late seventies, but was a well-to-do business man who'd been in the Chicago area since the mid-1940s. He has a close-knit, extended Catholic family and he is the youngest of three brothers."

"Any sisters?" Jen asked.

"He didn't mention any. He did speak rather unflatteringly about his brothers, though. Said that his brothers had been given better opportunities than he had and that they were operating more lucrative businesses in the Chicago area."

"Sounds like sibling rivalry. Maybe that's why he had to leave Chicago," Jen suggested, wondering if she should order dinner.

"One time at the tavern, he did mention that he had worked for one of his uncles in Chicago, but was asked to leave because of a 'personality difference' with his cousin, who was also involved in the same business."

"Did he say what the business was?" Jen asked.

"He was vague on that point. I don't even have a clue, except that it is some kind of business where he could apply his degree in business administration. He told me he finished his degree in 1971 at the University of Chicago."

"So, what did you do after dinner?" Jen asked.

"When we were waiting for the valet to drive the Porsche around, Tony asked if I'd like to hear some live music. Well, actually, he didn't ask. He just stated that we were going to listen to live jazz. More like an order. Good thing I like jazz," Allison said, adding in a humorous tone, "Actually, I didn't mind staying in Denver a little later, because I thought it would be easier to get rid of Tony once we got back to town."

"Where'd you go for jazz?" Jen asked, wanting all the details.

"We went to LoDo, near Coors Field. He took me to the Cambridge Club on Wynkoop Street. A blues band was playing and the place was packed. He asked if I minded whether he smoked a cigar. I said, no, and asked if *he* minded if I smoked a cigarette. From the look on his face, you'd have thought I'd offered him poison."

"Does his double standard surprise you?" Jen asked raising her eyebrows with a look of mock disdain.

"No," Allison answered, sipping her coffee. "After that, he ordered two brandies for us, without even asking me what I'd like. We listened to the music for a while and then he leaned over and asked me an unexpected question. A disturbing question," Allison said with a note of concern in her voice.

Jen leaned forward, resting her elbows on the table. "What?"

"He said, 'Who's your blondy-haired friend that drives the old white Bronco?' I tried to act like I didn't know what he was talking about. He told me that he saw us drive off in the white Bronco last Saturday morning. I can't believe he's been spying on me though his windows at the casino," Allison exclaimed. "I was angry, but tried to be casual. I said that you were an old friend from college visiting from Aurora and that we were going shopping in Boulder."

"Did he believe you?" Jen asked hopefully.

"No. Instead he wanted to know why we didn't just meet in Boulder, or somewhere half-way between Aurora and Dawson. I said that my truck was acting up and that my friend came to pick me up. He puffed on his cigar for a while and said, 'I thought she might be that reporter, Jen Slater, from *The Front Range Journal*.'"

Jen groaned and covered her eyes with her palms, thinking. Allison paused and Jen said, "If he can see your parking lot, maybe he could see my license plate number." She paused again, uncovering her eyes and resting her chin in her right hand. "Or maybe he was in contact with Fred Gray at the gaming division. Okay, so now maybe he knows that I'm investigating his business relationships. He still doesn't know about our interest in Steve's death and our suspicion regarding his possible complicity. Maybe he'll just focus on the financial aspect, and not connect our other activities with Steve's death."

"Maybe," Allison said, but she wasn't reassuring.

"Anything else happen Thursday night?" Jen asked as she pulled her hair behind her left ear.

"He invited me to visit his quarters again, for a night cap. I declined and I could tell he was irritated with me. Instead, I asked him to drop me off at the tavern, so that I wouldn't have to take him back to my place."

"Smart move," Jen said with approval.

"Yeah, he's like fly paper and I was afraid I couldn't get rid of him any other way. When we arrived at the tavern, I let myself out of the car and I thought he was going to break an ankle trying to get to my car door before I could escape. I made it safely inside the tavern and took off my fur coat. It's big and bunchy and I held it in my arms, so that he couldn't reach me."

"Another good move," Jen said with appreciation, "I'll have to remember that one." She added silently to herself, *if I ever have another date, desirable or otherwise.*

"I know the town will be abuzz with gossip today. Half a dozen of the regulars saw us come in," Allison said with a shrug. "Tony was really irritated with me, so I gushed what a fabulous time I had had and he seemed to relax some. Then, to make him feel better, I mentioned that we hadn't discussed any business yet and suggested that I contact him soon. He looked happier and agreed."

"Well, good job," Jen said with a smile.

"Yeah, except that he knows who you are."

"Oh, well. We'll just keep picking away until we find what we're after," Jen said.

Jen thanked Allison for her help and promised to keep in touch before she left for Morrison still wishing that she had ordered dinner.

Chapter Six

Jen was at home on Saturday morning and had time to call Deputy Manydeeds. She phoned the station in Dawson and asked for Charlie. He answered and she introduced herself. He was friendly and said he remembered her. Jen heard warmth in his voice.

"Charlie," Jen said, "I may have something relevant to Steve Myerhoff's death. Is there some time that we can discuss it? Since I spoke to Sheriff Beamer earlier in the week, and he considers the case closed, I didn't want to come the department to talk. Can we meet?"

"Sure," Charlie said. "Is there somewhere near your home that's convenient?"

"Yes. Do you know were Red Rocks Amphitheater is at Red Rocks State Park?" Jen asked.

"Yes. Are you free tomorrow?"

"Say 11:00 in the morning in the parking area overlooking the amphitheater?"

"I'll see you there," Charlie said.

❋ ❋ ❋

It wasn't really a date, it was business, but Jen felt a gleam of excitement as she loaded Sarah into the Bronco on Sunday morning. It's a nice day, she thought, and Sarah will enjoy the ride. Besides, it was Kaari's day off and Jen didn't like to impose on that if she could avoid it.

Jen drove north on Foothills Road and west into the entrance to Red Rocks State Park. She followed the signs to the famous outdoor amphitheater, constructed in 1939 with seating for 10,000. Jen liked this parking lot because the west side was flanked by red cliffs of the 300 million-year old Fountain formation deposited on top of the Precambrian Idaho Springs formation that was between 1.5 and 2 billion years old. This time gap always impressed Jen. She could walk up to the rocks and lay her hand on the contact between the older gneiss and the much younger sandstone, knowing that a billion years of the geologic record was absent.

The Bronco climbed the gravel road up to the parking area overlooking the amphitheater. As she entered the parking lot, Jen saw Charlie leaning on the front of a black jeep. The jeep's hard top had been removed and she saw the roll bar and worn seats. His arms were crossed and he was looking out over the amphitheater to the east where he could see downtown Denver and the high plains of eastern Colorado in the distance. It was a clear, sunny morning and the visibility from Red Rocks Park was 100 miles.

Except for the jeep and Bronco, the parking area was empty. Jen parked Wild Bill on the opposite end of the area because she didn't want Sarah to overhear their conversation.

"I'll only be a minute, sweetie," she said to Sarah, "Let's roll down your window."

"I can do it, Mama," she said confidently, as Jen got out and pulled the paper bag containing the cobble from under her seat.

"Okay."

As Jen walked toward Charlie, she noticed his trim, broad-shouldered figure. *He looks strong and must weigh about 180 pounds—not at all like tall, skinny Greg.* Charlie wore fairly new jeans, a belt with a large buckle, cowboy boots, and a blue and green checked shirt, open at the neck.

Charlie noticed that Jen walked in a business-like manner and had small feet. She wore jeans and a gray sweatshirt, pulled up at the sleeves. Today she was hatless and he saw her squint slightly with the late morning sun in her eyes.

Charlie removed his aviator-style sunglasses as she approached. The breeze gently touched his black hair and brushed it across his forehead. She smiled at him and could see the smile in his eyes. They greeted each other.

"Last weekend I went with Allison Henry to the scene of Steve Myerhoff's death," she said. "I climbed the cliff and took a look around. I found something hidden in the grass that may have a bearing on his death."

Charlie nodded for her to continue. Jen lifted the paper sack onto the hood of the jeep.

"I hope you don't think this is silly, but I found a rock at the top of the cliff that doesn't belong there. It's a stream-rounded cobble of gray granite. That's out of place on top of a red sandstone cliff. This rock is typical of those found in Darkhorse Creek."

"Maybe someone put it there intentionally," Charlie suggested.

He doesn't seem to think this is silly so far, Jen thought, relaxing slightly. Jen pulled the cobble from the paper sack, flattened the sack, and placed the rock on top.

"That's what I think, too. When I picked this up and turned it over, I saw these brownish stains on the side," she rotated the cobble for Charlie to see. He leaned on the hood and looked carefully at the rock.

"Initially, I saw several small dark hairs attached to the stain. Unfortunately, they rubbed off during my climb down from the top of the cliff." She didn't mention the fall or the bruised ribs. "Do you think these might be blood stains?"

"Possibly," Charlie answered. "If I may have this, I can send it to the state crime lab for testing."

"Oh, certainly," Jen replied. "It might be important." She paused. "Another thing I noticed was that there was no blood at the base of the cliff where Steve landed after his fall, and I thought that was curious. Surely, he would have bled some, don't you think? Head wounds usually bleed like crazy. I wonder if the head injury occurred elsewhere?" and I wonder, she silently added, whether the body was dropped from the cliff by the murderer.

"Hard to say," Charlie said noncommittally as he rewrapped the cobble in the sack and placed it on the front seat of the jeep.

Jen thought, he doesn't seem very interested in the rock. Maybe law enforcement has trained him to adopt a neutral attitude. Or maybe he is just naturally low-key or controls his expression. After all, he only smiles with his eyes. Maybe he is more interested than he lets on.

"I have a friend at the state crime lab who owes me a couple of favors and I'll send it to him to determine if the stains are human blood. Sheriff Beamer's made it clear he considers the case to be closed and that, in his opinion, there is no evidence of foul play. That means that I have no official role in any further investigation."

"Oh," Jen said, feeling disappointed and knowing it probably showed in her face. Everything did. "I don't want you to get into trouble over this, especially since the sheriff doesn't want you to be involved."

Charlie was unconcerned. "I'll be glad to help you out, if I can."

"I'm disappointed that the sheriff doesn't want to discuss the case further."

"Sheriff Beamer is run ragged right now trying to cope with tourists and traffic with a small staff. In his view, everything is in order and he can't spare staff for an investigation."

"Well, thanks for driving down today," Jen said, "I appreciate it."

"No problem. They do give me a day off occasionally," he said as his eyes sparkled. "It's a beautiful day for a drive."

"I better get back to my daughter," Jen said as she turned toward the Bronco. She and Charlie walked across the parking area toward Wild Bill.

"Would you and your daughter like to go for a walk?" Charlie asked spontaneously.

Jen stopped some distance from the Bronco and turned so that Sarah wouldn't hear her. She smiled and gently shook her head, saying, "I'd love to, but my daughter is wheelchair-bound and there are no paved paths at Red Rocks. Thank you for asking."

"Perhaps some other time, then?" he asked.

"Yes, that would be nice," she answered as they continued toward the Bronco, reaching Sarah's window.

"Sarah, this is Deputy Manydeeds, from Dawson," she said by way of introduction, and, "Charlie, this is my daughter, Sarah."

Sarah and Charlie smiled at each other and shook hands through the open window. Jen thought, this is the first time I've seen him smile—relaxed and happy as though he truly likes children. *Maybe impassive exteriors can hide a lot of feeling.* Sarah and Charlie chatted for a few minutes.

Charlie turned to Jen and said, "When will you be in Dawson again?"

Jen said she didn't know, but she thought soon. She explained that Allison was helping her with her investigation. Charlie nodded briefly in acknowledgment and they parted.

Jen drove south to Morrison in silence. She sighed and thought of her missed opportunity for a walk and a conversation with Charlie. She hoped that there would be another opportunity.

As a single parent, a handicapped child was a struggle for her. *Why can't Sarah be normal?* Jen asked herself for the thousandth time. Parents of normal children have no idea what it's like to live with and care for a handicapped child. Why does it have to be me? Why did her father leave us?

Jen's emotions were welling up again as she thought of how Greg had left them. *Why do these bitter feelings keep coming back? Why can't I put them behind me?* She knew the answer was that the cut was too deep. And there was her sweet daughter, Sarah, present every day of her life to remind her of Greg's absence. Her therapists had helped her work through a lot of the emotional baggage, but some remained.

Sarah interrupted Jen's thoughts and asked, "What are you thinking about, Mama?"

Jen paused, "Oh, I'm thinking about what a nice man Deputy Manydeeds is," she said, loath to express to her daughter the bitterness she felt for a situation that victimized the child, too. "What did you think?"

"I thought maybe you were thinking about going for a walk with him," Jen heard Sarah say, and knew that the rest of the unspoken sentence was, "but you can't because of me."

Damn, she has sharp ears. Nothing wrong with her hearing. "No, sweetie, I can walk with him some other time. This is my day to spend with you. That's more important to me." She reached over and patted Sarah's blond head and they looked at each other and smiled. "I love you, sweetie."

"I love you, too, Mama."

Jen felt sad and guilty for her thoughts. I'm not perfect, she reminded herself. I do have a life of my own, beyond Sarah somewhere, I just haven't discovered it yet. Sarah is my priority and a life of my own will have to wait. She sighed again. It could be worse. If I didn't have Kaari to depend on, it *would* be worse.

Cheer up, she thought. You met someone with a nice voice who invited you for a walk, and you will see him again. Now, that's something to look forward to. She smiled slightly to herself, as she pulled into her driveway.

Chapter Seven

Jen received a call from Allison at her office late Monday afternoon.

"Anything new?" Jen asked, anticipating another interesting story.

"Yeah, Prince Charming called me this morning about 10:30 and ordered me to the casino's barroom to have lunch with him at noon. He wanted to talk about buying the tavern," Allison said.

"Did you go?" Jen asked.

"Yes. We met in the barroom because Tony said he likes to sit where he can 'keep an eye on things.' Maybe he spies on his employees, too. When I entered the barroom, I saw Barbara Knowles, the Monarch County clerk, at the bar with Tony. As soon as she saw me, she whispered something to Tony and gave him this coy little smile. The look she gave me over her glass was something else, though.

"They'd make a great couple. Barbara's been divorced twice and she's the same kind of phony that Tony is. Only in her case that means a bleached-blonde hair-do, heavy make-up, and bright clothes. Barbara wants Tony for husband number three. I could tell you stories about her. I've known her for years, ever since she started as clerk 15 years ago. The small town gossips have a lot to say about her, let me tell you."

Jen, fearing that Allison would launch into local gossip, diverted her by asking, "How is she as county clerk?"

"Awful," Allison answered. "She's isn't popular with anyone. Barbara goes out of her way to make things difficult for anyone who wants help from the county clerk's office—unless they're a favorite, of course. I'm not a favorite, and neither was Steve. Last summer she blocked every one of Steve's attempts to acquire historical documents about the tavern and casino. Steve complained about her attitude. I still haven't figured out how she retains her job."

Jen, quick to find an opening, asked, "What was lunch like?"

"We ate in the barroom. Did you ever go into the barroom at the casino?" Allison asked Jen, who hadn't. "It's so ugly, but I guess it impresses the tourists."

Jen, always curious, asked, "What's it like?"

"It's done up like the inside of a mine from the last century with rough beams and fake rock. The walls are decorated with old mining equipment. The place is dreary and overdone."

"Kind of funny, don't you think," Jen said, "that he objects to a real mine underground, but has a fake one in his barroom."

"That's Tony, I guess," Allison said.

"Did Tony order your lunch for you?" Jen asked.

"Of course," Allison said as she described the meal, making Jen's mouth water as she listened. To change the subject, she asked, "Did you talk any business this time?"

"Actually, we did. He told me, in his know-it-all sort of way, that my business would improve if I'd install slot machines. I tried to explain that slots would mar the historic look and feel of the tavern with all that light and noise; and that preserving the tavern's authentic feel was important to me because it's been in the family practically since the town started.

"Tony proceeded to offer me a mere $100,000 for the tavern and claimed that was a fair deal. He must think I'm dumb as an ox," Allison exclaimed. "I mentioned as coolly as I could that the county assessor values the property at over $300,000 and that half a million was a more reasonable price. That rude bastard. He laughed in my face. It made me angry, but I controlled myself. I simply told him that I wanted fair-market value for my property and that the offer was too low. I suggested contacting an appraiser or realtor and my attorney before deciding."

"What'd he say to that?" Jen asked.

"He said, 'You don't need those people. All they'll do is take your money and inflate the price of the property.' Tony said we don't need middlemen and that we can work it out ourselves. I told him I'd think about it and went back to the tavern."

"Another delightful date," Jen joked. "Actually, I had a 'date' this weekend."

"Oh, tell me about it," Allison said with interest.

"Well, it wasn't really a date," Jen said shyly. "I met with Charlie Manydeeds on Sunday to show him the stained cobble."

"Lucky girl," Allison said. Jen thought she heard a note of envy in Allison's voice. "Charlie is such a nice guy. What did he say about it?"

"He said that the stains are possibly blood and that he would send it to the state crime lab for testing. He didn't seem too interested and said that the sheriff doesn't want him involved in reopening this case. Charlie wants to help us on the side, though."

"He would. He'll be a good resource," Allison said with a sigh.

"It's getting late and I have to head home soon," Jen said.

"Oh, that's true. So, what do you want me to do next?" Allison asked.

"If Tony has an office at the casino, maybe he has something in there that's relevant," Jen suggested. "Do you think you can get into his office?"

"Maybe. I can suggest that we meet in his office to discuss the tavern in more detail. I probably won't get to rummage through his files, but you never know."

"Well, give it a try."

❋   ❋   ❋

The next day, when Jen picked up her messages at noon, she had a call from Allison and she returned the call.

"This morning, I called Tony and told him that I thought over his offer and decided he was right—middle-men aren't needed. I asked when we could meet and he said to come to the barroom at 9:00 tonight and that he'd have a tentative contract drawn up," Allison said.

"Great," Jen said. "See if you can get into his office."

"Getting into his office won't be the problem," Allison said, "but getting him out so I can look around might be."

Jen was thoughtful. "You need a diversion." She gently stroked her eyebrows as she thought.

"You said 9:00, right? I can come to Dawson tonight and create a diversion," Jen said, thinking, how will I do that?

"Okay, maybe around 9:30?" Allison said. "What'll you do for a diversion?"

"I don't know yet, but I'll think of something."

"Well, just don't start a fire," Allison said lightly.

Jen smiled and said, "Don't worry, it won't be anything destructive or illegal."

"Then do you want me to call you if I find anything interesting? Or do you want to meet at the Mexican restaurant afterwards?"

"At the restaurant," Jen said. "After I create a diversion, I'll drive to Golden and wait for you until 11:00. After that, I'll have to go home. Work tomorrow, you know."

On her way home from her office, Jen thought of possible diversions. How would she get Tony out of his office, especially with his interest in Allison. Maybe I could pull the fire alarm or call in a bomb threat, she thought smiling to herself. No, that would never do, Jen decided, after all, I'm supposed to be a law-abiding citizen. *What can I do that would bug Tony enough to get him out of his office?*

As Jen pulled into her driveway and waited for the garage door to rise, she saw Moppet's golden eyes watching her from the far corner of the garage. Maybe I can put cat hairs in the food, she thought as she drove in and parked.

She gathered her things and climbed out of the Bronco.

"Hi, kitty-pie," she said walking over to where the cat squatted. Jen reached down to stroke Moppet as the cat rose with arched back in greeting.

"What are you doing in the garage?" she asked. "Catching crickets again, I see." Moppet liked crickets, but never ate the rear legs. On the garage floor around the cat, were several pairs of unconsumed legs.

Jen had a flash of inspiration. She recalled the sign at the casino that said free breakfast all day and imagined to herself the stir she could create by finding cricket legs in her scrambled eggs.

"Moppet, you're a genius," she said with delight as she picked up two of the legs and laid them on her palm. "I'll just take these with me and demand to see the manager when I find them in my food." Jen put the legs in Wild Bill's ash tray before going into the house.

❄ ❄ ❄

Around 8:15, Jen kissed Sarah and said goodnight to Kaari. She drove to Dawson and parked behind the sheriff's department. The lot was poorly lit at night, something Jen hadn't noticed when she had parked there during daylight hours.

Jen reached into the ash tray and gently lifted the cricket legs, dropping them into the pocket of her flannel shirt. Checking her watch, she saw it was nearly 9:00.

Jen got out of the Bronco and walked through the alley next to the fire station. She was directly across the street from the casino coffee shop that advertised free breakfast. Through the dimly lit windows she could see a steam table and a buffet line. A dozen diners were taking advantage of the free food. Good, Jen thought, the more people, the better for me to create a scene with bug parts. I can demand to see the manager and they won't refuse.

Jen had a few minutes before she needed to create a diversion and walked down the block, crossed the street, and entered the casino through the main doors. The casino floor was moderately busy and Jen decided to hide out at the end of a row of slots, hoping to be inconspicuous. She dropped nickels into one of the machines for about 15 minutes.

Rather than enter the coffee shop through the casino, where she might be seen by Tony, Jen left by the main doors and walked up the block to the coffee shop entrance on the street. She entered through the glass doors and saw a sign that said, "Please Wait to be Seated."

Jen quickly scanned the room to locate the most obscure booth and when the hostess approached with a smile, Jen said, "Hi. Would you mind if I sat over there away from the windows?"

The hostess led Jen to a booth at the rear of the coffee shop and asked if she wanted a menu. Jen said, no, that she was interested in the free buffet. The hostess said for Jen to help herself when she was ready.

The waitress served coffee and Jen, unzipping her jacket, rose to examine the buffet offerings. On the steam table she saw scrambled eggs, sausage links, bacon, toast, donuts, muffins, and fried potatoes. She picked up a plate, thinking, how am I going to make cricket legs look convincing in scrambled eggs? Any scrambled-egg cook would notice a black bug leg in yellow scrambled eggs. Maybe, I can put a leg in with the chunks of potatoes. She began to serve herself, taking eggs, sausage, bacon, toast, and fried potato, filling her plate.

Jen returned to her booth and seated herself so that she could see the patrons and staff. She checked her watch and saw that the time was 9:20. Perfect, she thought, casually reaching into her shirt pocket hidden behind her gaping jacket. She removed one of the legs, laying it on her thigh.

Jen began to eat eggs and potatoes. She picked up a piece of toast with her left hand to shield her plate from view. With her right hand she laid her fork down, carefully broke off a piece of the leg, and slid it into her potatoes. Watching the people in the restaurant carefully, she returned the remaining leg fragment to her pocket.

Taking a bite of her toast, she stirred the potatoes with her fork so that the leg looked like it had been fried with the potatoes.

I'm not much of an actress, she thought to herself, but here goes.

Carrying her plate to the cash register, the hostess asked Jen with concern, "Is something wrong, ma'am?"

Jen summoned her most indignant tone, hoping she was convincing, and plunked the plate down on the counter.

"I want to see the manager about my food. I can't believe you would serve food like this."

The hostess peered closely at the plate and gasped as she saw the cricket leg mixed in with the potatoes. She apologized profusely.

"I must see the manager about this," Jen said.

"I'll get Mr. Crocket for you right away."

"No. I want to see the casino manager," Jen insisted.

"Please wait here," the hostess said as she picked up the plate to carry it into the kitchen.

"I'll keep that here," Jen said taking the plate from the hostess.

"Of course," she said stepping into the kitchen with a look of embarrassment.

Jen felt bad that she had upset the hostess, but knew that if she didn't make a fuss, she'd never be able to draw Tony out.

A moment later, a tall, nicely built young man, dressed in the standard casino uniform, stepped through the kitchen door and up to the counter.

"Good evening," he said pleasantly. "I understand that there's been a problem with your food?"

"Yes, and I insist on seeing the casino manager. Mr. Delano—isn't that his name?"

"I'm Jim Crocket. I'm sure we can resolve this problem," he said apologetically. "We strive to maintain very high standards in our kitchen. I can't imagine how something like this might have happened." He looked carefully at the plate and lifted it from the counter to take it into the kitchen.

Jen stopped him, lowering the plate back to the counter.

"No," she said adamantly, "I want to see Mr. Delano." By now the other diners had an interest in the conversation. Crocket looked around and saw the diners looking back. He smiled slightly and said, "Mr. Delano encourages us to manage our problems independently. If you would just step into my office…"

"You don't understand," Jen said, deciding to reveal herself as she realized that Crocket was reluctant to disturb his boss. "I'm a reporter from *The Front Range Journal*," she said rather loudly, knowing that the diners where most attentive, "and I want to see Mr. Delano."

Crocket smiled to Jen and said, "Certainly. I'll get him, if you'll just wait at your table. I'll be right back."

Jen returned to her booth with her plate and Crocket left the room, entering the main lobby of the casino. Jen checked her watch and saw that it was 9:40 and hoped Allison had been able to reach Tony's office.

A few minutes later, Crocket entered the coffee shop behind a shorter, heavier man, who could only be Tony Delano. As Delano caught sight of Jen, she saw his eyes narrow perceptibly. He knows who I am, Jen thought, feeling his scrutiny. She rose from the booth and stood by the table as Delano approached with his jaw set.

"I'm Tony Delano, the manager here at the casino," he said quietly, not offering his hand. Mr. Crocket stood behind Delano, shifting his weight nervously. "Mr. Crocket mentioned a problem with your meal," he said in a neutral tone that belied his belligerent stance. "I'm sorry that this happened. Nothing like this has happened in my casino before," he said reaching for the plate and passing it back to Crocket without looking at the offensive potatoes. Crocket took the plate into the kitchen.

"You are…?" Delano asked.

Jen stood her ground and told Delano who she was, adding a comment on how shocked she was to find something so distasteful in her potatoes.

Tony demurred, saying he hoped that this would not reflect negatively on her opinion of the casino. He reached into the breast pocket of his suit coat and drew out a pair of show tickets, saying, "If you'll just accept these complementary tickets, I'm sure you won't have this type of problem again in the Golden Nugget."

Jen was unsure what to do next, but decided to accept the tickets as Delano walked her to the door. Across the street, she climbed into the Bronco, noticing that it was now 10:00. She started the engine and drove to Golden, where she waited in the restaurant for Allison to arrive.

Allison rushed into the restaurant as Jen was served coffee. "You won't believe this," Allison said as she sat in the booth opposite Jen and unbuttoned her jacket.

Jen heard Allison's excitement and asked, "What happened?"

"Your diversion worked—I saw inside Tony's safe."

"Tell me," Jen said, feeling some of Allison's excitement.

"When I got there, Tony said, 'Allison, do you want to talk business tonight?' as though he had other activities in mind. I said yes and asked if there were a quieter place to talk. He conveniently suggested his private office. We took the public elevator to the top floor and walked into a private hallway through a very squeaky security door."

"Maybe the squeak is part of the security system," Jen suggested with humor, relaxing a bit after her own performance in the casino.

"Tony's office was on the right and his private quarters were on the left. At the end of the hallway, I saw another elevator door."

"That must be the elevator to the private parking area you told me about," Jen said, sipping her coffee.

"We went into his office," Allison paused. "I looked through the miniblinds on his west-facing windows and saw right into the tavern's parking lot."

"Now you know how he spies on you," Jen teased.

"You know, I have to say that this guy always surprises me. He's never what I expect."

Allison looked around for the waitress and signaled for coffee.

"What do you mean?" Jen asked, wondering to herself how Allison really felt about Tony's intriguing aspects.

"His office is beautifully done with all sorts of masculine decor like a dark green oriental rug, and an enormous mahogany desk in the center of the room."

Allison's coffee arrived and she added sugar and cream.

"Tony has a wet bar and small fridge, too. Behind his desk, he has a mahogany bookshelf that fills the entire wall. The shelves are packed with beautiful pieces of African artwork."

"Sounds like a powerful room," Jen said.

"Yes," Allison agreed, "and I hate to admit this, but it was romantic, too, especially when he turned on a CD of soft jazz." Allison sighed.

"I sat in one of his big leather chairs and he poured drinks for us. Then he sat on the love seat and invited me to join him. I said I'd rather talk business. He was annoyed with me, I could tell. He moved behind his desk and sat down in an enormous leather chair, like a king on his throne."

Jen thought Allison was drifting and needed to refocus. "Did he have a contract for you?" she asked.

"Oh yes. He had it in a manila folder lying on his desk. He picked it up, but wouldn't let me see inside. He said, 'I think a reasonable price for the tavern is $150,000, cash.' I started to object that the offer was too low, but we were interrupted by a knock at the door."

"My diversion," Jen said with a smile. "The kitchen manager, Crocket."

"I guess. He didn't introduce himself. He just asked to speak to Tony in the hall. Tony was really aggravated and left the office in a huff. I could hear them in the hall, but I couldn't hear the words. Soon Tony stepped back inside and said he had some problem to manage and to sit tight— that he'd be right back. I could hear the security door squeak when they left."

"Good," Jen said. "Did you look around when he was gone?"

"Yes. First, I closed the office door some so that no one could see me from the hallway. Then, I snooped around. I sat on his throne and looked under his desk. He had a small safe on the right side with a goose neck lamp attached underneath the desk. I switched on the lamp so I could see better. The safe door was cracked about a quarter of an inch and I pulled it open."

"What did you find?" Jen asked leaning toward Allison in anticipation.

The waitress approached their table with the check, saying that the restaurant would close in 15 minutes.

"A handgun was sitting on top of a bunch of manila folders," Allison said quietly, moving closer to Jen so that they wouldn't be overheard. "I moved the gun and looked through the folders. The second one down said 'Destroy' on it, so I looked inside. The first document was the coroner's report on Steve. The historical maps from the county clerk's office were underneath the report. They were folded up and clipped together."

"County clerk's aren't supposed to give out original historical maps," Jen said.

"Well, it looks like someone gave these to Tony."

"Maybe it was your county clerk, Barbara."

"Yeah. They seem to be friends."

"Find anything else?" Jen asked.

"Yes. Get this. The last set of clipped papers were all of Steve's documents."

"You mean the ones we saw at the cabin and photographed?" Jen asked.

"Yes, but I don't know how they got into the safe."

"Tony must have taken them from the cabin," Jen suggested. "Maybe he wanted to compile all the evidence about the gold so no one else could use it. After all, you said it was in a 'destroy' file. I'll have to think on this a bit... Did you put it all back before Tony returned?"

"I was putting everything back in the safe, when I heard the security door squeak. I closed up the safe door like I found it and hurried back to my chair."

"That was a close call," Jen commented. "Did you remember to turn-off the light over the safe?" she asked.

Allison paused, confusion clouding her features. She replied in an uncertain voice, "I don't know. I think so, but I'm not sure. I was in a rush."

"Well, maybe Tony didn't notice in the midst of the distraction."

"Maybe," Allison said doubtfully.

"You don't know," Jen said reassuringly. "You did a terrific job and discovered a great deal that supports our suspicions. We should re-visit Steve's cabin to make sure everything is in order. Can you go up there with me this weekend?"

"Ooh. Not this weekend. I'm out of Dawson this weekend. Can you go by yourself? I can leave the key in the flower boxes in front of the tavern and give you directions."

"Sure," Jen said, "Let's have 'em." Allison gave the directions to the cabin. They walked to the cash register and paid for their coffees. As they walked to their vehicles, Jen told Allison about her diversion and Allison laughed, saying she could just imagine Tony in his conversation with Jen regarding her complaint about the food.

Jen had one more question. "How did you get away from Tony?"

"Easy," Allison said with a flourish, "Before he walked in, I picked up his telephone and pretended like I was finishing a conversation with Rick. I told Tony I had a water pipe break at the tavern and Rick was swamped."

Jen smiled and told Allison she thought her ruse was clever as they said goodnight.

✳　✳　✳

Very early Thursday morning, Jen woke to the sound of her telephone ringing. She brushed her hair out of her eyes and looked at her digital clock, seeing that the time was 1:53 a.m. Who would call at this hour? I hope nothing's wrong with my mother, she thought as she answered.

"Hello?" Jen said. At first she heard nothing. "Hello?" she said again.

A husky male voice said, "Ms. Slater, I understand that you have been making inquiries into the affairs of a certain casino manager."

Jen said nothing.

The voice went on in a threatening manner. "I would advise you to desist. Your situation can be made uncomfortable, should you chose to continue your inquiries, you know. I'm sure you would find a difficult personal situation if the Immigration and Naturalization Service were to suddenly realize that your Swedish nanny was here illegally on an expired tourist visa. The IRS has an interest in seeing that taxes are paid on wages provided to domestic help. Wouldn't it be a shame if you had to explain your housekeeper to the IRS and pay back taxes and penalties? Think about it," the voice advised. The line went dead.

Jen was stunned. She wondered how much else they knew and what they would do with the information. Was she safe? What about Sarah and Kaari?

Chapter Eight

On Saturday, Jen headed for Dawson. She stopped at the tavern to retrieve the keys to Steve's cabin from the flower box.

The road to Steve's cabin was rougher than Jen had remembered and she hoped that she was following the directions correctly. It was early afternoon and she didn't want to waste her time lost in the forest. After giving thought to the problem of Steve's maps and papers, Jen decided that she would collect them for safe-keeping if they were still in the cabin. She felt a twinge of conscience as she thought of crossing a police line and taking something that wasn't hers.

She drove Wild Bill up the rutted drive toward the cabin. As she approached, she saw that the yellow tape forming the police line was down on the ground. *Strange. Maybe it blew down in the wind.* She stopped the Bronco and considered the cabin before climbing out. Jen noticed that the front door was slightly ajar. She felt disconcerted. *Why would the door be open?* There were no other vehicles around and no evidence of recent tire tracks in front of the cabin. *Better take my pepper spray, just in case,* she thought as she rummaged in the glove box for the canister.

Jen got out of the Bronco slowly and approached the front door. She saw that the shutters on the windows were still open from their last visit. Jen carefully pushed the door open wide enough to see inside. She could easily see the interior and wondered why the room was so bright. Jen stepped back from the door and peered in through the window, noticing that the curtains were down and light was streaming into the cabin through the uncovered windows. *Why are the curtains down? They were in place when I was here before.* She listened, but the cabin was quiet. Jen felt sweat on her palms as she clutched the pepper spray more tightly.

Jen stepped back to the door and opened it wide enough to step inside. As the door swung open, Jen drew in a sharp breath at her first sight of the destruction. She was shocked by the condition of the cabin's interior. The mess was unbelievable. So was the smell of something spoiled. When she stepped inside, a small ground squirrel darted between her feet, startling her badly. The kitchen cupboards and pantry contents had been emptied onto the floor. Cans of food had been mauled and bitten, glass jars were broken open and remnants of food were scattered everywhere. The bread box was torn open and the mice had been into it. The cabinet doors were scratched and the sofa slashed.

The kitchen table and chairs were overturned. Jen stepped up to an overturned chair and saw a tuft of brown fur caught between the leg and seat, as though a large animal had brushed past. *A bear! A bear has broken in and caused this damage.* Jen felt some relief that the disaster was natural rather than the result of vandals. She plucked the tuft of fur from the chair and carefully wrapped it inside a tissue to save for Sarah's nature collection.

She moved through the debris toward the lean-to part of the cabin, where Steve had kept his cot, desk, and papers. Jen stepped over the torn curtain that had once hung between the rooms, and into the office area. The desk that had held the papers was knocked on its side and the papers scattered over the floor. Jen picked her way through the mess. *Steve's maps and cross sections should be here. Surely, the bear wouldn't selectively eat maps and cross sections.* As she drew closer, she saw bear scat sitting on top of the papers. Ugh, she thought, as she carefully shifted the offensive droppings to the side of the room so that she could get to the papers.

Jen examined all of the papers and could not find Steve's maps or cross sections. *Gone. Where? In Tony's "Destroy" file, of course, just as Allison had said.* Jen felt shaken. Now she knew that the cabin had been ransacked by someone, who had disguised the damage to look like that caused by a marauding bear.

Jen felt herself shake as she climbed back into the Bronco and started toward Dawson. As she drove along the jeep trails, she considered the implications of her discovery. *So, the cabin has been made to look like a bear searching for pre-hibernation goodies to cover up the theft of the maps and cross sections. All of the food packages are torn up and bear fur and scat are conveniently placed to provide authenticity. If I hadn't seen the cabin before, and known what papers to look for, I'd be convinced that this was the work of a bear.*

When she was more composed, she pulled her cell phone from her jacket pocket and called the sheriff's department, asking for Charlie.

When he answered, Jen said, "Hi, Charlie, this is Jen Slater."

"Hello, Jen," he said, "Nice to hear from you."

"Well, you wanted to know when I'd be in Dawson again, and here I am. I have something I want to tell you about, but not over the cell phone. In person would be better. Are you free for a few minutes?"

"Sure. Can you stop by the station? I'm on duty now."

Thinking of the small size of the town and that Tony might somehow observe her Bronco again, she hesitated, "Is there somewhere else, maybe outside of Dawson? Isn't there a picnic ground near Darkhorse? Would that be too inconvenient for you?"

"No, not at all. It's called Darkhorse Picnic Grounds and is just inside the national forest. Where are you now?"

"I think I can be there in about 30 minutes," Jen said. "Can you meet me at the table that's the furthest from the road?"

"Sure. I'll see you there," Charlie said.

Jen felt relief as she drove eastward. Charlie was so polite. He didn't question her about why she wanted to meet or ridicule her evidence, even though she had presented a rock as a potential murder weapon. What would he think of the ransacked cabin? Or the bear fur and scat? She would soon find out.

The half hour passed quickly, and Jen found herself turning north into the picnic grounds. She drove down the gravel road to the end and saw Charlie sitting inside his black jeep. Well, she thought, he didn't come in an official vehicle, just his private jeep.

Jen parked and climbed out of the Bronco. Charlie, dressed in his deputy's uniform and official fleece-lined leather jacket, had gotten out of his jeep and stood leaning against the end of a picnic table.

They said hello and sat down on opposite benches facing each other.

Jen felt nervous, but decided to tell all about her experience at the cabin.

"You know the cabin where Steve Myerhoff lived in good weather? The one up on Master's Creek in the national forest?" she asked.

Charlie nodded once.

Jen continued, "You know that there's a police line around the cabin to keep people out?"

He nodded again.

"Well, I've crossed that line twice and entered the cabin both times," she confessed.

Jen watched Charlie's face for evidence of disapproval. He simply nodded for her to continue and appeared unperturbed by her confession.

"The first time I visited there was on Saturday, September 24th, and the second time was this afternoon. On my first visit, the cabin was tidy, clean, and orderly. All of Steve's maps and cross sections were laid out on his desk in the lean-to part of the cabin. Today, the cabin was totally trashed! The curtains were torn off the windows, the furniture was slashed, tables and chairs overturned, cabinets opened and food containers all over the floor. There was even a tuft of bear fur and some scat left behind. It looked just like the work of a bear." She watched his face and thought she saw a look of surprise in his eyes.

"It wasn't, though. The bear would not selectively eat certain maps and cross sections and the ones relevant to Allison's property were gone." She paused, adding, "However, I know where they are."

Another nod from Charlie.

"Tony Delano has them."

Charlie's impassive expression changed slightly. *Finally, a look of interest.* "How can you be sure that Tony has them?" he asked.

"Allison saw them in his office along with the coroner's report on Steve's death," Jen answered. "There's no question that they're the same documents that Steve had in the cabin." She paused. "He also had the county clerk's original documents relevant to the tavern and to the Golden Nugget Casino in his office."

"The county clerk isn't authorized to release original or historical records," Charlie said. "How did Allison manage to search Tony's office?"

"I'd rather not get into that story," Jen answered, drawing a wadded tissue from her pocket and placing it on the rough wood of the picnic table. "I saved this from the cabin," she said as she carefully opened the tissue to reveal the clump of fur. "I didn't collect the scat, though," she said apologetically.

"May I handle this?" Charlie asked.

Jen nodded and Charlie picked up the fur and examined it closely, gently pulling it apart, studying the fibers.

"I'd say this bear has been dead for a number of years," he said as he continued to examine the fur.

Jen looked at Charlie quizzically, then realized the implications of his statement.

"You mean that it came from a dead bear, like a bear rug, or stuffed bear?"

"Exactly. The fur has been clipped with a knife or scissors. Fur torn from a live bear would have the root of the hair attached. This doesn't.

The fur is missing the natural oils I would expect on a living bear, too. It looks like evidence planted by the thieves as proof that the cabin was looted by a bear.

"It's not black bear fur, either," Charlie continued. "In fact, it looks more like grizzly. Black bears are common bears along the Front Range. There are no grizzlies in Colorado. The closest grizzlies live in Yellowstone National Park in Wyoming. If a live bear had been inside the cabin, it would have been a black bear."

Jen was impressed by Charlie's powers of observation, knowledge, and deductions based on a simple tuft of fur.

He folded the fur carefully into the tissue, asking, "May I have this?"

"Certainly," Jen answered, knowing now that she had removed potentially critical evidence from the cabin. "Do you think the sheriff's department can check out the cabin?"

"I'll go up there later and have a look around," he said. "Do you and Allison think you can write up a list of the documents that are missing from the cabin?"

"Actually," Jen answered, "the first time I visited the cabin I was with Allison. After we had gone to the cliff where Steve's body was found, she took me up there. We found all of the maps and papers inside on Steve's desk. I had one of my daughter's disposable cameras with me, so we moved everything outside and took pictures of the most important documents. Then we put the papers back inside on the desk like we found them, so they would appear undisturbed."

"Do you have the photographs now?" Charlie asked.

"Not with me, but at home. Would you like copies?"

"I'd like copies of the photographs and the negatives for safe-keeping, if I may," he said.

"Sure. How about if I bring them next time I'm in Dawson?" Jen suggested.

Charlie nodded.

They sat for a moment. Jen asked tentatively, "Did you find out anything about the rock I gave you?"

"Yes. My contact at the crime lab ran tests on the stains and he confirmed that they were human blood. He couldn't give me any more information because of the small amount and the condition of the sample."

Jen sighed. She felt vindicated, as though she had found something important. This time she nodded to Charlie in acknowledgment.

"I'm off duty now," Charlie said, "Can I buy you dinner in Darkhorse? I know a nice, quiet little diner."

Jen was surprised. "I'd like that, but how about coffee, instead? I'll need to leave soon to get back home."

Charlie nodded. "The diner's on the north side of the main street across from the church. The best parking is around back. You can follow me, if you like."

"Thanks," Jen said, "I'll do that."

Fifteen minutes later they were seated across from each other in a booth at the diner. Daylight savings time would soon be over, and it was growing dark earlier now. Jen and Charlie ordered coffee. They chatted a bit about how pleasant the fall weather had been and the possibility of an early winter.

"How's your daughter?" Charlie asked.

"Oh, she's fine. She's spending the day with Kaari, my live-in nanny, and her favorite kitty, Moppet. I need to get back soon so that Kaari can have the evening off. I thought about bringing them with me for a drive in the mountains. After seeing the cabin, I'm glad I didn't."

"Kaari is an unusual name. Where's she from?"

"Well," Jen said hesitantly, "she's from Sweden, here on an expired tourist visa. She could pass for my sister, except she still has an accent. Kaari's been with us practically since Sarah was born. I couldn't live without her. She does everything for me at home and loves Sarah. She takes Sarah to her physical therapy lessons and just does everything. You won't report me to the INS, will you?" she said pensively, as she thought of the threatening phone call she had received.

Charlie's eyes twinkled and she saw his amusement. "You can depend on me to hold your secret."

Jen realized how tense she had become. *Maybe that phone call made me more nervous than I thought.* Jen wondered why she was reluctant to tell Charlie about the call, and had no answer. Instead, she made a concentrated effort to relax some and smiled.

"Doesn't Sarah's father help you out?" Charlie asked quietly.

Jen's smile changed to a look of disappointment. "No. He left me shortly after Sarah was born. Now he lives in South America."

Charlie's face became impassive. "Dead-beat dad?" he asked in a neutral tone.

Jen flinched and she saw that he was immediately sorry he had asked.

"I'm sorry," he said. "None of my business." He retreated to sip his coffee.

Jen managed another smile, thinking, why am I still so sensitive about Greg? "No, that's okay. I guess I have trouble still believing that he left us. I've spent a lot of time trying to put it behind me and haven't managed to completely let it go yet," she said.

"You will. It takes time. I had a past to let go of, too," he said empathetically.

They looked into each other's eyes and saw common experience there.

Jen glanced at her watch. "Oh, I've got to go. I'll be late. Thanks for the coffee and the help. I really appreciate it. I better run. May I pay for my coffee? Or leave the tip?"

"No," Charlie said, "you can get it next time." Jen finished her coffee as Charlie pulled out a small, black leather-bound notebook. "Let me give you my phone numbers in case you need to call me." He neatly wrote down numbers for home, the sheriff's department, and police radio phone. He tore the sheet from the notebook and slid it across the table to Jen.

Jen said, "Thanks. How about if I write down my numbers for you?"

Charlie handed the notebook and pen across the table to Jen. She scribbled her name and phone numbers for office, home, and cell phone. Jen flipped the notebook open to the second page and jotted down her address. As an after thought, she included Kaari's pager number, saying, "This is Kaari's pager number. I sometimes call her and leave a voice message."

Jen passed the notebook back to Charlie and he scrutinized her notes, with a barely perceptible rise of his eyebrows. Jen suddenly realized that her handwriting, never the best, was probably illegible to him.

Feeling slightly embarrassed, Jen asked, "Can you read it? I can rewrite it for you. I can be a sloppy writer sometimes."

Jen felt herself blushing. He folded the notebook and tucked it inside his jacket.

"It's fine," he said, smiling with his eyes. "I can make it out just fine. Please call me if you need anything at all."

"You do the same," Jen said as she rose from the booth. Charlie started to rise, too, but she stopped him. "Oh, don't get up. You haven't finished your coffee yet."

Charlie settled back into his seat and nodded. They said good-bye and Jen walked out through the front door and onto the sidewalk. As she turned, waving to him through the window smiling, she saw him lift his coffee cup in response.

✶ ✶ ✶

The drive back to Morrison seemed long to Jen. Her mind was filled with thoughts of past, present, and future. Why couldn't she accept Greg's deficiencies and let him go? She had her own life now. Would she really have another chance for coffee with Charlie? *He did say that I could get the check next time.* Was the threatening call something she should be worried about?

It was dark when Jen arrived home and the temperature had dropped with the setting sun. She entered through the kitchen door and found Sarah and Kaari watching the Disney channel in the family room. They greeted each other as Jen picked Sarah up.

"Where's you kitty?" Jen asked.

"Gone all day," Sarah said with disappointment.

"Well, I'm sure she'll be home in time to eat," Jen said. Turning to Kaari, Jen asked her if she'd checked the mail and she said no.

Jen, snuggling Sarah inside her unzipped jacket, carried her outside to check her rickety curb-side mailbox mounted on a steel post. Years ago when the box was installed Jen was sure that it had been stable. Now, every time something heavy was placed inside, the box tilted slightly. Under the street light, Jen saw that the box was listing toward the house.

"Look," Jen said to Sarah as they approached the mailbox, "Somebody must have sent us something."

"Maybe it's for me," Sarah said with excitement.

"Well, maybe," Jen said shifting Sarah to her left hip and opening the front of the steel box. She kissed Sarah's cheek as she reached inside with her right hand.

What happened next was a blur to Jen because the events seemed simultaneous. As she reached toward the back of the box, she heard a distinct buzzing rattle from the box's interior. A stale, acrid odor rose from the mailbox as it shifted slightly. Jen began to withdraw her hand in alarm. As she did, she felt the shock of pain in the heel of her palm and the weight of something dragging along the bottom of the mailbox with a rasping sound.

Sarah cried, "What's wrong, Mama?"

Jen felt Sarah slipping from her arm and heard her scream as the rattlesnake fell from the mailbox. Jen dropped to her knees, whipping her right arm away in an attempt to shake the snake loose. The rattler released its grip on Jen's hand and landed in the street on its back. The snake twisted its body onto its belly and moved quickly across the asphalt, disappearing into the neighbor's shrubbery.

Jen felt light-headed, but managed to lay Sarah on the grass. The child was still screaming in fright and Jen was aware that Kaari was there, asking what happened.

"A snake! A snake! In the mailbox," Sarah shrieked. "It bit Mama!"

Jen, still on her knees, began to tremble with pain and anxiety. *I mustn't panic.*

Kaari, unsure whether to attend Sarah or Jen first, knelt down beside Jen and asked, "Are you all right?"

"I got a snake bite," she said through gritted teeth. "Take Sarah inside and call 911."

Kaari scooped Sarah up and hurried into the house with the crying child. Jen held her arm below waist-level and applied pressure to her wrist in an attempt to prevent the venom from circulating too quickly. She was aware that her neighbor from across the street had come to her side. John put his arm around her, helped her to her feet, and guided her to the curb.

"There was a rattler in my mailbox," she said faintly, "it went into your bushes."

"It's okay," John said, helping her to sit on the curb. "I saw the snake—it was a prairie rattler, about a foot and a half long. Let me see your hand."

Jen held her hand palm up as John examined the two small puncture marks oozing blood. "These aren't too bad, Jen. You aren't swelling much yet. Let me hold your wrist." Jen felt John apply moderate pressure to her lowered wrist as she heard distant sirens drawing closer.

"I feel so light-headed," Jen said.

"It's just the shock," John said reassuringly. "You'll be fine, Jen. Try some deep breaths."

The ambulance, police car, and fire truck arrived together, amidst sirens and flashing lights, drawing the neighbors out onto the street.

Kaari had wrapped a blanket around Sarah and had carried her out to the curb.

Jen heard John telling the police and paramedics about the snake bite as they knelt before Jen to examine her hand.

One of the paramedics said, "We're going to take you to the emergency room." Jen nodded, as they placed her on the gurney. Kaari brought Sarah over and Jen could see the tears flowing down the child's cheeks.

Jen smiled weakly and said, "I'll be okay, sweetie. I'll be home before too long. You stay here with Kaari." Sarah nodded her head, but Jen could see her distress as Kaari stepped back so that the paramedics could load her into the ambulance.

John said, "Jen, they want to take you to Swedish Hospital. Is that okay?" Jen nodded. "I'll follow you in my car." She nodded again and said, "Thanks, John." She waved to Sarah as two paramedics lifted her into the brightly lit ambulance and closed the door behind them.

The younger paramedic smiled at Jen and said, "Good thing it was cool out tonight, otherwise your rattler might have been more lively."

"Yeah," the other paramedic added, wrapping an ace bandage around her wrist to restrict the circulation of the venom, "Good thing, too, you didn't look in the mailbox first—a snake bite on the nose is worst than on the hand," he teased. Jen smiled through her pain.

"Aren't you going to slice me open and suck out the poison?" she asked, trying to distract herself from the pain in her palm.

The younger paramedic applied a sterile bandage to Jen's palm. "Naw," he said, "that's only for cowboy movies."

"Besides, we might do more damage with a razor blade than the snake did with its fangs," the other added.

As they prepared to take Jen's vital signs, the older medic said, "I've seen a lot of snake bites. This one doesn't look too bad. Not much swelling. That means a small amount of venom was injected. About 20 to 30 percent of bites don't inject venom at all. Bet it hurts, though."

Jen nodded.

"Well," he continued, "Not to worry. More people die from bee stings and lightening strikes every year than from snake bites."

"You're a comfort," Jen said.

"Snake bites are usually superficial. If you tend them right away, anti-venom takes care of most of the problems."

"Well, I'm ready for my shot of anti-venom," Jen said, "especially if it'll stop the pain."

"Not until we get to the ER," he said, taking her pulse. "First the poison control medics will test you for an allergic reaction."

"Oh," Jen said, "that's sensible."

"Then the doctor gives you two aspirin for the pain," the other joked, adding, "We're almost there."

After three hours in the emergency room on an IV drip of two units of antivenin, Jen was told to see her doctor in four days, administered aspirin, and released.

John drove Jen home. She felt exhausted and sore. Her hand was bandaged and supported by a sling to keep the snake bite below heart level. She wondered how two little punctures could hurt so much.

John walked her to her door and Kaari let her inside.

"How's Sarah?" Jen asked.

"Crying a long time. I sat with her in my arms until she was sleeping."

"Poor thing," said Jen. "John said he called from the emergency room." Kaari nodded. Jen added, "I think I'll wake her up to let her know I'm all right."

Jen went into Sarah's bedroom and woke the child, kissing her face and reassuring her that she was fine.

Jen and Kaari chatted for a few minutes and Kaari said she wanted to go out with friends for a few hours, if Jen was okay and didn't need her. Jen realized that the events had been stressful for Kaari, too and said fine.

Jen retired to her room feeling drained and sat on the edge of her bed for a few minutes before reaching for her phone. On the second ring, Charlie answered.

"This is Jen," she said, hoping that her voice didn't sound strained.

"What's wrong? Has something happened to Sarah?"

Jen heard the concern in his voice. "No, Sarah is fine for now. When I got home tonight, I went outside to check my mailbox and there was a rattlesnake inside. It bit me. I just got home from the emergency room." Jen drew in a deep breath to keep from crying, but knew that tears were near the surface. "Sarah was with me at the mailbox and saw the whole thing." Jen began to cry.

When Jen was calmer Charlie said, "I'm sorry that your daughter witnessed such a shocking scene. I can understand how upset you must be." He paused, to let her grieve. "This is potentially serious. Tampering with mailboxes is a federal offense. I want you to call the postal service on Monday and file a report with them. Can you do that?"

"Yes," she said as she gained control over her tears, saying in an embarrassed voice, "I'm sorry to be so upset. It was a shock. And it hurts. My arm's in a sling."

"Don't apologize," he said kindly. "You have a reason to be upset."

"Sarah's cat was missing all day, too," Jen said. "She finally came home. I'm just glad someone didn't catch her and stuff her inside my mailbox."

Charlie hesitated a moment until Jen was more composed. "Do you have any idea about who might have done this? Anything unusual happen recently? Any threats?" he asked.

Now Jen hesitated. "Actually," she said, "I did get a strange call at 2:00 a.m. on Thursday from someone who knew my name. It was a husky male voice who addressed me as 'Ms. Slater.' It wasn't a voice I recognized."

"What did he say?" Charlie asked, his voiced hardened.

Jen heard his tone change and felt disconcerted. "Well, he apparently knew that I had done some investigation into Tony Delano's licenses issued by the Colorado Division of Gaming, although he didn't name Tony. He said, 'a certain casino manager.'

"He knew about my personal situation, about having Kaari here illegally. He threatened to make my situation 'uncomfortable' by exposing her to the INS and me to the IRS if I chose to 'continue my inquiries.' He didn't mention anything about snakes."

"The snake is a warning," he said flatly. Jen thought she detected a note of anger in Charlie's usually calm voice.

"Why didn't you tell me about the threatening phone call earlier? You should have reported it to the police right away."

Jen felt upset with herself. She knew he was right. "I didn't think it was for real," she answered lamely. "I guess I wasn't being very sensible about it."

"You need to be very careful," he said more gently. "This kind of thing can get more serious. Is there somewhere your daughter and nanny can stay for a while? With a friend or relative?"

"Yes," Jen answered. "Sarah's father has an aunt living in the Springs who loves to see Sarah. I can call her."

"Good," Charlie said. "My advice is to call her now and take Sarah and Kaari there tomorrow morning." He paused, and added, "Would you like me to come down tonight to help you with anything?"

"Oh," Jen said, "I think I'll be all right. It's such a long drive for you to come here. We'll be okay. I appreciate the offer, though. You're very thoughtful."

"Please call me if there is anything else I can do. Let me know what happens. You try to get some rest tonight."

Although it was after 11:00 p.m., Jen decided to call Aunt Norma in Colorado Springs, hoping it wasn't too late. Jen explained that she was involved in a case that was potentially dangerous and told her about the snake bite.

Jen asked if Sarah and Kaari could stay with her in Colorado Springs for a while. Norma said she would love the company and that they could stay as long as they liked. Jen arranged to drive Sarah and Kaari down to the Springs, expecting to arrive late the next morning. Norma was upset about the snake bite but said she would be delighted to have Sarah and Kaari, helping to raise Jen's spirits somewhat.

Kaari was still out, so Jen jotted a quick note for her so that she would be prepared to leave in the morning. Jen lay down on her bed, trying to relax. Soon she was sleeping in her clothes with the lights on, her bandaged hand and sling lying across her chest. Hours later, she hardly stirred when Kaari covered her with a warm blanket and turned out the lights.

Chapter Nine

Monday morning was overcast and drizzly. The temperature had dropped 20 degrees over night as a cold front moved through the Denver metro area. Jen knew it would return to bright sunshine and crisp fall weather by Tuesday afternoon. *That's fall in Colorado—summer one day and winter the next.*

Jen drove to work, and when she reached her desk, she dialed Allison at home as she shed her calf-length, dark taupe raincoat. Allison answered and, this time, she sounded sleepy.

"Have a nice weekend?" Jen asked.

"Yes, thanks," Allison answered. "Every fall a group of my cousins and I have a small reunion at Yellowstone before the winter sets in. It was gorgeous this year. How was your weekend? Did you visit Steve's cabin?"

"I had one of the worst weekends on record," Jen sighed.

"What happened?" Allison asked, now more alert.

Jen told Allison about her experience at the cabin, including the details regarding the bear fur and scat.

"The maps and papers were gone?" Allison asked. "Well, at least we know where they are."

"Yes, but for how long? They were stashed in a 'Destroy' file. Someday Tony will get around to burning the file."

"What did the cabin look like?" Allison was curious to know. Jen gave a full description.

"Did you tell anyone?" Allison asked when Jen was finished with her methodical description of the cabin's interior.

"Yes," Jen said and described her meeting with Charlie.

"Wow. You have had a busy weekend," Allison remarked. "Anything else?"

"Yes, lots," Jen answered. "I asked Charlie about the rock with the stains on it that I had found at the cliff. He said the state crime lab confirmed that the stains were human blood, but couldn't provide any other details."

"The murder weapon," Allison said with excitement. "You found the murder weapon."

"Well, we can't be sure," Jen said cautiously. "Let me tell you about the rest of my weekend. When I got home on Saturday night, someone had put a rattlesnake in my mailbox and it bit me."

"Oh! That's awful. I'm so sorry! Are you all right?"

"I'm okay."

"Who would do such a thing?"

"I don't know," Jen said, "but I reported it to the police and postal service. I think it's related to a threatening phone call I got earlier that told me to cease and desist my investigations of a 'certain casino manager.' Guess who that might be? Charlie said that the snake was probably a warning from the same person. I was afraid for my daughter and nanny, so I took them to Colorado Springs yesterday to stay with a relative."

"It's him. I know it's him. Mafia does that kind of thing. They threaten and then push to let you know that they mean it, so you get the point," Allison said, and added thoughtfully, "Although, I have to say he did a creative job with the cabin, you know, to make it look like a bear attack. Very clever. Wonder where he got the bear poop from?"

"Don't know," Jen said, with a tinge of humor. "I doubt he followed a bear around in the woods with a pooper-scooper."

They both laughed and it helped to relieve the tension.

"I'm glad that you sent your daughter somewhere safe, but it tells me that you intend to pursue the case," Allison said.

"Yes, I do. Are you interested in continuing?"

"You bet. Now I just have more reasons to pay that slimeball back—for wrecking the cabin and your personal life, the gag-me dates I've endured on behalf of the investigation."

"We don't know that Tony trashed the cabin," Jen reminded her.

"I feel it in my bones," Allison replied.

"We need to check out the county clerk's office to see if the historical documents are missing," Jen said. "Since Barbara Knowles knows you, we might get better results if I went."

Allison agreed.

"I can come up to Dawson on Friday afternoon," Jen said, pausing before continuing and considering the best approach for presenting her idea. "Now, I have a suggestion for you to consider. Since we have copies of the documents, I think that we can stir the pot if we can find a mining company that is interested in reopening the claims. It'll be harder for Tony to kill off a big corporation than it was for him to nail Steve. I have the training to put together a package that will interest a mining company, and I have a person in mind who will be happy to see the prospect.

What do you think of that idea?"

"Sounds great," Allison said with enthusiasm. "You can pick up where Steve left off. Since our public authorities, with the exception of Charlie, are uninterested, maybe we can provoke Tony into revealing himself. I love your idea. Let's do it!"

"Good," Jen said. "Let's meet at the Darkhorse diner for dinner on Friday, say 5:30? I can tell you what I saw at the clerk's office and explain the details about reopening the claims."

"See you then."

❋ ❋ ❋

Jen had her evenings free during the week. Although she missed Sarah and Kaari badly, she had plenty of time now to study the documents and write up a prospect that she knew would appeal to gold mining companies. She had the photographs enlarged and painstakingly reconstructed Steve's maps and cross sections. Jen contacted the assay company and had copies of Steve's assays sent to her overnight so that she would have originals to include in her report. Jen enjoyed the work, although the hours were long, often keeping her up until 1:00 a.m., and the snake bite was painful when she typed. She found that she remembered a great deal about her former work as a gold geologist and it brought back happy memories of the years before Greg when she had actively looked for gold.

By Thursday night she had a draft of the prospect and maps ready for a presentation, and copies of the photographs and negatives for Charlie. She called Charlie at the station to let him know that she would be in Dawson on Friday afternoon and had the photos for him. He agreed to meet her at the same picnic table at 4:30, after he was off duty for the day.

Jen left work at noon on Friday, drove home, and changed into her jeans and a flannel shirt. She gathered up her prospect and the items for Charlie before driving to Dawson. She was hesitant about driving the white Bronco into town, knowing that Tony was familiar with the vehicle, but she had no choice. She decided to park the Bronco behind the fire station again, as the location couldn't be seen from the street.

Jen walked around the fire station and south to Grand Street. She took the stairs from the street to the double-door front entrance of the City Hall and County Court House, an historical wood frame building with a red brick exterior. As she entered the building, she noticed that the main hall was large and poorly lit with a high ceiling and squeaky wood floors. Jen spotted the marquee on the wall behind an antique glass case and found the location of the clerk's office on the first floor.

Jen walked into the clerk's office in the northeast corner of the building. The large room, partitioned into sections, had enormous windows along the north and east walls filling the room with natural light. The small waiting area was divided from the office and storage area by a six-foot high partition located across from the doorway. An old worn credenza sat against the partition, and to her right was a scratched and nicked counter that nearly reached to Jen's shoulders. Behind the counter were shelves, filing cabinets, and map drawers. To her left around the end of the partition, she saw desks and more storage for documents.

Jen approached the counter and reached for the bell to attract the clerk's attention. She was curious to see Barbara Knowles, now that she had heard about her. To her disappointment, a young woman in her early twenties came to the counter and said, "May I help you?"

"Yes," Jen answered, "is the county clerk in today?"

"Barbara Knowles? No she's off this afternoon. I'm the assistant clerk. Can I help you?" she asked politely.

Jen, hoping that her disappointment didn't show in her face, answered, "Sure. I'm looking for the historical documents relevant to the gold mining claims for these two lots."

She handed the assistant a piece of paper with the lot numbers for the tavern and casino and the claim numbers relevant to the properties. Jen had gotten the numbers from Steve's notes so that she wouldn't have to look them up in the clerk's plat book.

The assistant frowned. "Hmm. The Miner's Tavern and the Golden Nugget Casino," she mused. "Deputy Manydeeds was in here earlier this week quizzing Barbara about documents for the same two lots." She smiled at Jen and said, "Just a second, I'll get the documents for you."

I guess Charlie is more interested than he lets on.

The assistant was gone a long time, and Jen heard the sounds of cabinet and file drawers opening and closing and the assistant walking over the wood floors in search of the documents. When she returned to the counter, she was empty-handed and looking distressed.

"I can't find any of the historical documents on the claims. The information filed under these claim numbers is missing. I know we have historical documents on these claims. I saw them myself last summer when a local miner was in here looking for the same information. I remember, because he and Barbara argued over access to the information. I guess they didn't get along well," she added.

Jen was not surprised that the clerk was unable to locate the historical claim documents. "You're sure?" she asked. The clerk nodded. "Did Barbara give anything to Deputy Manydeeds?"

"I don't think so."

"Thanks for looking," Jen said. She walked back out onto Grand Street and returned to Wild Bill.

Jen drove to the picnic area for her rendezvous with Charlie. She was an hour early and decided to take the hiking trail along the stream. She returned to the picnic grounds at 4:30 and saw Charlie's black jeep. The hard top was on the jeep, as the weather was now too cool in the mornings and evenings for open-air driving. Charlie stood leaning against the jeep with his arms crossed over his chest, looking up the trail. The late afternoon sun filtered through the pine trees and speckled the picnic table. Yellow aspen leaves littered the ground.

They greeted each other, Jen with a smile and Charlie with a nod, and Jen retrieved the photographs and negatives from the Bronco. They sat down at the table as they had during their last meeting.

Charlie asked, "How's your snake bite?"

"Oh, better," she said raising her right hand to show the bandage. She was out of the sling now and had more freedom of movement. "I went to the doctor on Wednesday and it looks good. There's little tissue damage but I have to keep the bandage on a few more days. It's still swollen."

"Hurt much?" he asked with concern, pursing his lips together.

Jen nodded and smiled weakly. "Some," she said, "but at lease I have been able to prepare copy for the *Journal*."

"Is everything okay at home?" he asked. "Did you find a place for your daughter to stay?"

"I took her to visit her great aunt in Colorado Springs. She'll stay there for as long as needed." Jen sighed. "I miss her, though. Kaari, too."

"Hopefully, they can come home soon," Charlie said encouragingly.

"Well, anyway, I brought you copies of the photos we took of the documents at Steve's cabin. And the negatives." She slid a 9-by-12 inch envelope across the table to Charlie. He picked it up and looked inside.

"Thanks," he said, "I'll take good care of these for you." He closed the flap on the envelope, laid it on the table, and rested his folded hand on top. "I visited the cabin last Sunday. The destruction there appears typical of that caused by a bear. I collected the scat and had it analyzed along with the fur you collected."

Jen, curious, leaned toward Charlie and asked, "What did you learn?"

"Our bear is a hybrid," he said with a sparkle of amusement. "The fur is from a Kodiak brown bear and the scat is from a polar bear, neither of which exist in the wild here in Colorado. The fur was clipped from a cured bear hide. I don't know anyone in the county who has hunted big game in Alaska or who might have a Kodiak bear skin."

Jen wondered if Allison knew anyone with a stuffed bear, since she had so many stuffed animals at the tavern.

"Maybe it belongs to a newcomer to the county," Jen said, thinking of Tony Delano.

"Possibly," he agreed.

"What about the scat?" Jen asked.

"I can't be sure of the individual bear, but there are several zoos along the Front Range that have polar bears. The Denver Zoo, for one. Another is the Cheyenne Mountain Zoo in Colorado Springs. I called both zoos, but no one seemed to know of recent requests for polar bear scat."

Charlie must think this is quiet a twist on his usual police work, Jen thought. *He thinks it's funny.*

"I guess, when you went into police work, you weren't aware of the importance of bear scat identification as an investigative tool," she suggested with a smile.

"You take what evidence you find and use it, scat or not," he responded. "I also photographed the cabin and dusted for fingerprints. Hope you didn't touch too much when you were there."

"No, I don't think so," she said seriously, before she realized that he was teasing her gently. She hoped she wasn't going to blush. She rested her chin in her left hand, spreading her fingers over her cheek hoping to cover any blush. "Do you have the results yet?" Jen asked.

"Not yet. On Monday, I called the Colorado Division of Motor Vehicles to see if I could get Tony's thumb print from his driver's license. He doesn't have a Colorado license. I also learned that there are no vehicles registered under the name of 'Tony Delano.' I knew he was from Chicago, so I called Illinois motor vehicles, with the same result."

"Maybe his name's an alias," Jen said. Charlie nodded.

"I guess you didn't get any fingerprints to compare with those from the cabin," Jen said.

"Actually, I did, but I think Allison would enjoy telling you that story," he said, running his finger along the edge of the envelope.

Jen was certain that he wouldn't tell her anymore and she would have to wait to ask Allison how Charlie managed to fingerprint Tony without his knowledge.

"On Sunday," he continued, "I also went to the Elbert's property and saw the location where the body was found. Just as you suggested, there wasn't any visible evidence of blood on the boulders at the bottom of the cliff. I went further up the canyon and found a game trail leading to the top of the cliff."

I wished I'd thought to look for a trail, then I wouldn't have fallen and lost precious evidence.

Charlie continued, "I conducted a systematic search of the area, walking a grid starting 200 feet back from the cliff face. I found a discolored area in a clump of dried grass and collected a sample of the soil for analysis to determine if human blood factors are present."

"You've been busy," Jen said. "I was at the county clerk's today, looking for the historical maps."

"I went, too, on Monday. Barbara gave me the usual run-around," Charlie said. "The maps are gone." Jen nodded.

❀ ❀ ❀

Charlie didn't tell Jen the full details of his experience with Barbara Knowles. Now that he'd had some time to think about it, the experience was both humorous and irritating. He had stopped into the county clerk's office during his off-duty lunch hour.

"Hello, Barbara, how are you today?" he had asked politely.

"Fine. Nice fall weather," she had said and he'd nodded in agreement.

"What can I do for you today?" she had asked sweetly.

"I would like to see what documents you have on the Miner's Tavern and the Golden Nugget Casino, please. I'm interested in any historical documents that might be in your possession. What do you have?" Charlie had asked, anticipating little cooperation.

Barbara had shifted her weight back on her heels and said, "I'll have to look the lot numbers up in the plat book first and then see what we have."

She was gone for a short time and returned with two files, marked with the lot numbers, placing them on the counter for Charlie to look at.

"Thanks," he said as he reached for the documents, wondering if this had been too easy.

"Excuse me, I have to make a phone call," she said over her shoulder as she walked out of sight behind the partitions.

Charlie had opened the first file to discover recent tax and assessment documents for the tavern, a surveyed plot plan for the lot, a yellowed newspaper article about the antique bar, and other legal documents regarding the transfer of property to Allison upon the death of her uncle.

The second file contained similar information about the earlier buildings that had occupied the site of the present-day casino, prior to their demise. Recent documents relevant to the casino were included, such as the tax assessment, a surveyed plot plan, and a note stating that architectural blue prints were on file. There was nothing in the files regarding historical mining information.

When Barbara had returned, he had said, "I'm interested in the historical information on these lots with respect to gold mining. Isn't there information on gold mining for these?"

"All of the historical information we have on the two lots is contained in these files," she had answered with a smile, tapping her pencil impatiently on the counter top.

Something didn't seem right to Charlie. "The county has historical gold mining records. I thought that they were stored here."

"Yes, some are," she had continued to smile, but Charlie could see that she knew where the documents were and was not going to offer him any clues as to how to find them.

"How do I access them?" he had asked, starting to feel irritated.

"You must have the claim numbers."

Charlie realized that Barbara had given him information based on the lot numbers, which were used to describe the locations of surface structures. Claim numbers were used to identify subsurface mining rights.

"I need the claim numbers, then?"

"Yes, I said that," she had snapped.

Charlie had leaned over the counter and, inches from Barbara's face, had said, "May I have them, please?"

"Well, all right," she had said, taking a step backward, "but you'll have to look them up yourself, it's my lunch break and I'm leaving in a few minutes, so you'll have to hurry because we close for lunch, as you know."

She led Charlie behind the counter to a large reference book containing lists of claim numbers cross-referenced to the plat book. Barbara walked away after showing the book to Charlie and without offering him any guidance on how to use the book. After a few minutes of exasperating search, Charlie located the claim numbers and jotted them down in the black leather notebook he carried in his pocket. He returned to the counter and tapped the bell for assistance. Barbara reappeared. He tore the page from his notebook and handed her the list of claim numbers, saying, "I would like all historical documents relevant to these claims, please, including maps or plans that you may have."

"I'm sorry. You'll just have to come back after lunch. I can't possibly find them for you now." She had walked in front of the counter, taken Charlie by the elbow, and ushered him to the door, saying, "Come back in an hour." She guided him through the doorway and closed the door in his face.

One hour and twenty minutes later, Charlie had returned to the clerk's office to find the door still closed. He tried the doorknob and it was locked. He knocked on the door and there was no answer. Charlie walked down a narrow hallway to the rear entrance and knocked lightly on the open door. Barbara's assistant clerk came around a bookshelf and looked surprised to see Charlie standing in the doorway.

"Charlie, need some help?" she asked.

"Yes, your main door is locked and Barbara was supposed to help me locate some documents."

"Sorry. I didn't know it was still locked. Come on in through this way." She led Charlie around to the front counter and unlocked the main door.

"Is Barbara here?" he asked.

"Oh, yes. She just stepped into the ladies' room. She'll be right back."

Charlie had waited patiently for 10 minutes until Barbara walked up to the counter.

"Can I help you?" she had asked, as though this were her first meeting with Charlie.

"Yes. I would like historical information on the claim numbers I left with you before you closed for lunch."

"Claim numbers?" she asked as if a claim number was a foreign concept.

"Yes, the list of claim numbers I handed to you before you closed for lunch," he repeated, his face impassive.

She looked puzzled, "I'll look around. I'm sure they're here somewhere."

Barbara was gone for another 10 minutes. When she returned, she said, "I can't seem to find them. You'll have to look them up again." She beckoned for Charlie to follow her behind the counter and she led him back to the reference book. Charlie repeated the process and found the claim numbers, handing them once again to Barbara.

"Please wait for me in the waiting area," she said, as she turned away from him.

Another 10 minutes had passed by. Charlie stood at the counter. Barbara entered the waiting area suddenly through the main door and came up behind him. As Charlie turned, he saw her blanched face and anxious look.

She had said to him quietly, "I can't find them. I just don't understand. We haven't lost documents before, in the 15 years I've been the county clerk. They're missing! Oh, I'm so upset! Someone must have stolen them. Maybe it was that awful man, Steve Myerhoff, who stole them. I haven't seen them since last summer when he insisted on having full access to the documents for these claims." She had wrung her hands and looked anxiously into Charlie's impassive face, as if hoping for reassurance.

Charlie had looked Barbara right in the eye, and said evenly, "I can take your statement on the loss of the documents, if you want to report them missing."

"Oh, yes," she said.

"I'll go next door to the sheriff's department and get a report form. I'll be right back."

Charlie had left the Court House through the back door and walked into the front door of the sheriff's department located in the adjacent building. He made it back to the clerk's office in four minutes. Barbara wasn't behind the counter, so he tapped the bell. The assistant clerk came around the counter and smiled at Charlie.

"Is Barbara here?" Charlie asked.

"No, she left just a minute ago. She said she had an emergency at home."

Charlie, exasperated, had thanked her and left. He'd fill in the report himself at the station and turn it in for investigation when he was ready.

❄   ❄   ❄

The sunshine was gone now and the air was growing cooler as Jen and Charlie sat across the picnic table from each other. Jen glanced at her watch and saw that it was time to meet with Allison.

"I have to go, now. I'm having dinner in Darkhorse with Allison. We have some business to discuss," Jen said. She wondered briefly if she should invite Charlie along and decided against it, considering how clear his boss had been about his involvement in the case.

They rose from their seats and climbed into their respective vehicles. Charlie turned his jeep west, back toward Dawson, and Jen turned east toward Darkhorse.

Chapter Ten

Charlie said you helped him get Tony's fingerprints. I'm curious to know how. What happened?" Jen asked Allison after they were comfortably seated in the booth farthest from the door. Jen had parked off the main street in Darkhorse so that her Bronco wouldn't be so noticeable. She had entered the diner carrying a legal-sized expanding file and had sat opposite Allison, facing the back wall.

"Oh, I've been meaning to tell you about that," Allison said, leaning toward Jen and lowering her voice in a confidential manner. "Charlie came into the tavern on Tuesday morning just after we opened and asked for a private chat in my office. He wanted to know if Tony ever came in. I told him about Tony's regular Tuesday night visits around 9:00 p.m. I wondered what Charlie was up to and asked if he was tailing Tony. He had said, 'No, not exactly, but I'd appreciate it if you didn't mention my visit or my questions about his habits.' I remember thinking I could hardly wait to tell you."

"Did Charlie come in at 9:00, too?" Jen asked.

"No, later. Not until Tony was about two-thirds finished with his beer. Charlie came in, dressed in dark-colored street clothes, and sat in a booth behind Tony."

In her imagination, Jen pictured Charlie lurking in some dark doorway within sight of the casino, waiting for Tony to nip across the street and into the tavern.

"How did Tony act?" Jen asked.

"At first, he was his normal, obnoxious self. Do you know how he greets me?" Allison asked. Jen shook her head.

"He just says, 'Allison,'" she mimicked in a flat monotone, "as though my name were a statement."

"Well, that seems better than a term of endearment," Jen suggested with a smile. "What I really mean is, did he act any different, like he noticed that you'd looked in his safe?"

"No, not that I saw. If he thought I'd been in his safe, I know he would've been really angry. He just seemed, well, normal—like nothing was wrong."

"Let's hope it wasn't an act," Jen said with a sigh.

"I served Tony a glass of beer," Allison continued. "We chatted for a few minutes before Charlie arrived. As soon as he saw Charlie, he swallowed the rest of his beer, nodded to Charlie, and said goodnight. After Tony left, I stashed the dirty glass under the bar and wiped down the bar top.

"Charlie moved to Tony's bar stool and I offered him a beer. But, you know, Charlie's sworn off drinking. Says it isn't good for him. He had coffee instead. After I served him coffee, he said, 'That glass that you just put under the counter? I'd like to have it, if I may.' He's so polite.

"When I reached for the glass, he asked me to pick it up by the rim with a napkin and slip it in a plastic bag that he pulled out of his pocket. Then he asked me to carry the bag back to my office without anyone noticing. I nodded and walked down the hall, followed by Charlie. When we got there, Charlie asked to have the glass. That's when I asked him if he was looking for fingerprints.

"He gave me a stern look and said, 'Not a word to anyone, please, or I may be out of a job for insubordination.' He left by the back door."

Jen leaned on the table with her chin in her hand and quickly told Allison what Charlie had learned from his visits to the cabin and climbing site; and about his attempt to acquire fingerprint information from Tony's driver's license. Jen added, "I suspect that Tony's name is probably an alias."

"Really? This guy gets more and more creepy," Allison said with surprise, her gray eyes wide. Jen thought, does she mean creepy or interesting?

The waitress stopped by for the third time and Allison said, "Maybe we should order."

They studied their menus. After they ordered, Allison asked, "What did you find at the county clerk's office?"

"First of all, Barbara Knowles was off for the day, so I didn't get to meet her," Jen said.

"Too bad," Allison said. "You missed a real treat."

Jen smiled at Allison's humorous tone and continued. "The assistant clerk tried to help. She recognized the lot and claim numbers and mentioned that Charlie had been in earlier asking about the same ones. When she looked, she couldn't find any of the historical documents on the claims. She also remembered that the last time she saw them was when a 'local miner' had asked for them last summer."

"That would've been Steve," Allison said, adding, "Big surprise that the documents aren't in the clerk's office, since I saw them in Tony's safe." Jen agreed.

"So, tell me more about your idea for taking the claims to a mining company," Allison said.

"As I mentioned, I thought we should see if we can get some action by finding a mining company to reopen the claims."

"What do we have to do?"

"I took the first step already by preparing a prospect for presentation to a mining company. I used the photos of Steve's documents and the historical information you gave me to develop a written narrative and economic analysis. I also had the assay company send me hardcopies of the assay results for inclusion in the report. I redrafted the maps and cross sections and put together a package." Jen pulled out her file to show Allison her work just as the waitress arrived with their meals.

The dish of venison stew and fresh corn bread smelled delicious and momentarily distracted Jen until Allison asked again, "What do we have to do?"

"Since you are the owner of the claims, you need to prepare a letter for the mining company offering them the prospect."

Allison looked puzzled, "How do I do that?"

"Don't worry. I drafted a letter for you. If you'd like, you can read and sign it after we eat. If it's all right with you, I'll call up my old boss, Dr. Paul Case, tomorrow. I'll ask to meet with him, saying that I have a hot prospect and that I want him to be the first to see it."

"What happens after he sees it?"

"If he sees it and likes it, he'll sign a contract with you as the owner and begin exploratory activities on the claims. If they find an economically viable deposit, they'll proceed with production, meaning that the buildings overlying the mine will come down. Of course, the owners of the buildings are compensated for the structures and loss of income."

"Why would Tony object to that?" Allison wondered.

"If Tony is running a legitimate business, he'll receive full compensation," Jen answered. "However, illegal income from drugs, prostitution, money laundering, or restricted gaming are not compensated, and that may affect his standing with his 'investors.' If this is a hot issue with Tony, he's sure to react."

"I love it," Allison exclaimed, "it's perfect."

"Let me explain a bit about the gold exploration process. After the contract is signed, the mining company sends out registered letters to the property owners of the surface rights to notify them that they wish to begin exploration on their land. They have a legal right to proceed in this state, with or without the surface owner's permission. Because mining has had such a long and spectacular history in Colorado, mining rights have precedence over surface rights. The law states that the mining company is required to compensate the surface owner, but that the surface owner cannot prohibit mining."

"That means that they'll pay me?" Allison asked. "I'd hate to see the Miner's Tavern destroyed. It's rich with my family's history, you know, and I love the old place. Do you think I could get them to move the tavern to another foundation so that I could continue to run it?"

"I think so. The mining company is interested in historical buildings and doesn't like to destroy them needlessly. If they can save an historical building by relocating it, I'm sure they'll consider it. It'll be a while before they would start mining operations anyway, so you have some negotiation time. First they have to invest in additional exploration to determine the extent of the gold deposit. It may be large enough to affect other adjacent properties, too," Jen explained.

"Okay, first they see the prospect, then they sign a contract. After that they send out registered letters saying they want to explore. They explore and then decide if they want to open a mine. The next step is to compensate the surface owners and tear down their buildings. Last, they start the actual mining operations."

"That's a good summation," Jen answered, pleased at how quickly Allison caught on to the process.

"I can hardly wait to see them take a wrecking ball to the Golden Nugget. I'll be out there with my camera," Allison exclaimed, and added, "what do they do to explore?"

"They look at the historical information, assuming that Barbara Knowles hasn't lost it all," Jen said. "They might take surface soil samples and stream sediment samples. The company's geologists will re-enter open shafts and re-sample the veins for assay. They'll bring in drill rigs and drill a series of holes on a grid and collect the cores for analysis. The company's geologists will use all this information to develop a three-dimensional map of the potential ore body using computer models. It'll be fun to see the information shape up into a 3-D picture of the gold deposit."

"How long will all this take?" Allison asked.

"I'll try to get an appointment with Dr. Case next week," Jen answered. "Depending on the availability of funds and staff, the process could take months or years. I'm hoping I can get him moving right away, though. I'll just have to wait and see."

"This is exciting," Allison said. "Where do I sign?"

Jen smiled at Allison's enthusiasm and drew the letter from her file for Allison to read and sign, which she did. Jen placed the letter back in the file and asked Allison if she would like to see the maps. Allison declined, saying that they wouldn't mean anything to her. Jen was disappointed, but understood Allison's lack of interest in the technical issues.

They finished up their dinner with coffee and headed back to their homes, Allison to Dawson and Jen to Morrison.

❋   ❋   ❋

On Saturday morning, Jen decided to try calling Dr. Case at home. He said how happy he was to hear from her and was curious to know how her career as an environmental reporter was developing.

Dr. Case had laid Jen off from her job as an exploration geologist in 1989, shortly before his own dismissal by the owners, prior to their public declaration of bankruptcy. He'd always felt that she was the most talented geologist on his staff and he'd hated to let her go. Jen knew he had always felt especially guilty about her layoff because she'd been seven months pregnant at the time and unmarried. They had been friends and had stayed in touch over the years.

"Can I come in and see you early next week?" Jen asked. "I have a prospect that you should see. In my opinion, it's economically viable and worth your consideration."

"Certainly, Jen, how about Monday morning?"

"Can we make it early, so I'm not too late for work?"

They agreed to meet at 7:15 a.m. and hung up.

❋   ❋   ❋

Jen drove into the parking lot of the Rocky Mountain Mining Corporation in Lakewood at 7:10 on Monday morning and took her file up to Dr. Case's office. They chatted and poured coffee for themselves. Dr. Case invited Jen to spread out her data and maps on a large table in a conference room adjacent to his office. Jen laid out the maps, cross sections, assay data, her own neatly prepared geological interpretation, written analysis and economic evaluation, and Allison's signed letter. They spent an hour reviewing the information and Dr. Case was impressed with the prospect.

Jen excused herself and called her office to say she would be late.

When she returned to the conference room, Dr. Case said, "Jen, I would like to accept your prospect for presentation to the vice president of exploration. He'll be here tomorrow for a general review of our best prospects. I can slip this one in for presentation with the others we have identified. Your timing couldn't be better. Rocky Mountain Mining just happens to have money available right now because some of our South American exploration activities have been delayed. That's freed up funding for additional domestic exploration. The funds have to be spent this quarter."

"Great," Jen said. "Should I call you later in the week? I know this prospect will interest them. Just look at the assay data—one ounce of gold per ton. If the ore body is large enough, you'll have a 'gold mine,'" she joked.

Jen left her documents with Dr. Case, they shook hands, and Jen drove into Denver to start her work day. Jen sighed as she drove, thinking about how much she missed her past life as a geologist and wishing she could turn back the clock. *Can't be done*, she reminded herself.

When she arrived in her office, she called Allison to let her know that she had seen Dr. Case and had given him the documents.

"He was really interested," Jen said and relayed the details of the meeting, adding, "things could move quickly if they like the prospect."

"Good," Allison said. "Call me when you have more news."

❄ ❄ ❄

At her office on Wednesday morning, Jen received a call from Dr. Case.

"Good news, Jen," he said. "The vice president reviewed your prospect and accepted it for funding. You did a great job putting it together."

Jen said, "Thank you," feeling a bit guilty that she hadn't done all of the work herself. She had added to Steve's work, and had failed to provide him the credit—an unethical use of another's work. However, considering the circumstances, it was best to keep things simple in the eyes of the mining company, and anyway, Steve would be vindicated if they were able to prove that he was murdered by Tony.

"I wonder if you and Ms. Henry are available to sign an exploration contract with Rocky Mountain Mining Corporation? This prospect is so strong that we want exclusive rights for the next six months to initiate our exploration program. Can you come in this week?" Dr. Case asked.

"I'll call Allison and ask when she is available. Shall we say Friday morning, tentatively?"

They agreed on a time and place and Jen called Allison to confirm her availability.

* * *

On Friday morning, Jen and Allison walked into Dr. Case's office. He greeted them, shook hands, and served coffee. The mining company's head exploration geologist from California, Mike Lang, and several contract representatives were present. They sat around Dr. Case's conference table and discussed the details of the exploration contract, which cited Allison Henry as the owner of the subsurface rights to the properties underlying the Miner's Tavern and the Golden Nugget Casino; and Jennifer Slater as the prospector. Additional documents had been prepared for notification of owners of the affected surface properties, namely Allison Henry and Tony Delano.

Allison innocently asked, "When do you start mining?" bringing smiles to everyone in the room.

Dr. Case answered, "First, we'll assess the prospect through an exploration program. Once those data are assimilated, we will decide if the ore body is large enough to mine economically. The process can take years."

Allison looked disappointed, but her enthusiasm wasn't dampened. "When will you notify Mr. Delano?" She asked.

"Our legal department will act right away, considering our interest in the prospect. I imagine both of you will receive registered letters sometime next week," Dr. Case said.

"Your exploration activities won't affect my building will they?" Allison asked.

"No," Dr. Case answered. "If we decide to drill test holes and collect samples, we will drill around the existing buildings. We'll want to enter the shaft on your property, though, and some of the documents you'll be signing today will grant us permission to do that."

"I'd hate to see anything happen to my tavern. It's been in the family a long time. We've had some famous visitors there. My Uncle Ralph always claimed that the venerable Alferd G. Packer, cannibal extraodinaire, visited the Miner's Tavern. Only for drinks, though. No meals," Allison added as they laughed.

"Packer was quite a character," Dr. Case said, "or should I say, 'several characters'? After all, you are what you eat." They laughed again.

Jen smiled and said, "Packer certainly represents one of the more lurid aspects of Colorado mining history."

"Cannibals are a curious subject," Mike Lang said. "I know about

California's most famous cannibals—the Donner Party—but I don't recall the details associated with Alfred Packer."

"Ah, yes. The Alferd Packer story," Dr. Case said with amusement, turning to Mike.

"I'm missing something," Mike suggested, obviously curious and wishing to share in the amusement.

"Packer was a strange person," Dr. Case said. "Just about every Colorado resident knows about Packer. Would you like to hear the Alferd Packer story?" Dr. Case asked Mike. "We have time to digress briefly."

"Sure," Mike said.

"Well," Dr. Case began, "he was born in 1842 in Pennsylvania and christened 'Alfred' However, he idiosyncratically referred to himself as 'Alferd' all of his adult life. Packer was a shoemaker by trade. He served in the Union Army during the Civil War and was honorably discharged early for epilepsy."

"Is that when he came west looking for gold? In the 1860s?" Mike asked.

"Yes," Dr. Case said. "Packer worked his way westward for several years, until he found himself in Utah in the 1870s, working in the smelters and unsuccessfully mining for gold.

"He learned of gold strikes in Breckenridge, Colorado, and managed to join a party of aspiring gold miners headed into southwestern Colorado to prospect on Ute lands. It was quite a crew, ranging in age from less than 20 to nearly 60, and included Packer's future meals—he didn't have to pack in his food, his meals walked into the San Juan Mountains voluntarily," Dr. Case joked.

"I thought that they left Utah really late in the season and were caught in snow storms," Jen said.

"They set out from Bingham, Utah, in the late autumn of 1873 but were really poorly provisioned for the journey, especially so late in the year. Mike, both you and Jen have been down to the San Juans and you know what conditions can be like, even during the summer months."

Jen nodded in agreement, feeling an involuntary shudder run up her spine. Cannibals had always secretly fascinated and repelled her. "The group that left Utah was fairly large, wasn't it?" Jen asked as she brushed her hair behind her ear with her right hand.

As usual, Dr. Case's knowledge was thorough. "There were 21 members in the party. They didn't get along well and made some poor choices en route that caused delays, resulting in further depletion of provisions. A bad combination, especially since game was scarce.

"The Utes took them into camp near Delta, Colorado, where they were protected from the bitter winter weather. At this point, the group broke up. Packer and ten of the men elected to proceed. However, Packer had a dispute with one of the other members and the party was divided again, with five men accompanying Packer. A unfortunate choice, indeed, for those poor souls," Dr. Case said as he shifted in his chair. Jen saw that he was pleased with the interest he'd generated in his audience.

"Packer's party left the Utes on February 9th, 1874, with provisions supplied by their hosts. Packer wasn't seen again until mid-April, when he arrived on foot at Los Piños Indian Agency, located near Lake City. There he had the misfortune to encounter a member of the original party of 21 men. This gentleman became suspicious of Packer because he was carrying items belonging to other members of his party, including a hunting knife and a bank draft. Packer started drinking and telling conflicting stories regarding the deaths of his traveling companions and the exact nature of his ordeal."

"I think every student in the state knows something about Packer's activities between February and April," Jen commented recalling her first exposure to cannibals as a grade-school child.

Dr. Case nodded and smiled. "Packer eventually made two confessions, admitting that he had lived off the flesh of his five fellow travelers for nearly 60 days when he was lost between the Los Piños Agency and Lake San Cristobal.

"The details of the confessions were conflicting, although the bottom line remains the same—four of the men were murdered by hatchet blows to the head and the fifth was shot first and then axed. Packer ate his deceased companions while camping within 20 miles of the Indian agency."

"The press had a field day with that story," Jen said, silently asking herself how she would have felt about writing up such a gruesome tale. "Gory headlines appeared all over the world and titillated readers with eye-catchers such as, 'Human Jerked Beef' and 'Fiend Became Very Corpulent Upon a Diet of Human Steaks.'"

Jen saw Allison shudder.

"Packer was arrested," Dr. Case said, "but escaped under suspicious circumstances and became a fugitive for nearly nine years. He was finally captured in Wyoming in 1883. Maybe he stopped in Allison's tavern for a whiskey before heading to Wyoming."

"Maybe," Allison agreed in amusement.

"Packer was tried for murder in Lake City that same year, found guilty, and sentenced to death by Judge M. B. Gerry. The case was appealed to the Colorado Supreme Court and dismissed due to a technicality," Dr. Case said, shaking his head. "He was re-tried in Gunnison in 1886, again found guilty, and sentenced to 40 years in the state penitentiary."

"I wouldn't want to be his cell mate," Mike commented.

"Nor I," agreed Dr. Case smiling amicably. "Packer did time until 1901, when he was paroled by the governor. Packer resided near Littleton, Colorado, until his death in 1907. He is buried in the Littleton Cemetery and thousands of people visit his grave every year. Anyone ever visited there?" he asked, but no one had.

Dr. Case continued. "The National Forest Service has a Packer Victim Memorial Plaque located a few miles south of Lake City; and a marker on Cannibal Plateau showing visitors the way to Deadman's Gulch. The victims were buried near the site of their demise and their graves can be visited, if one so desires," he said nodding his head.

"Incidentally," Dr. Case continued, "Packer continues to generate controversy to this day. Recently, there has been proposed legislation afoot to grant him a posthumous pardon on the grounds that he was a victim of circumstance."

Allison said, "Packer's left quite a legacy. Not too long ago students at the University of Colorado in Boulder declared their dining facility the 'Alferd Packer Memorial Dining Hall.' Not much of a recommendation for the fare, if you ask me."

"Yeah," Jen said, "and how about their annual Alferd Packer Day celebration every April, where they have Packer look-alike contests and onion eating contests."

"An onion-eating contest doesn't sound very tasty," Mike said and the group agreed.

"My favorite Packer story has to do with The Packer Club," Jen said. "Have you ever seen their membership card? It contains the quote by Judge Gerry, who presided over Packer's first trial and who ordered him hanged in 1883. It says something like, 'There were seven Democrats in Hinsdale County, but you, you voracious, man-eating beast, you ate five of them.'" The group chuckled. Jen added, "I heard that when you join

The Packer Club, you receive a membership card with Packer's photograph on it, and a sandwich."

The group laughed.

"There's a mountain café up in Silverton that serves a 'Packer Special' to unsuspecting tourists and then informs them regarding the origin of the special's name. They do a brisk business," Dr. Case said.

"I'll have to remember all these details," Mike said. "I have several youngsters at home who'll find the story fascinating."

"Well, shall we continue with our business?" Dr. Case asked.

"Yes," said Allison, "where do I sign?"

They spent the next hour reviewing the documents and signing papers, clearly explaining the details to Allison before she signed. When she and Jen left the office, they stood outside in the parking lot for a few minutes.

"I wish I could be there to see the look on Tony's face when he receives the letter notifying him of impending doom," Allison said with glee.

Jen, more conservative in her response, replied, "I hope he doesn't come after us with a rock. I know this may sound silly to you, but we need to be careful. Lock our doors at night. Look over our shoulders. Try not to be alone."

"You worry too much, Jen," Allison admonished.

Jen shifted her feet and changed her brief case to her other hand. "You think you know Tony because you've seen him socially a few times," Jen said. "But you know he can't be trusted. We aren't even certain about his name. What if everything he told you about himself was a lie? If he murdered Steve because he didn't want a gold mine under his casino, what's to stop him from harming you or me for getting a large mining company involved?"

"I just don't think he will. Besides, he doesn't know about this, or that you even knew Steve. He doesn't know that I saw his files. He doesn't know that you and Charlie saw the trashed cabin. Since you didn't see Barbara Knowles when you went to the county clerk's office, he won't know that you have been asking for the missing claim documents."

Jen interrupted, "He's sure to know that Charlie was asking for the same documents earlier. When Charlie went into the clerk's office to get the same information, Barbara waited on him. If those two are involved in this, then Barbara would have told Tony about it."

"True. Well, I'll keep my head down," Allison said with a shrug. "You, too. How's your daughter doing?"

"Good, although we miss each other. I'm going down to the Springs this weekend to see her. Call me when you get your registered letter and let me know what happens."

Allison assured Jen that she would call and they parted.

❋ ❋ ❋

On Friday afternoon, Allison called Jen at the office. "Jen," she said with excitement, "I received my registered letter. I know Tony got his, too. Rick, my bartender, found out from one of his friends who works at the casino. His friend just happened to be present when the mailman delivered the letter for Tony to sign. Rick's friend said Tony turned purple when he saw who it was from."

"Okay, so now he's really mad. Maybe he'll do something rash," Jen said hoping it wouldn't be anything deadly.

"The letter had our names in it—mine as the owner of the mineral rights and yours as the prospector."

"Oh, well, he would have found out anyway," Jen said.

"I know you're going to see Sarah this weekend, but maybe we can get together next weekend and review our case," Allison suggested.

"Okay, I'll see how things go. We have to watch the weather, though, the long range forecast shows storms for late next week. I'd hate to take my Bronco into a blizzard."

Chapter Eleven

On Friday afternoon, Jen left work early. When she returned home to her empty house, she saw that she had a call on her answering machine. The message was from Barbara Knowles saying, "This call is for Jennifer Slater from the Monarch County clerk. I understand that you were looking for the information on gold mining claims associated with the Miner's Tavern and the Golden Nugget Casino. That information is now in our office. I can make it available to you on Friday afternoon or evening, before I pass it along to the sheriff's department. If you would like to review the information, please call the county clerk's office before 4:30 p.m."

Jen didn't remember leaving her name with the assistant clerk when she visited the Court House, but she was feeling stressed, and she knew that stress affected her memory. On the phone that morning, Sarah had cried to come home, and Jen knew she had to resolve this case soon.

She looked at her watch. The time was 4:36. Quickly, she dialed the number for the Monarch County clerk's office. It rang once and was answered by a woman, saying, "Monarch County clerk's office, Barbara speaking."

"Hi, this is Jen Slater, returning your call. Your message said that the documents I'm looking for are in your office?"

"Yes, they'd been misplaced. I have to turn them over to the sheriff's department and thought you might like to drive to Dawson before the storm hits, have a look, and drive home. I can hold them for you, but only for a few hours. I'll be here until about 6:30 p.m."

Jen's thoughts raced. "I can be there before 6:30. I'll leave right away. Thanks," she said and hung up.

Jen quickly called Norma in Colorado Springs, spoke with her daughter explaining that she would be coming on Sunday instead of tonight, and gave a series of instructions to Kaari. Next, she called the tavern. Allison wasn't in, but she spoke with Rick.

"Rick, I'm coming to Dawson and want to stay at Allison's house tonight. Can I leave a message for you to pass along?"

"Sure," he said, "Allison won't mind. She loves company. Do you know how to get there?" Jen didn't, so Rick gave her directions. "Do you know where the key is?" he asked. Jen said she didn't know that either. "You'll find it under the bird feeder on the front porch. There's a storm watch for tonight, you know, and it could be a bad one," he reminded Jen.

"Yes, I know. Thanks."

Jen threw a few essentials into an overnight bag and changed clothes. She knew it would be growing colder, the pleasant fall weather about to change, and Wild Bill had a poor heater. Leaving her hosiery on, Jen put on a pair of heavy wool socks, flannel-lined jeans, a tee shirt, turtleneck shirt, and sweater vest. She put on her gray boots, picked up a parka, and slipped her cell phone into her coat pocket.

Jen arrived in Dawson by 6:00. It was dark and the temperature had dropped to around 45 degrees after sundown, a comfortable evening temperature for a mountain town in early November. The sky was clear and there was no evidence of an impending storm. Jen had lived in Colorado long enough to know how deceptive the weather could be, especially under the erratic conditions of late fall. She parked Wild Bill behind the fire station and locked the Bronco. She approached the front of the County Court House and walked up the steps, wondering if the door would be locked. Reaching for the doorknob, she saw light coming from the clerk's office, and opened the door.

Jen entered the clerk's office and tapped the bell on the counter. A blonde, slightly overweight, heavily made-up woman in her early forties came from the rear of the office and stepped up to the counter.

"May I help you?" she asked, as though these were regular business hours and she was not expecting anyone in particular.

Jen thought the woman had to be Barbara Knowles, based on the descriptions she had received.

"I'm Jen Slater. You called me about documents for mining claims affecting the Miner's Tavern and the Golden Nugget Casino?"

Barbara looked puzzled, and answered, "Well then, I suppose I did. I'll get them for you. But you have to use them here because the sheriff's department wants to see them next. And you can't copy them because the copier's turned off for the night."

Barbara walked to the rear of the office, out of Jen's sight. She was gone about 10 minutes, during which time, Jen heard nothing except the creaks and groans of the old building. Finally, she heard Barbara's steps as she returned to the front counter. She was carrying a neat stack of folded papers, which she set on the counter across from Jen.

"Here you are. You only have until 6:30, about 15 minutes," she said as she walked to her desk. Jen heard her chair squeak as she sat down.

Jen examined the maps, noticing that they had been folded to a size where they would fit inside a manila file folder. Jen knew that, normally, important historical maps would have been stored flat inside a map drawer, or rolled inside a map tube. Folding large maps was discouraged, as the creases sometimes obscured critical data. She carefully unfolded the maps and examined each one. They were interesting and confirmed her own interpretation of the ore bodies and claims. No wonder Tony didn't want them available to the public. She could understand why Steve Myerhoff had wanted to see them as well.

Exactly 15 minutes later, Barbara returned to the counter and began folding the documents, pulling one from Jen's hands.

Jen watched her a moment, and asked, "Why are these maps folded? The one's I've seen are usually stored flat or rolled."

"This is how we do it here," Barbara snapped as she stacked the folded documents neatly on the counter. "Goodnight," she said abruptly.

Jen mumbled a thank you and left through the main door, thinking how unpleasant Barbara Knowles was and that Allison was fully justified in her comments about her.

It was chilly on the Court House steps and Jen zipped her parka up to her neck. She reached in her pocket for her keys and returned to Wild Bill. Jen thought of stopping at the Miner's Tavern but decided to call Allison from her home instead. She knew that Friday nights were busy for Allison and Rick and didn't want to distract them from their work. She started the Bronco and drove north on Fourth Street toward Allison's home. As the Bronco climbed the gravel road into the mountains, Jen noticed that Wild Bill seemed sluggish.

She found Allison's home, pulled into the secluded drive behind large evergreens, and looked at the porch for the bird feeder. She turned off the headlights and engine. As she reached for her overnight bag, she felt the Bronco shift independently, as if a weight were moving. She froze as she felt the cold muzzle of a handgun press against the base of her skull.

A husky male voice said quietly, "Turn on the engine."

Jen was unable to move.

"Do it," the man said sharply as the gun's muzzle was thrust against her neck.

Jen's breathing was shallow and her body flooded with adrenaline. Her hand shook as she reached for the key and restarted the engine.

"Drive back down the mountain to Dawson."

Jen somehow managed to put the Bronco in reverse and return to the road.

"Drive very carefully and follow every instruction," the man said.

Jen was terrified and gripped the steering wheel so tightly that her knuckles were white. She drove back onto the paved portion of Fourth Street and into town. They approached the north side of the Golden Nugget Casino.

"Turn left on North Street." Jen turned east on North Street and saw the back of the Golden Nugget Casino looming on her right.

"Turn right onto the delivery ramp." She turned the Bronco onto the casino's downward sloping ramp.

As Jen entered the delivery ramp, the garage door opened automatically. She drove slowly into the deserted underground delivery area and saw another garage door open on her right leading into a parking area the size of a double garage.

"Turn right and park. Turn off the lights and engine."

Jen did everything she was told and was aware of the garage door closing behind her, trapping her inside an underground parking garage with her unknown assailant. She sat with her hands clenched on the steering wheel.

She croaked, "Are you going to shoot me here?"

The man sniggered. "No. We have something else in mind."

Jen listened to his voice. It wasn't a voice she recognized, although it reminded her of the threatening phone call.

"Get out," the man said, as she heard him opening the rear door behind her. She slipped out of the Bronco and looked over her shoulder at her captor. The harsh neon light revealed a muscular man wearing dark clothing. His face was obscured by a black ski mask and he wore tightly fitted black leather gloves. He motioned with his gun for her to move toward a small, private elevator that opened into the garage. They entered the elevator and rode to the top floor. The door opened into a long, dimly lit hallway with a security door at the far end.

The man used the gun to guide Jen down the hall to a door on her right that had a sign saying "Private." Across the hall was a door marked "Manager's Office." The man reached around Jen and tapped quietly on the door. It was unlocked from within and opened by Tony. He was dressed in a black suit, white shirt, and red tie.

Tony motioned them inside and indicated for Jen to sit in a chair across the room from the sofa. The main room of the living quarters was outfitted with western decor, including furniture made of knotty pine and western paintings on the walls. Jen moved across the polished wood floor of the room, stepping onto a thick rug. Once seated she looked down at the floor and into the enormous, snarling face of a huge bear, its expression permanently fixed in a look of hatred, its glass eyes stared outward and nostrils flared. The lips were drawn back for effect, exposing the canines. The mouth was large enough to swallow a small dog. The fur was a golden brown color, with a grayish wash. In life, the bear must have been huge. Jen stared. *So, here is the bear rug that had provided the tuft of fur.*

Tony left the room through the door Jen had entered and the man with the ski mask stood across from her, as though on guard. Jen had looked around the room and the decor made her think of Ronald Reagan's personal quarters at the White House, when he was in office. She began to notice that bear motifs were everywhere—in the paintings on the walls, as sculptures on the shelves. *This man has a bear fetish. No wonder he would think of a bear to cover his intrusion into Steve's cabin.*

Jen continued to unobtrusively scan the living quarters. To her right was a dining room set. She was attracted to a bone-colored object sitting on the table and turned her head slightly to see more clearly. The enormous skull of an animal with huge canines was sitting on the table. After a moment of puzzlement, Jen realized that the object was the skull of a bear. From where she sat, Jen couldn't tell if the skull was real or a plastic replica.

As a center piece, Jen wondered how it could possibly serve to enhance the appetite. *Maybe Tony took the skull with him when he trashed to cabin and used it to crunch open the food cans.*

The television was turned to the cable weather channel and Jen was vaguely aware of the forecaster's comments. She glanced at her watch and saw it was 7:30 p.m. Jen was wearing her parka and thought of the cell phone in her pocket, wondering if there were a place she could make a call without being observed.

"May I use the bathroom?" she asked, her voice sounding strained and unnatural.

The man said, "Stand up. Turn around. Feet apart and hands behind your head."

The man approached her from behind and began to frisk her, finding the cell phone immediately. He took it from her parka pocket, tossed it onto the sofa, and finished his search.

"No," he said. "Sit down." He returned to his guard position.

❋   ❋   ❋

Shortly after 10:00 p.m., Jen heard a loud squeak in the hallway and wondered if someone were entering the hallway through the noisy security door Allison had told her about. A minute later, she heard a light tapping on the door and it was opened by the man in the ski mask. Jen was surprised to see Tony thrust Allison into the room. Leaving the door to his private quarters open, Jen heard him lock the security door and the door to his office.

Jen and Allison exchanged glances. Tony entered the living quarters and closed the door behind him, saying sarcastically, "Ladies, let me take your coats." Neither one of them moved. Tony's voice hardened as he said, "Now!"

Jen took off her parka and Allison removed her fringed buckskin jacket. The man in the ski mask collected them. Tony indicated that Ski Mask should frisk Allison, which he did, finding only her car keys. With a nod from Tony, he left the room.

"What do you want?" Allison demanded in a firm voice.

"Shut up, bitch," Tony sneered. "Sit on the floor. The bear rug is very comfortable." Tony motioned with the gun for them to sit together on the bear rug. "No talking," he said as though he were a school teacher and they were the students.

Jen and Allison sat side by side on the bear rug, their shoulders touching. Even though she was afraid, Jen couldn't help noticing the thick, warm fur and faint, musky odor. She dug her fingers deep down into the fur, clenching, grasping clumps between her fingers and sweaty palms.

Jen stared at Tony as he relaxed on the sofa across from them. He loosened and removed his tie, keeping his gun trained on them.

"I saw you admiring my bear rug," Tony said to Jen in a conversational tone. "Beautiful, isn't he? *Ursus horribilis*. Kodiak brown bear—a subspecies of grizzly." Tony smiled to himself. "I shot this bear in the Aleutians five years ago and had him made into a rug as a reminder of his power. Guess how many trained dogs this bear killed before I shot him," Tony demanded. Jen had no idea how to answer this question. "Guess," Tony demanded again in a menacing tone.

Jen whispered, "Two?"

Tony grinned and said, "This animal killed four hunting dogs before I shot him. I killed him with a single bullet—right to the heart." Tony patted his chest for dramatic effect.

He's bragging, Jen thought, just like some tough guy.

"He was about 10 years old," Tony continued, "in the prime of life. Was over nine feet long and more than five feet at the shoulder." Tony paused, recalling the scene with pleasure, impressed with his prowess over the enormous and frightening bear.

"You know how much this bear weighed?" he demanded waving his gun at Jen.

"Five hundred pounds?" Jen said.

Tony laughed. "You stupid bitch," he said, "look at the size of him— a thousand pounds."

He's trying to humiliate me.

She imagined a scenario where Great White Hunter Tony Delano arranged a trip to the Aleutian Islands off the coast of Alaska with a group of poachers who had caught the bear in an illegal steel-toothed foot trap. She pictured Tony shooting the trapped bear without endangering himself. The dogs, of course survived the experience, having been trained not to approach within the range of an enraged bear. Jen decided that Tony thought the story about the dogs being killed by the bear added to the drama of the scene. *If he ever did hunt, it was probably without a license.*

"Grizzlies have ugly claws. Five-inches long on their front feet," Tony said raising his left hand and curling his fingers. "They can easily tear open a fallen tree to reach grubs and termites. One blow to the head can bring down a bull elk in his prime." He suddenly lunged toward Jen with his claw-like hand. Jen flinched and turned her face away from Tony, instinctively raising her hand in self-defense.

Tony's laugh had a disturbing quality that truly frightened Jen. *He's depraved. He wants to be as frightening as the bear.*

"They're tough animals," Tony continued. "When I was hunting in Alaska, the rangers at Denali National Park were relocating bears. They had one large male grizzly in a cage and were ready to release the bastard when he tried to escape. The ranger shot that son of a bitch five times at close range with a .357 magnum. The last bullet stopped him only because the shot was lucky enough to sever the spinal cord."

Tony narrowed his eyes, staring at Jen. "A female grizzly is a fine mother. Ever wonder why she's so fierce about protecting her cubs?" Jen shook her head, wondering where this would lead.

"She'll take on a male twice her size and drive him off if he comes near her young, even if he was the cubs' father. Why?" Tony demanded of Jen.

Jen shook her head and whispered, "I don't know."

Tony answered with an air of satisfaction, "Because the male will eat the cubs if he catches them. Did you know they were cannibals? They'll catch and eat black bears, too. Black bears are wimps," Tony said smugly.

"Can't shoot a bear between the eyes. Just makes him mad. You know why? Huh?" Tony demanded again. Jen shook her head again.

"Because the bone of the bear's skull is so thick that it's impenetrable to bullets. The original bonehead." Tony said laughing at his own joke.

Tony continued his recital. "Climbing trees is no guarantee that you're safe from a bear attack. All bears climb trees, even grizzlies. Climb a tree and the bear comes right up after you, biting into your calves and thighs and trying to pull you down.

"You can't outrun a bear on open ground. Bears have been clocked at 35 miles per hour. You run from a bear and he'll think you're food. Old bear'll take you right down and crush your skull with one bite." Jen thought of the snarling bear rug and the ferocious look permanently frozen on the animal's face.

"Ever see what a bear can do to a human body?" he asked Jen in a friendly tone as though they were discussing a benign subject. Jen made no response. "Grizzlies might not wait until you're dead before feeding," Tony said, he voice becoming hushed and ominous. "They usually start with your thighs and work their way up. They bite into your flesh and pull upward, yanking strips of muscle and fat from your legs. Bears like breast meat, too." Tony leered at Allison. "When they finish there, they move to your arms. Sometimes they take the viscera, especially the liver and other organs. Their claws are like knives and they open you up with one stroke."

As Tony talked, Jen felt the blood drain from her face as she realized she was watching the veneer of civility slip away from Tony, revealing the true nature of a cruel and inhumane man. *He's enjoying this.*

"Bears will eat anything. Humans are food, too. What they like best, though, is a rotten, stinking carcass. The riper, the better. Imagine what a winter kill carcass is like in the warm days of spring," Tony said, gloating. "Grizzly comes out of his den, thin and hungry. He raises his nose to the air and sniffs, locating that ripe carcass. He just can't wait to sink his teeth into the rotten remains."

Ski Mask returned to the living quarters, dropping Allison's keys onto the sofa beside Jen's cell phone. Tony picked up the cell phone and turned it over. "You won't need this anymore," he said, as he crushed the phone with the butt of his gun as Jen watched in dismay.

Tony rose from the sofa, letting the pieces of the phone fall to the floor, and walked into his bedroom, closing the door behind him.

Jen and Allison both turned their attention to Ski Mask, as he stood guard by the door.

"How did you get here?" Jen whispered to Allison when Ski Mask was concentrating on the weather report.

"Tony called me at the tavern about 9:30 and told me to come over at 10:00, saying that he had a new contract for me that was 'generous.' He told me to come up to the top floor and into his office through the security door. When I tapped on his office door, he yanked it open, shoved a gun in my face, and grabbed me by the wrist. He spun me around and twisted my arm up behind my back. What do you think he'll do?"

"Shut up," Ski Mask ordered.

Jen glanced at her watch—the time was 10:40. A few minutes later, Tony returned to the living room dressed in expensive outdoor attire and warm boots. *These must be the clothes he wore when he shot the bear. Now he's going to wear them to shoot us.*

Chapter Twelve

Tony took two warm parkas from his living room closet and tossed one to Ski Mask. Jen and Allison watched from the floor as the men put on the jackets. Tony moved behind Allison, squatted behind her, and reached for her wrist, tightly twisting her arm up behind her back.

He leaned over her shoulder and said through clenched teeth, "You're such a stupid bitch. You can't fool me. I see right through you. You'll suffer. I'll have your tavern and I'll tear it down. It'll be gone and all your pitiful family history with it."

Allison was frightened by Tony, but she managed to say bravely, "Let go of me!"

Tony laughed harshly and reached for her other wrist. Allison struggled against Tony as he tied her hands behind her back with cord, cutting into her skin. He took a fistful of her hair and yanked her head back so that she looked straight up into his face. Tears came to her eyes.

Tony smiled. "That's better. I'd rather see fear than anger in your face. I've known what you've been up to for some time. I'm smarter than I look, bitch."

"So am I," Jen heard Allison say in a strained voice, admiring her nerve.

"I seriously doubt that," Tony sneered and released her hair, saying to himself, "Revenge is sweet." He gagged her mouth with a kerchief, knotting it tightly behind her head.

Tony moved to Jen and tied her hands behind her back and gagged her mouth.

"And you, little Miss Reporter. Your snake bite wasn't enough warning? You want your defective daughter to be next?" Tony mocked. "I know everything about you and your little family. You should have kept your nose out of my business. You're such an amateur," he said with disdain.

Jen was frightened, her eyes opened wide.

"Oh," Tony said. "You're afraid. Good. I like that in a woman. Are you afraid for your precious daughter? The cripple? You should be. I don't have to break her legs," he laughed, "they're already ruined. What kind of mother are you, anyway, producing a physically defective brat?" He laughed again as he stood up.

"Let's go, girls. On your feet."

Jen and Allison looked at each other, afraid to move.

"I said, let's go!" He reached down and took a handful of Allison's hair and dragged her to her feet. "Now!" he said to Jen. She struggled to stand. Tony kept a hold of Allison's hair and motioned for Jen to precede them through the door Ski Mask held open. Jen walked into the hallway, followed by Tony and Allison.

Ski Mask locked the door to Tony's private quarters behind him as he entered the hallway. He took Jen by the arm and pushed her down the hallway toward Tony's private elevator. The elevator door was open and they entered the dim interior. Tony used his key to unlocked the control panel below the elevator floor buttons. He flipped several switches, one of which shut off the elevator's interior lights, and re-locked the box.

The only light in the elevator was from the floor buttons. Tony pushed the button for "Roof." They rose one floor and the elevator opened into an unlit sheltered lobby with one window facing toward the helicopter. It was dark on the roof. The air was cold, but the stars were still visible. The storm front had not yet reached Dawson.

"Sit down," Tony ordered. Jen and Allison sat on the cold lobby floor looking up at Tony has he held his gun on them. Ski Mask left them for the helicopter and was preparing for their departure.

"Isn't he wonderful?" Tony asked in a mocking voice, motioning toward Ski Mask with his gun. "He can do just about anything. I arranged for him to fly a helicopter here from Las Vegas to help me take care of you two girls. He gave me a hand with your geologist buddy, too. Uncle Mario loaned him to me. My uncle runs the Desert Dunes in Vegas and he's smooth," Tony said in admiration. "He has no criminal record and is a respectable community member with sons and grandchildren. The perfect setup."

Mafia... Allison's intuition was right. How much of what he says is true? Probably most of it—why lie to people who are about to die? And his reference to "geologist buddy..." Did he mean Steve? Is Tony saying that he and Ski Mask murdered Steve?

Tony continued, "My uncle is a good businessman and never lets competition stand in his way. He has a reputation among our family as a man who overcomes every obstacle. When I get out of this dump, I'll be joining Uncle Mario in Vegas as his right-hand man."

It was clear to Jen that Tony held his uncle in high esteem, but she wondered if he would have to compete with his cousins, Mario's sons, for the coveted position.

"Uncle Mario is proud of my performance here," Tony bragged. "I'm reporting close to $18 million every month in business to the state—and that's barely scratching the surface in terms of my overall profits from 'associated businesses.'"

Jen, looking up at Tony from where she sat on the lobby floor, wondered why, when he was so clearly in control, he still felt the need to impress them. *Maybe he just can't resist the desire to brag.*

Ski Mask returned to the lobby.

"On your feet," Tony ordered.

Tony and Ski Mask guided Jen and Allison through the lobby door and toward the helicopter. Ski Mask opened the door on the co-pilot's side and released the seat, sliding it forward. He motioned with his gun for Jen to climb in. She hesitated and he struck her with the back of his left hand, knocking her head against the helicopter. She was slightly dazed, more from the shock of having been hit than from the blow itself.

Jen turned to face the helicopter but knew she couldn't climb into the cramped space with her hands tied. She motioned with her fingers and felt the cold blade of a sharp knife against her hands as the cord was severed.

She heard Tony's voice ordering her to get in and she struggled into the rear seat. Allison climbed in next, her hands also free of bonds. Even in the dark, she sensed Allison's mutual fear. Ski Mask entered the pilot's seat and Tony climbed into the co-pilot's seat.

"Put on your seat belts, girls, I wouldn't want you flying around the cockpit in case we hit turbulence. We're going for a ride," Tony told them over his shoulder as he and Ski Mask adjusted their headphones. Ski Mask started the engine as Jen and Allison fumbled with their seat belts and harnesses in the dark. The only light inside the helicopter was from the dials and digital displays in the cockpit. Jen saw some of the lighted dials and noticed the clock. The time was 11:20.

Ski Mask lifted off from the roof of the casino without using landing lights and rose straight into the air before turning west toward the Roosevelt National Forest. Jen felt the cold and began to shiver slightly. She looked toward Allison, but the interior was too dark for Jen to see her face. Jen reached behind her head and untied the gag. Why would Tony object now? she thought. No one could hear them scream. She reached behind Allison's head and untied the knot, letting both gags drop to the floor of the helicopter. Jen and Allison reached for each other's hands in the dark and grasped tightly.

Jen saw the digital clock in the cockpit and watched minutes slipping away, wondering if they would really be her last. Twenty minutes had passed since the helicopter had departed the casino. Jen felt their air speed decrease. Suddenly, the pilot turned on landing lights and began to search for a suitable landing site. He hovered briefly and gently set the helicopter down on a rocky outcrop above the tree line, slowing the rotors.

Tony unbuckled his harness and seat belt, shouting over his shoulder for Jen and Allison to unbuckle. He removed his headphones, opened the door, and jumped out. Jen felt the blast of cold air enter the interior of the helicopter. Tony unlatched the seat and slid it forward so that Allison and Jen could climb out. Allison slid out first and Tony shoved her downslope, away from the helicopter's rotors. Jen dropped to the ground and slipped on the icy rocks. Tony kicked and pushed her downslope.

Allison helped Jen to her feet. *He'll shoot us and fly away. I'll never see my daughter again.* To her surprise, Tony climbed back into the helicopter and slammed the door. The helicopter lifted off from the side of the mountain, flew overhead, and was soon gone from sight, the sound of the rotors quickly fading away.

Abandoned.... So, he isn't going to shoot us and fly away. He's going to leave *us and fly away.* Jen and Allison looked at each other in the dim starlight. Both had wrapped their arms around themselves trying to conserve body heat.

They stood on barren, windswept rocky ground above the tree line somewhere in the Roosevelt National Forest. The stars shone in the moonless sky, but Jen knew it wouldn't last. Soon the temperature would drop further, the wind would pick up, clouds move in, and snow fall. And fall. Ending some time on Sunday, according to the weather forecasters.

"That sorry son of a bitch," Allison exclaimed, her breath visible in the icy air. "He left us! He didn't even have the courtesy to shoot us. Now we'll freeze to death. He likes bears so much, maybe he thought it would be a great joke to leave us for spring bear food."

Jen's eyes adjusted to the dim starlight. "We won't freeze," she said calmly as she quickly removed her vest.

"What are you doing?" Allison asked with astonishment, "It's 10 degrees out here."

Jen began to wrap the vest around her head and neck, leaving an opening through which to see. "Thirty percent of your body heat is lost from your head and neck. I'm going to protect my head and neck with my vest. Do you have any clothes you can use to cover your head and neck?"

Allison looked down at her cowgirl outfit. She was wearing her boots with acrylic socks, a blue denim calf-length skirt with a cotton half-slip, a long-sleeved blue check flannel shirt, and a leather vest.

"My slip might work," she said as she reached up under her skirt, pulling her slip down to her ankles. She stepped out of the slip and picked it up, not sure what to do. Jen reached up and wrapped the slip around Allison's head and neck, leaving a place for her to see through. They were both shivering.

Jen sat on a rock and unlaced her boots, mentally reviewing her clothing. *Hosiery and boots will protect my feet and flannel-lined jeans will protect my legs. I have on a tee-shirt and turtleneck that will keep my upper body and arms from exposure. My head, neck, and face are covered.*

Jen slipped off her boots and removed her heavy wool socks. She put her boots back on and laced each the best she could with her cold fingers. Allison had begun to move around to help warm herself.

"Do you have anything to cover your hands with?" Jen asked as she pulled the socks on over her hands and up her arms nearly to her elbows. *Make-shift mittens, but they might work.*

"No. Nothing," Allison replied, "well, except my socks."

Jen considered Allison's thin boots and said, "Better leave them on. Keep your hands under your arm pits."

Jen stood up. "I have an idea," she said. "We need to move down to the tree line and look for shelter." She studied the stars. *My survival skills are rusty.*

"Why are you looking up?" Allison asked as she watched Jen. "I thought you wanted to go downhill?"

"I do, but I want to go downhill on the north side of the mountain and look for a drift of last year's snow."

"Snow? That's cold! Why don't we look for a cabin or something?"

"We could wander a long time and find nothing before the storm hits. I want to find natural shelter if we can. Besides, there's a chance that Charlie will find us."

"How? No one even knows we're missing. Charlie doesn't know where we are and Tony isn't going to tell anyone."

Jen studied the stars and found the Big Dipper. She looked for the two pointer stars located on the outside of the dipper. She knew that these two stars point to the last star that makes up the handle of the Little Dipper. This was the Pole Star, and told her where the north side of the mountain was.

"This way. Let's head downhill this way," Jen said, feeling the cold through her clothing as if they were no more substantial than paper. They started downslope, angling to the left toward the north side of the mountain. The tree line was visible and loomed larger as they picked their way over the icy rocks and tufts of alpine vegetation. As they approached the tree line, their progress was hindered by low-growing, stunted shrubs and ground-hugging evergreens. About 500 feet downslope they reached the tree line.

Jen kept her fix on the Pole Star, but realized that the stars would not be visible long, as wisps of high clouds had begun to drift in overhead, harbingers of the coming storm.

"I'm looking for a medium-sized evergreen, like a Douglas fir or Colorado blue spruce that still has a ring of snow about the base," Jen told Allison.

They entered into the tree line on the northern side of the peak. Jen saw lodgepole pine trees, but nothing like what she had in mind. Patches of snow still showed in some of the low areas, and she saw an old drift preserved in the lee of outcropping rock. At least there is a chance of finding snow, she thought. Good thing there was lots of snow in the high country last spring and a cool summer this year.

"I see a spruce, Allison. It's down in that hollow," Jen said through clenched teeth. She wished she could run but was afraid of stumbling. Allison followed Jen downslope to the base of a large spruce tree. The low-lying, broad branches fanned out from the base of the tree, tapering upward gracefully. The tree, still and black in the dark, towered 50 feet above them. In the dim starlight, Jen saw a snow ring preserved around the tree, rising up to the base of the lowest branches.

"What luck, we're saved," Jen exclaimed.

"How?"

"Follow me." Jen motioned for Allison to follow her to the downslope side of the tree. The old snow drift on this side of the tree was shallow, as though more snow had collected on the upslope side than on the downslope side.

Jen stooped down and peered under the branches where the snow ring was shallowest. "If we crawl in here," she said to Allison, "we can survive until Charlie finds us."

"Why do you think Charlie is going to find us? Are you delirious already?"

Jen stood up and began to kick away the hardened snow with her boot and Allison stooped to help move away the snow and enlarge the opening. Jen reached for her shoulder, saying, "Your hands aren't protected. I have mittens and I'll remove the snow. Stand back a ways."

When the hole was big enough for Jen to enter, she said, "I'll check it out."

Jen crawled underneath the evergreen boughs, sliding down the snow ring on her belly into the trough formed between the snow ring and tree trunk. Jen couldn't see anything underneath the dense branches over her head. She felt the tree trunk and found that the opening was about two feet high, with a space of about three feet between the trunk and the ring of snow. The trough was a good shelter. The ground near the base of the tree was free of snow and covered with spongy pine needles and dried pine cones.

"Are you all right?" Allison called. "Are there animals in there?"

"No animals," Jen answered. "It's perfect." She began to crawl clockwise around the tree trunk, back toward the opening on the downslope side of the tree. Soon Jen's head, swathed in her vest, appeared at the opening. She slid over the crest of the snow ring and out of the shelter.

"Crawl inside and make yourself comfy," she told Allison. "The clouds are already covering the sky and the wind is picking up."

"Is it safe?"

"Yes. And there're no animals. It smells just like a Christmas tree. You'll be warmer inside."

Allison stooped down to the opening and slid over the crest and under the tree.

"Are you coming?" she asked Jen.

"Yes, but I want some branches for insulation. I'll be back."

Jen moved back upslope toward the tree line. The closer she walked to the tree line, the smaller the trees were. She located young fir trees less than six feet tall and began to strip branches from the smallest ones, her make-shift mittens protected her hands from the rough tree bark. Jen dropped the branches into a pile near her feet. When several of the trees were stripped of boughs, Jen gathered an arm load and struggled back toward the shelter.

When she reached the entrance, she dropped to her knees and began to push the branches underneath the tree, saying, "Allison, I want you to put these branches underneath you. We need about six inches of thickness between us and the ground surface. Make a nest and we'll curl up together. I'll be back."

"Okay," Allison responded. Jen heard Allison crawling around the tree trunk and toward the entrance to reach the branches.

Jen returned to the small fir trees. She heard the sound of the wind in the treetops and felt the tug against her clothing. She didn't have much time. Wind chill would rapidly cause hypothermia if she were exposed for long. She picked up the remaining branches and carried them back toward the shelter. Snowflakes fell, obscuring her vision. She stumbled downslope from the tree line, thinking *I must be near the shelter. Why can't I find it?* Jen began to feel a touch of panic. *Where's the spruce?* She heard the sound of trees in motion and felt the strength of the wind against her body. I have to find the shelter, she thought.

"Allison! Allison!" she called out, afraid she wouldn't be heard over the rising wind. She stopped and listened for a response.

"Jen! Where are you?" Jen was relieved to hear the faint voice, but surprised that the sound was behind her. In her disorientation, she momentarily thought Allison had left the shelter and had tried to follow her.

"Allison, I'm lost. Start counting slowly."

Allison paused briefly and began to count. Jen walked toward the sound of Allison's voice and knew that she was nearing the shelter as the counting grew louder. Suddenly she was at the base of the tree. Jen kneeled down and began to push the branches underneath the protective boughs of the spruce. Allison moved around in the trough and reached for the branches. When they were all inside, Jen slid into the shelter on her belly.

By now, her hands, face, and feet were numb. She began to shiver.

"I made a nest," Allison said. "Can you crawl up here? You poor thing. You must be freezing." Jen heard the concern in Allison's voice.

Allison had done a fair job of constructing a nest in the dark. The activity had helped to warm her, too, Jen realized; Allison wasn't shivering as much now.

Jen crawled up onto the nest. "I'm all right. I think we'll be safe in here. Curl up around the trunk, but don't hug it. Stuff some branches between yourself and the tree trunk," Jen said. Allison struggled with several branches and managed to wedge them between herself and the trunk.

"I'm going to snuggle in behind you to conserve body heat." Jen crawled up behind Allison, pulling several branches over her friend. She pulled branches up behind her back to insulate herself from the snow ring and dragged other branches over her legs and shoulders. Jen placed her body against Allison's, tucking her knees up behind Allison's knees.

"It's a lot warmer in here than outside," Jen said.

"Are you sure?"

"Yes, neither one of us is shivering as much and there's no wind inside our shelter. Maybe we can prevent hypothermia and severe frostbite," Jen said hopefully.

My famine guard is finally going to be useful.

"I can't feel my feet anymore, or my fingers. How 'bout you?"

"No," answered Jen, "but we'll be fine."

❋ ❋ ❋

They were quiet for a long time, shivering occasionally to stay warm. Although they heard the trees in motion outside of their shelter and felt their spruce move and creak in the wind, the thick boughs and snow ring blocked the wind and snow.

"Why do you think that Charlie is going to rescue us?" Allison asked.

"When I got home this afternoon—I guess now it would be yesterday afternoon—I had a message on my answering machine from Barbara Knowles saying that the documents I wanted had been found. I could see them if I hurried to Dawson before 6:30 p.m. It was the only time I could look at them because she said she had to turn them over to the sheriff's department."

"Weren't you afraid it was a setup?" Allison asked.

Jen was thoughtful for a moment. "Yes. So I called my daughter's nanny, Kaari, in Colorado Springs and told her I'd beep her every four hours from my cell phone until I could get down there. I told her to contact Charlie if I missed a check-in. I hope she did and that my plan works. We'll have to wait out the storm, first, before anyone will come for us." Jen sighed.

"The storm is supposed to last for two days. Think we'll make it?" Allison asked anxiously.

"We have to," Jen said with determination. "What would Sarah do without me?"

They listened to the wind in their tree. Jen said, "It was snowing when I crawled in here. Now the wind is picking up. Maybe we'll get more snow on our tree and the insulation will be better."

"I know snow is supposed to be a good insulator, but I always think of it as something cold," Allison said with a shiver.

Jen's shivering had become less severe and more intermittent.

"We aren't shivering so bad now. I wonder how long you can shiver?" Jen asked trying to remember from her training in basic survival skills.

"Until you die, I think," Allison answered, "or until you get bad hypothermia, anyway." After a pause, she added, "I have to use the bathroom."

"Can you wait?" Jen asked with concern.

"For two days?"

"I mean that you should try to prevent dehydration," Jen answered. "One way to do that is not to pee. It keeps the moisture inside you for longer. It's just a suggestion. If you really have to go, please use the other side of the tree."

"Maybe I'll wait," Allison said. "Worse things have happened to me."

"Jen," Allison said after a pause, "how did you know to look for a spruce tree?"

Jen was thoughtful, recalling her experiences with Steve. "When Steve and I were graduate students together, one of our favorite activities was to work with a Boy Scout Explorer's High Adventure Post. We spent a lot of time training teens how to rock climb and rappel. We also participated in survival training and taught kids how to build snow caves and shelters. Colorado blue spruce trees are nearly perfectly designed as ready-made shelters. A snow ring completes the shelter by providing a wall around the base of the tree. We were incredibly lucky to find this tree, because they're not abundant." Jen paused, adjusting a pine branch to cover her shoulder.

"I was also thinking about making a snow cave for us, but the snow at this time of the year is crystalline and icy, not fresh and fluffy. I did see one old snow drift when we were looking for trees, but we didn't have anything to break through the ice or to dig a cave with."

"Oh," Allison answered.

Jen wondered what the time was. Her watch was buried under the long sleeve of her turtle neck and her sock-mitten.

"Allison, can you see your watch?" Jen asked.

"I can, but I don't have a lighted dial."

Jen used her right hand to pull the sock down from her forearm to her wrist. She scooted her sleeve up over her watch and held the lighted dial up close to her face.

"It's nearly 1:00 a.m." she told Allison as she replaced her clothing. "Do you feel any warmer now?"

"Yes, but my feet and toes are still numb."

"I feel warmer, too," Jen said. "Maybe we should rest."

Chapter Thirteen

Jen and Allison lay quietly together. Allison stirred and said, "That Tony… You know, I'll never forget him as long as I live, which might not be too long. He's a murderer and kidnapper. What a cruel man, taunting you about your daughter's handicap. He has facets I never expected. Some things about him were obvious—like his machismo and braggadocio. Other things were more subtle, like his fetish for bears. I never would have guessed he had a thing about bears. Maybe they secretly terrify him. I wish a bear would eat Tony."

"Unfortunately, he intended us to be the bear food," Jen said.

"We'll be ripe carcasses by next spring, as Tony so delicately pointed out in the comfort of his own home," Allison said with a shudder. "The bears will come out of their dens starved and sniff us right out. At least we'll be dead so we won't have to be eaten alive, even by a wimpy black bear. A 300-pound bear is big enough to scare me. It doesn't take a half-ton bear to do the job."

Jen, thinking that Allison was becoming morbid, changed the subject by asking, "So, you were married?"

"Yeah. Jack. Maybe Jack wasn't such a bad husband, after all. He had his problems. He had cared about me. Too bad he also cared about Debbie and Sue, those little tarts. Jack is best left behind. So is St. Louis and all those attorneys, for that matter."

Jen thought that Allison made it sound so easy to leave her past behind. *Why can't I do the same?*

"What about you? Have you been married?" Allison asked.

"No. I lived with Greg Myerhoff and we had Sarah. Greg couldn't deal with a child and left for South America. We haven't heard from him since."

"Greg Myerhoff? Any relationship to Steve?"

"Brothers, but they were incompatible personalities," Jen said. Still curious about Allison's relationship with Steve, Jen said, "Mind if I ask you a personal question?"

"No, go right ahead. Our secrets aren't going anywhere."

124

"Were you and Steve lovers?" Jen asked.

Allison hesitated before she answered. She sighed and said, "I wish we had been. We seemed perfect for each other, but Steve had an unrequited love for a woman he had known when he was a graduate student."

Jen couldn't think of anyone Steve had dated seriously when they were students together.

"I can't think who that might have been," Jen said, puzzled.

"Well," Allison said, pausing again, "all he would ever tell me about her was that she preferred his older brother..."

Jen was shocked. "Me?" she whispered. "He loved me? I never knew... he never said. There was no indication." Jen felt a rush of emotion and felt the color rise in her cheeks, despite the cold. *I never knew.*

Jen recalled how steadfast their friendship had been, until she had started seeing Greg. She never thought that they had drifted apart for personal reasons—she just assumed that Steve's long absences from her life with Greg were due to his activities as an independent exploration geologist. He had been working in Nevada and California during her years with Greg. Before that, he worked in Colorado. *Maybe it was too painful for him to see me with Greg.*

❋ ❋ ❋

Jen and Allison periodically dozed and woke shivering. Jen had no idea how long each doze-shiver cycle lasted because she couldn't see her watch easily. When she started to doze, her thoughts drifted into the twilight world between reality and dream, confusing and disturbing her. When she was shivering, she was alert. It seemed to Jen that her thoughts were crystal clear when she was awake and shivering. As she warmed and relaxed, her thoughts drifted into bizarre labyrinths of people, places, and events.

Jen's conscious thoughts centered around the practical aspects of survival and rescue. *We have a good shelter and it seems to be above freezing in here. Eskimos who live in igloos strip down to their undies when the interior temperature reaches 40 or 45 degrees so they don't overheat and allow moisture to collect in their clothing. If they can survive nearly naked at 40 degrees, we should be able to make it with our clothes on. Our shelter is like an igloo but not as well insulated.*

We can use snow for water. There's no food. What about food? A body can last two weeks without food, but only about two days without water.

Rescuers should be able to find us in two weeks, hopefully sooner. Rescuers should come by air. I'll have to listen for helicopters and airplanes. Maybe the Civil Air Patrol will find us.

How will Charlie find us? No one knows where to look. There must be hundreds of peaks in the Roosevelt National Forest. Every passing day, we'll grow weaker. After the storm clears, I'll try to make a fire to attract attention. Maybe someone will see it from the air and report it.

I can't make a fire. No matches. Flint and steel? No, we don't have those, either. How will I find dry tinder under these conditions? How will I attract attention, if I can't make a fire? A sign in the snow? How deep is the snow? Will I be able to walk through the snow without exhausting myself?

What if I survive and I'm disabled? What if I lose digits or limbs to the cold? We should be better off than some of those unfortunate arctic explorers whose toes were so badly frozen that they turned black and had to be amputated on the spot with a pen knife. Ugh, what a thought. Where did that come from? How will I care for Sarah if I'm disabled? Kaari can't care for both of us.

What about my daughter? Poor Sarah. If I die, she will be motherless. Parentless, for that matter. Who will care for her? Kaari and Aunt Norma? Would her father come back for her? Never. He has no interest in his daughter. He's a deadbeat. Why do I deny it? Greg and his stupid plants and leaves. I need to accept that Greg sees Sarah and me as burdens. We both deserve better.

Bears again. Jen wished Allison hadn't mentioned bears because Jen couldn't get them off her mind. *Bears eat everything. I guess people do, too, if they're hungry enough. Bears eat other bears. People eat other people. Those in the know say human flesh tastes like chicken, or maybe it's pork. Of course, people always say mild-flavored meat tastes like chicken. I wonder if people have dark meat and light meat, like chickens do?*

Would I eat another person? I have more famine guard than Allison does. What if I survive longer than she does? If I had to eat another person to stay alive, would I be a victim of circumstance, just as Alferd Packer was thought to be? I guess the legal aspects have to do, really, with whether or not you killed the person for food or if they died of natural causes before you ate them. I wonder what the legal aspects were for the two Alferd Packer trials? I'm sure Allison would be interested in the points of law because she used to be a paralegal.

Jen considered the case of the ill-fated Donner Party. The pioneers, originally from Illinois, had made it into the Sierra Nevadas in November 1846, and were forced into camp by heavy snows. The group broke up and some of the members attempted to reach civilization by pushing on into California. Some of those folks made it, but did so fueled by human flesh. They did have rules—nobody was required to eat a loved one, for example.

Of those who remained behind with the wagons, one man was found alive in the spring. He was accused of murdering the last surviving woman in the group, whom he had consumed. When on trial for murder in California, he was asked to explain why he didn't eat the haunch of oxen found at the camp site instead of the woman. He replied that the victim was more tender and juicy than the dried oxen meat. Later, after he was acquitted of murder charges, he sued his accusers for defamation of character and won his case.

❄ ❄ ❄

Jen's twilight thoughts were emotional and complex. *My daughter. Love of my life. Sweet girl. How she has enriched me.* In her mind, Jen saw Sarah's smiling face and shining eyes turn to sadness and tears. She saw Sarah playing in a field, running and jumping just like any normal child. Suddenly she collapsed and called out "Mama! Mama! Help me." Jen saw Sarah holding out her little arms to her but she couldn't move. She was frozen in time and space, watching but unable to reach for her daughter.

Jen and Sarah sat together on the floor of their family room, playing with Moppet, the child giggling as the cat chased a piece of string. In her mind, Jen saw the cat lying motionless in Sarah's arms, her furry head twisted backwards in an unnatural pose and her daughter looking down into the staring eyes of the upturned, lifeless face. Sarah anxiously repeated over and over, "Mama, what's wrong with my Moppet?" Instantly she saw herself holding Sarah in her arms, lifeless, with the child's face twisted upward staring into her eyes.

Greg was in her twilight thoughts, too. He smiled at her and grew smaller and smaller, as though he were receding into the distance. Jen watched him as he finally reached the vanishing point.

Greg held tiny infant Sarah in his arms and released her. Jen struggled forward and grasped the bundled infant before she struck the floor, folding her into her arms as Greg turned away. Jen saw only his back.

Bears. Snarling silently, their small glass eyes pressing close to Jen's face, the weight of their feet bearing down on her chest, their coarse fur red, the color of blood. Their mouths were open and their lips pulled back away from their yellow canines. The faces of the bears became unnatural, distorted, almost human-like, until she recognized the essence of Tony Delano, a man she would never forget.

When Jen dozed more deeply, her dreams were of cold. She dreamed she was in a box, like a freezer, and there were no openings. When she touched the side of the box, the cold seeped through her fingers, chilling her to the marrow. She would shiver awake in the dark and remember her whereabouts.

Sleeping again, she dreamed of being on the top of a mountain peak in the sunlight, but the sun wasn't warm. The light grew dimmer and the cold increased. She became aware that she was naked, exposed, chilled through. There was nowhere to seek shelter. The light continued to dim and Jen shivered awake in the darkness beneath the protective boughs of the spruce.

Masked figures lurked on the fringes of her dreamscapes, bobbing their heads, shuffling their feet. Always, they were dressed in black suits. Their eyes were narrow slits, cold and heartless. Ski Mask was there, faceless, threatening.

Jen felt herself flying through the air, frigid wind tearing at her hair and clothing. Suddenly, she began to fall, the cold air rushing past her, freezing her legs and feet. She landed on an icy plateau that she knew to be Cannibal Plateau.

Jen saw herself standing in front of a log fire roaring in a large, cavernous fireplace, but she could feel no heat. Steve stood by her and they smiled and chatted. As the fire grew brighter, Jen became colder. Steve began to melt, the smile on his face replaced with a look of disbelief and then terror. Jen reached out for him and felt only ice. He was gone.

❊   ❊   ❊

Jen shivered awake and noticed that there was faint light sifting through the boughs of the trees, lifting the darkness from her eyes. She struggled to see her watch. Allison stirred as Jen moved the watch into view, but said nothing. It was almost 8:30 a.m. Jen listened and realized that the wind in the trees was silent.

"Allison, I think the wind has died down and it seems brighter in here. Do you think that the sun could be out? The storm was supposed to last for two days. Maybe it's a lull between storm fronts. I'm going to look outside."

Jen moved the pine branches to clear her way and crawled around to the shelter entrance. She heard Allison moan and say thickly, "You are so nice and warm. Hurry back."

"Don't worry, I will."

Jen pushed the fresh snow away from the entrance and squinted as the light reached her eyes. "It isn't snowing anymore and the sun's out," she said.

Jen allowed her eyes to adjust to the light and then slid over the snow ring and out into the fresh snow. The snow was about a foot deep near the entrance and she tried to rise quickly, but felt dizzy. As she sat, she looked up and saw clear blue sky directly overhead.

"Allison, it looks like a break in the weather. The snow is about a foot deep out here, near the tree. I'm going above the tree line to mark the snow with an arrow so they can see where we are from the air."

"Okay," Allison responded, sounding groggy. "Be careful and hurry back. You know how fast the weather can change."

"I'll be careful," she said, hoping she sounded reassuring and wondering if her voice sounded as thick and frozen as Allison's did.

Jen rose from the snow and felt the cold, still air on her face where her eyes were exposed. She started for the small fir trees she had stripped earlier. The closer she came to the tree line, the deeper the snow was, reaching up to her knees. She found her trees and began to strip the remaining branches from them. *My arms are weak, this seemed easier before.*

Jen mumbled an apology to the trees. "Sorry little trees, but I need these branches more than you do. Every time I see a Christmas tree, I'll think of you." *What am I saying? Am I losing it already?* Peripherally she wondered what the penalty was for stripping trees of their branches in a national forest. *Jen*, she told herself, *put these thoughts out of your mind and get on with the job at hand. Concentrate.*

As soon as she had as many branches as she could carry, she picked them up and struggled back toward the shelter. *At least, this time I can follow my own footsteps and won't be lost.* She found the spruce, turned upslope, and moved above the tree line, aware that the snow was deeper here. Snow had gone down inside her boots and she couldn't feel it. A bad sign, she thought.

Jen dropped her armload of branches and climbed about 30 feet upslope from the edge of the tree line, struggling over the low shrubs and rocks underlying the snow. She turned around and put her feet together and shuffled downslope, plowing the snow before her, shoveling the fresh powder out of the way with her hands and arms.

When the trough behind her was about 18 feet long, she turned to her right and shuffled back uphill at an angle, leaving another trough about six feet long. *Why is this so much more work?* she wondered as she turned around and walked in the trough to the junction between the two troughs. She realized her answer was that shuffling snow downhill was less work than shuffling snow uphill. From the other side of the trough, she walked through the snow uphill at an angle and shuffled back downhill toward the junction. *Much easier*.

Jen had plowed three troughs in the snow, forming an arrow. She walked downslope to her pile of branches and picked them up. She walked back to the point of the arrow and followed the shaft uphill to the top. Jen began to lay the branches down in the trough, working her way back downslope, until she reached the point. She laid branches in the other two troughs forming the arrow's point. When she was finished, she felt exhausted.

She looked up into the sky. Conditions were still calm and clear. Maybe there is no more storm, she thought as she turned downslope toward the spruce. *No. It isn't over yet. Another 24 hours or more before they reach us.* She followed her own footsteps back to the shelter. *At least I made an arrow so that they can find us from the air.*

Although Jen was warmed some by the exercise, she began to shiver as she reached the tree and slid underneath the boughs. Before she crawled back into the pine branch nest, she struggled to remove her boots. Her fingers were cold, numb. She finally removed the boots and emptied the snow out of each one. She held her feet in her hands for a moment hoping to warm them some before she slid the boots back on. Jen knew that she shouldn't rub feet that may be frostbitten because the tissue might be damaged. She pulled her boots on but didn't try to tie the laces. Jen crawled back into the nest, resuming her place beside Allison.

"It was so quiet, I didn't hear you coming," Allison murmured.

"It's the snow," Jen responded. "It insulates the sounds. Unless a helicopter lands on top of us, we might not hear it. How are your toes and fingers?"

"Can't feel 'em."

"Me neither. I wonder how long before we become hypothermic?"

"Long before we're rescued," Allison said.

Jen worked her clothing around so that she could see her watch again. It was almost 9:30. She was amazed that she had spent nearly an hour outside. No wonder she felt cold. She began to shiver against Allison, hoping she would soon be warm enough to doze again, yet dreading the bizarre thoughts and dreams that she knew would come.

Chapter Fourteen

Charlie had spent Wednesday, Thursday, and Friday in Adams County assisting in the difficult apprehension of a suspect wanted for automobile theft in Monarch County. The young man was tough to catch and he had led Charlie and two Adams County deputies on a car chase in the stolen vehicle and involved them in a foot race, stand-off, and fist fight. The chase and capture had reminded Charlie of a triathlon event.

They had gotten their man, but didn't finish their paperwork until after 9:00 p.m. Friday evening. Charlie was tired, and the long drive from Adams County, east of Boulder, to his home in the Roosevelt National Forest, northeast of Dawson, would take nearly an hour. As Charlie drove, he thought over the events of the past three days and was glad they were behind him. He was looking forward to the next two days off, even though it was supposed to snow heavily. For now, though, the moonless night was still and clear, and the stars shone brightly.

His thoughts turned to local issues. Jen and her investigation came to mind. Charlie decided it was time to check with Jen to see if everything was under control and if she and her family were safe. *I'll call her tomorrow*, he thought, as he pulled into the front drive of his rustic one-bedroom cabin. Through the evergreens, Charlie could just see the lights from the cabin of his nearest neighbor. He had animal neighbors, too, and often found evidence of raccoon, puma, and mule deer.

Banshee ran to the garage from her doggy door at the front of the cabin, her tail wagging and face smiling.

Charlie stepped out of the jeep and greeted his pet, "Banshee, old girl. You miss me?"

He stroked the long, black and white fur of the mixed-breed border collie he'd had for seven years. He wasn't sure of her age, but thought she was about 10. He'd gotten her from the Dumb Friends League in Boulder and she reminded him of the working sheep dogs he'd had on the reservation as a boy. Often, they were his only company in a life largely characterized by solitude. As a young man, he wanted nothing more than to leave the reservation. Now, although he didn't consider himself a follower of the Blackfeet way of life, he recognized his heritage and felt enriched by his cultural background.

Charlie was older now, and had developed an appreciation for his people, whose ways he had rejected as a young man. Someday, he thought, he would take the time to learn more about his heritage from his maternal uncles who practiced the Blackfeet ceremonies and traditional ways.

Charlie unlocked the kitchen door and reached for the light switch set into the yellowed pine paneling. Banshee scooted inside the small kitchen and dashed for her favorite begging position in front of the old round-topped refrigerator.

"You must want a treat," Charlie said as her tail thumped on the worn green and white linoleum floor. Charlie walked past the tiny dinette set and reached for a box of dog biscuits hidden among the clutter atop the refrigerator.

Banshee whined with excitement as Charlie fished two biscuits from the box and fed her.

He pulled his boots off and dropped them by the kitchen door, draped his jacket over one of the two dinette chairs, and laid his gun and other gear on top of the newspapers stacked haphazardly on the table. He called his neighbor to let him know that he was home and to thank him for caring for the dog. As Charlie hung up the phone, he reached for his kitchen radio and switched on the weather station for news on the approaching storm. Charlie depended on his radio for news and weather, as he didn't have a television.

He fed Banshee a bowl of kibbles and fixed himself a sandwich and glass of milk. Charlie walked from the kitchen into the vaulted combination living-dining room to the sofa placed in front of the fireplace.

Even though the heat was on in the cabin, Charlie built a fire in the fireplace. He sat on the large, comfortable sofa with his feet propped on a footstool in front of the fire and finished his sandwich and milk. Banshee joined him on the sofa, curling up at his side and laying her head on his lap. Charlie stroked her ears and yawned. Before long they had dozed.

The ringing of the telephone woke both Charlie and Banshee. Charlie rose from the sofa, stretched briefly, and walked into the kitchen to answer the phone. The clock over the ancient two-burner gas range showed 12:30 a.m. and he wondered who would be calling at this hour, hoping there was no emergency for him to attend. He switched off the kitchen radio as he reached for the telephone.

When he answered the telephone, he heard an excited female voice, but couldn't understand her words clearly.

He interrupted, saying, "I'm sorry, I can't quite make out what you're saying. Please slow down and repeat your message."

She paused, and then spoke more slowly, "This is Deputy Manydeeds?" she asked.

Charlie heard her more clearly now and recognized a Scandinavian accent, thinking immediately of Jen's Swedish nanny.

"Yes, speaking," he responded. "Who's calling, please?"

"This is Kaari. I live with Jennifer Slater as nanny for her daughter," she said.

"Is anything wrong?" he asked.

"I don't know," she answered, "but I follow her instructions to me. She says that she calls me on my beeper every four hours so I know she is safe. She was calling at 10:00 tonight, but she did not call and I waited, thinking maybe she forgot. But now it is two and a half hours late. Jen gave me this number to tell Deputy Manydeeds if she missed a call every four hours."

Charlie heard the worry in Kaari's voice. "Where is Jen now?" he asked.

"She is gone to Dawson to stay with friend Allison."

Charlie's first thought was that, with impending bad weather, Jen must have had a compelling reason to stay overnight in Dawson. "When did she leave?"

"I am not sure, but she call me in Colorado Springs, hmm, about 4:45 in afternoon. She says she would see us Sunday."

"Did she say anything else? Give you anymore information?"

"No, only to call you if she miss four-hour check in. I am worried. Can you find her at friend's house?"

"Sure," Charlie said, "I'll call over there and see if they're in. Don't worry. You did the right thing. I'll take care of everything and call you when I know where she is. What's your telephone number there?" he asked.

Kaari gave the number to Charlie, and he said, "Thank you for calling."

"Okay," Kaari said, sounding relieved. "I go to sleep now. Goodnight."

"Goodnight," he said.

Charlie dug the telephone book from the pile of newspapers on the dinette table and dialed Allison Henry's home number. It rang five times and the answering machine clicked on with a recorded message. He left his phone number and a brief message for her to call him, thinking that Allison and Jen might be at the tavern, closing up. Next he dialed the tavern, but there was no answer. Because they might be enroute to Allison's cabin, he decided to drive over to make sure everything was okay.

Charlie walked through the living-dining room to his bedroom that opened into the dining area, passing by his second-hand oak dining room table overflowing with magazines, bills, empty coffee mugs, and police reports and paraphernalia, and into his bedroom. He turned on the bedside lamp sitting on the night stand. Banshee followed him, jumped onto the smoky-blue down comforter covering the double brass bed, and made herself comfortable on the mismatched pillows at the head of the bed. Charlie changed from his uniform into civilian clothes, warm boots, and heavy leather jacket.

Charlie switched off the lamp and left his pet sleeping on his bed. As soon as he stepped out the back door, Charlie noticed the change in the weather. The temperature had fallen at least 20 degrees and, though the air was still, the stars were blocked by heavy snow clouds.

He took the mountain roads over to Allison's cabin, listening to the weather reports as he drove. The forecaster issued a severe winter storm warning and advised against high-country travel over the next 24 hours. Chain laws were in effect for mountain passes along the Front Range and the forecaster urged everyone to prepare for the worst.

Charlie drove up to Allison's cabin at 1:15 a.m. Allison's carport was empty and Jen's old white Bronco was not in the drive. Charlie turned off his headlights and engine and observed that there were no lights on around the cabin. He picked up his flashlight before stepping out of the jeep. Charlie walked up on the front porch and knocked on the door. There was no answer and he decided to check the back door. He walked around the cabin and tried the back door with the same result.

Maybe they're still at the Miner's Tavern, he thought. I'll stop in there before the 2:00 a.m. closing.

The first snowflakes were falling as Charlie drove the jeep south down the mountain and onto the paved portion of Fourth Street. He encountered no other vehicles on his drive into Dawson. He approached the tavern from the north, turned into the lot at the back of the building, and parked. Charlie walked along the west side of the tavern, looking for Allison's truck and Jen's Bronco, thinking they might have parked on the side of the building, since their vehicles weren't in the back lot. He didn't see either vehicle.

Charlie entered the tavern through the double front doors and brushed snow from the shoulders of his leather jacket. Rick was behind the bar serving last call. It was 1:45 a.m. when Charlie seated himself on a bar stool and nodded to Rick.

"Snowing already?" Rick greeted Charlie. "Get you anything?"

"Sure. How about coffee?"

Rick poured coffee for Charlie and said goodnight to the departing patrons.

"Allison in tonight?" Charlie asked.

"No, she left for the evening," Rick said as he began to wipe down the bar. "She had overnight company tonight."

"Do you know who?"

Rick nodded. "Her friend Jen is staying with her at her cabin tonight. Actually, that's not true. Jen left me a note stuck to the mirror by the cash register saying that they had decided to spend a few days up at Steve Myerhoff's cabin."

"Did you talk to either one of them or see Jen when she left the note?"

"No. I found the note stuck on the mirror. Must have put it up when I wasn't looking. As busy as I was tonight, that wouldn't have been too tough. I didn't even have time to answer the phone. I guess the girls just wanted to let me know that I should take care of business for the next few days. Seems to me, though, that Steve Myerhoff's summer cabin is a bit remote for a weekend visit with a severe storm brewing."

Charlie was thinking the same thing. Jen, he knew, was sensible and wouldn't want to be stranded in a summer cabin with a storm imminent. And Allison, though somewhat less predictable, had lived in the mountains most of her life and certainly knew from experience that traveling to a remote cabin was a poor choice this time of year.

"When was the note left?" Charlie asked.

"Around 11:00 p.m., I think. I didn't notice it right away."

Charlie's mind began to piece together information on time and place. It was nearly 2:00 a.m.—eleven o'clock was three hours ago. If they had gone to Steve's cabin, they would have arrived two hours ago, giving Jen plenty of time to call Kaari on her cell phone, even if she were late for her scheduled call at 10:00. *Perhaps, Jen's cell phone isn't*

*working or maybe they were involved in an accident. I should drive
up to Steve's cabin before the storm is worse,* Charlie thought impul-
sively, *and see if they were in an accident.*

"Did you keep the note?" he asked Rick, who nodded yes. "May I see
it?"

"Sure," Rick said as he drew a folded sheet of paper from his vest pocket, laying it on the bar top.

Charlie unfolded the note, prepared on a half sheet of white photocopy paper, and read the brief message written in large, flowing script.
The message read, "Rick, Allison and I are driving to Steve Myerhoff's
cabin for the weekend," and was signed, "Jen."

Charlie didn't have to examine the message closely to know that the
large, flowing handwriting wasn't Jen's. He pulled his wallet from his hip
pocket and opened it, finding two pages torn from his police notebook.
He flattened these pages and placed them on the bar top next to the note.

Rick leaned over the bar and looked at the papers. "Is that Jen's handwriting?" he asked pointing to the two sheets Charlie had spread on the
bar top. "How can you read that?" he asked with amusement. Charlie
saw Rick frown as he compared the papers. "It can't be the same 'Jen,'"
he said, "this handwriting is totally different."

Charlie nodded. "Your note is a fake," he said, looking up at Rick.
"Any idea who might have left it? Anyone unusual in the tavern tonight?
Think, Rick, it could be important."

Rick looked puzzled, concentrating, and shook his head. Charlie folded the note and the two pages torn from his notebook and placed them
inside his wallet.

"May I use your phone? Let's try Jen's cell phone number and see what
happens," Charlie suggested.

"Sure," Rick said, "the phone's in Allison's office. That's why I can't
answer it when it's busy in the barroom and I'm the only one here." They
walked back to Allison's office and turned on the overhead light. Charlie
easily found the telephone sitting on Allison's tidy desk and dialed the
cell phone number. After several rings, a recorded message cut in, saying
that the phone was temporarily out of service. He held the phone so that
Rick could hear the message, too.

Charlie hung up and asked, "Have you seen either Jen's Bronco or
Allison's truck tonight? I looked around the parking lot when I came in
and didn't see either one."

"Not that I noticed," Rick answered.

"I stopped by Allison's cabin on my way here and neither vehicle was at the cabin and I didn't see any other drivers on the road as I drove into town. I can't think why they would take both up to Steve's cabin, unless they had intended to return at different times."

Rick shook his head and smiled, "They would have taken only one," he said, adding as a joke, "Maybe they took the Golden Nugget's helicopter up there."

Charlie's interest was aroused, although his face remained impassive. Charlie had been out of Dawson for three days. Perhaps he was missing something. He asked, "Did you hear a helicopter tonight?"

"Yeah. Actually, a helicopter came in on Thursday, late afternoon. I saw it arrive when I was out at the dumpster. Allison asked if it was a Flight-for-Life helicopter. I said, 'No, just lazy rich folks who can't be bothered to drive.' The helicopter sat on the helipad all day Friday. I heard it finally leave about 11:00 p.m. It's so loud that I can hear it coming and going from inside the tavern. Can't miss it," Rick answered as they turned off the office light and walked to the barroom.

Charlie sat on a bar stool, mentally reviewing what he knew about Jen and Allison's investigation of Tony, while Rick locked up the front and back doors. Jen missed her check-in call with her nanny. Jen and Allison's vehicles were missing. A decoy note was left indicating that Jen and Allison had gone on an impractical trip to a summer cabin with a severe storm about to descend. A helicopter had left the Golden Nugget Casino helipad at about the same time the note was left. Jen's cell phone was out of order.

Charlie surmised that Jen and Allison were in the helicopter.

"Did the helicopter return?" he asked Rick.

"Yes, about 11:40. It stayed on the helipad for only a few minutes and then flew off down the valley."

"When it went out earlier, at 11:00, which direction did it fly?"

"Well, it flew west, over the tavern. I noticed because it usually flies east toward the Jefferson County Airport. This was different. Strange, too, because it was flying west, into the storm. Not your best choice, I would think," Rick said.

Charlie decided it was time for action. He said, "Thanks for the coffee," and Rick let him out through the back door.

He stood in the falling snow and decided that he wouldn't go to Steve's cabin, because he knew Jen and Allison wouldn't be there. Instead, Charlie drove three blocks east to the sheriff's department.

He pulled his jeep into the visitor's parking place and entered through the front door, again brushing snow from his jacket and hair. Charlie heard the door buzz when he entered, surprising Pete Cane, the deputy on duty.

Pete rose from his chair, greeted Charlie, and asked, "What's up? I thought you'd be home sleeping off your latest adventures. Why you out so late? Want some coffee? I just made some fresh."

Charlie shook his head and said, "I think Allison Henry and the *Journal's* environmental reporter Jen Slater may have been taken for a joy ride by helicopter into the high country tonight. I want to look at some maps."

"Bad night to be out," Pete said. "Look at that snow fall. Roads will be pretty rough going by morning."

Charlie and Pete headed for the map drawers where the topographic maps were stored.

"Which maps do you need?" Pete asked.

"Local and west, northwest, and southwest of Dawson," Charlie said. They worked together to select the correct maps and spread them on top of the map cabinet.

"Have any idea where to look?" Pete asked.

"Yeah. I have a hunch. Rick Ansel over at the Miner's Tavern said that he had heard a helicopter leave from the Golden Nugget helipad. It was west-bound and returned in about 40 minuets."

"A helicopter travels at about 100 miles per hour," Pete commented.

"So," Charlie said, picking up a ruler from one of the desks and tapping his palm, "a 40-minute trip means about 20 minutes out and 20 back. Twenty minutes is a third of an hour. A third of 100 miles is 33 miles. Subtract 10 minutes to land. My guess is that they are between 25 and 33 miles from Dawson."

Pete held the maps in place while Charlie used his pencil and ruler to draw two arcs on the maps—one with a radius of 33 miles from Dawson and the other with a radius of 25 miles. The arcs, reaching from northwest of town to southwest, lay within the Roosevelt National Forest.

Charlie and Pete studied the area between the arcs. "Where would a helicopter go?" Charlie asked himself. "If the helicopter landed, it would have to be above the tree line, since there are no safe landing areas within the forest accessible at night."

Charlie and Pete began to search the map inside the arcs for mountain peaks that exceeded 11,000 feet, the average elevation of the tree line in Monarch County, spotting three candidates.

"It's one of these," Charlie said as they rolled up the maps and placed a rubber band around them.

Pete asked, "Are you going to attempt a rescue tonight?"

"I'm not sure. Let's check the weather first. I'll contact the Jefferson County Airport for the latest weather conditions," Charlie said.

Charlie used the police radio to reach the airport weather station. The dispatcher on duty answered the call.

"This is Deputy Manydeeds with the Monarch County sheriff's department. What can you tell me about this storm?"

"There are actually two storm fronts moving in from the west over the continental divide," the dispatcher said. "The first storm front is moving eastward quickly and will be out of the area in about six hours' time. Around 9:00 Saturday morning, according to the progs. This storm is expected to dump up to two feet of snow in the high country. There will be a brief abatement in conditions between storm fronts with sunshine and clear, but cold weather. The second front will be preceded by strong, gusting winds sometime before noon. Clouds will be moving in during the early afternoon, bringing another two feet to Monarch County before Sunday."

Charlie thanked the weather dispatcher and signed off.

The deputy asked, "What support do you think you'll need?"

"Given the weather conditions, I think I can act more quickly by myself, rather than wait for a search and rescue team to gather."

"That's true," Pete agreed. "They'd want to wait until Sunday because of the weather."

"Unless Jen and Allison have shelter, they won't survive. By 9:00 a.m., they'll have been exposed for nearly 10 hours. Their chances aren't good, but I need to try. I have a two- or three-hour window at the most to find them. The only way I'll be able to search is with a helicopter."

"Call Jimmy Best," Pete suggested. "He loves harrowing rescues."

"Perfect," Charlie agreed as he reached for a list of emergency search and rescue contacts taped to the wall next to the telephone. He read down the list, looking for the name.

Jimmy Best had been a helicopter pilot in Vietnam. After his discharge from the service, he worked in Alaska for years flying service helicopters to offshore drilling rigs for large oil companies. Flying in 60 knot winds over Cook Inlet was dicey work, requiring skill, talent, and nerve. Now Jimmy worked along the Front Range of Colorado, flying helicopters for medical evacuations and search and rescue operations.

The time was nearly 3:00 a.m. when Jimmy answered his telephone with a sleepy voice.

"Jimmy, this is Charlie Manydeeds," Charlie said.

"Charlie, how the hell are you?" Jimmy asked.

"Good, except that I have an emergency search and rescue operation that I need help with."

"Sure. What do you need?"

"I think I've located the whereabouts of two women stranded above the tree line in the Roosevelt National Forest, approximately 30 miles west of Dawson."

"Jesus, in this weather? How did they get into that predicament?"

"I think that they were kidnapped, transported by helicopter, and abandoned above the tree line on one of three peaks."

"Are you assembling a search and rescue team?"

"No. I don't think there's time to assemble a team. If I do that, we won't get out until late Sunday, after the storms pass through. Their chance for survival is low. Sunday is too late. But I have a plan I think might work. This is where I need your help."

"Shoot," Jimmy said.

"According to the weather dispatcher at the Jefferson County Airport, there are actually two storms, back to back. The first storm should let up about 9:00 a.m. for two or three hours. During that time, conditions will be clear and cold. As the second storm moves in, we'll get gusty winds, then clouds and more snow."

"You want to fly in the window between the storms?"

"Yes."

"I'm your man," Jimmy said without hesitation. "Meet me at the Jefferson County Airport at 6:00 a.m. and bring your maps. We'll watch the weather and see when we can leave. We'll take Jefferson County's rescue helicopter. I'll call ahead and make the arrangements."

Charlie hung up the phone, confirmed that Pete understood the plan, and headed for the door with his roll of maps. He glanced at the wall clock and saw that it was about 3:20 a.m. Charlie walked out the front door and into the heavily falling snow. The temperature was near zero and there was no wind.

Charlie drove home. A sleepy Banshee greeting him in the kitchen, stretched, and wagged her tail shyly. Charlie stroked her head, thinking that he now had less than two hours to prepare his gear and drive to the airport, a trip requiring an hour or more under these weather conditions.

Upstairs in the loft area overlying his kitchen and bedroom, Charlie turned on the overhead light. He looked over his neatly ordered search and rescue equipment. Charlie was proud of his equipment and took pains to keep it accessible and in top shape. He could, at a moment's notice, be prepared to initiate search and rescue activities in the high country. The sheriff's department maintained adequate equipment, but Charlie preferred to have his own. The rest of his house was impassable, but he didn't mind—his only concern was for his equipment.

Taking a large canvas army kit bag, Charlie placed wool blankets, ropes, hats, socks, gloves, and a first aid kit inside. He picked out a pair of snow shoes and carried both downstairs and into the living room, setting them on the sofa. In the kitchen, he made a large thermos of hot chocolate, filled two insulated canteens with hot water, and took chocolate bars from the cupboard. He placed the items inside the kit bag.

Charlie walked into his bedroom and took off his clothes, tossing them onto the bed. He put on thermal underwear, insulated socks, and a heavy wool turtleneck sweater. He put on his orange thermal jumpsuit with attached hood, pulling the zipper up half way. He wore the jumpsuit during official search and rescue operations and knew from experience that it would give him the most freedom of movement and keep him warm without a bulky parka. He put on his best thermal boots and took his gloves and goggles from the closet shelf, tucking them inside his breast pockets.

Charlie loaded his gear into the jeep, said goodbye to Banshee, locked up his cabin, and drove down the mountain toward Dawson. The snow was falling and visibility was poor. The roads were barely passable in some areas. When Charlie entered Dawson, he saw that the county snow plows had been at work trying to keep the roadways clear. He drove eastward on Darkhorse Canyon Road, watching for snow plows moving against the traffic, and into the Jefferson County Airport parking lot by 6:15 a.m. Jimmy was already there, waiting for him.

Chapter Fifteen

The time passed slowly for Charlie, as he waited with Jimmy for the weather to improve. Patience, however, was one of Charlie's virtues. He had explained the situation to Jimmy regarding Jen and Allison and their investigation of Tony Delano and how he had arrived at his deduction regarding their whereabouts.

It was about 7:00 a.m. They sat in the weather station at Jefferson County Airport with the forecaster who was monitoring conditions on the weather radar.

"I can see the trailing edge of the first storm on the radar," he told Charlie and Jimmy. "At the rate the storm is moving, I expect clear conditions to prevail in western Monarch County between 8:00 and 9:00 a.m. Snow will probably taper off here in Jefferson County about 9:00 and we'll be clear about 10:00 a.m. As soon as the snow lets up a bit, you can prepare for departure. You'll be airborne by 9:00."

"Great," said Jimmy. "I'll start my pre-flight ops now."

Jimmy prepared the flight plan paperwork and contacted the control tower for pre-flight instructions. The flight manager told him that flights were grounded until cleared by the weather station.

Charlie and Jimmy finished their coffee. They walked into the hangar adjacent to the weather station and picked up a snow shovel and broom before heading for the helipad where the county's search and rescue helicopter was parked. Snow plows had been out on the runways for several hours and crews had cleared the area around the helipad with snow shovels. Charlie and Jimmy used the broom to brush snow from the helicopter and the shovel to remove snow from the helicopter's skids. They checked the fuel tanks and performed the pre-flight check.

Charlie looked at his watch and saw that an hour had passed. He watched the snow and noticed that the storm's intensity had lessened in the last hour and visibility had improved. The other hangars and buildings at the airport were now visible and Charlie saw the morning light growing brighter as the cloud cover thinned.

Charlie and Jimmy loaded the gear into the helicopter, climbed in, and started the engine. They put on their headphones, harnesses, and seat belts.

Jimmy contacted the weather station on the radio and the forecaster said, "Conditions are good enough for departure. You are cleared for take-off. As you head west, conditions will improve. Expect the break in the weather to last two or three hours. When you return, you'll be in front of the second storm which should hit Jefferson County in mid-afternoon. Good luck, gentlemen."

"Thanks. We'll maintain radio contact with the control tower. We may need medical support when we return."

The air traffic controller acknowledged Jimmy's request for departure and granted permission to depart at will. When the helicopter was ready, Jimmy lifted off from the helipad and headed west. The time was 8:45 a.m.

As they traveled west, the helicopter gained altitude. Visibility was poor and Jimmy remained in contact with the control tower. He gained altitude and flew parallel to the hogbacks along the Front Range until he reached the entrance to Darkhorse Canyon where he turned west. With each mile, visibility improved and the snow decreased. By the time they flew over Dawson, the snow had stopped, the clouds had begun to break up, and weak sunlight filtered through.

Jimmy flew toward the northern-most peak Charlie had identified on his topographic maps. The bald mountain stood tall among the other peaks in the range, rising more than a thousand feet above the tree line and reaching an elevation of 12,400 feet. Conditions were now clear, calm, and sunny with a spectacular, cloudless blue sky. On the peak, Charlie saw brilliant white snow, gray rock, and snow-covered evergreens below the tree line, but no signs of human activity.

They flew around the peak twice searching methodically near the tree line for evidence of Jen and Allison's presence. Charlie felt that Jen and Allison would have sought shelter in the trees or looked for a cabin. He saw no cabins or smoke from a fire to alert him. Charlie knew that cabins were sparse in this part of the national forest and were located further downslope, below 9,000 feet. The time was 9:40 a.m.

"Let's head south to Mt. Scott," Charlie said into his microphone. Jimmy nodded and flew south over the snowy mountains, reaching the peak in 20 minutes. They repeated their search, finding no evidence of Jen and Allison. The time was 10:20 a.m. as they flew south toward Bear Mountain, the third peak Charlie had identified as a possibility.

As they approached the mountain from the north, Charlie saw the majestic peak standing silhouetted against the blue sky to the south. The windswept gray rocks on the north side of the summit lay in the shadow cast by the peak. Further downslope, snow lying in the shadow looked faintly blue. The scene was cold, desolate, barren.

Charlie felt anxiety grow in the pit of his stomach. Had he failed to guess correctly? Would he find them before they died of exposure? Bear Mountain, he mused. Of course they would be here! Hadn't the cabin been made to look like a bear attack? Charlie silently berated himself for not searching this peak first. Every hour was critical and the time was nearly 10:45. On the ground surface below, he saw the wind beginning to pick up snow and blow the powder eastward.

"The wind speed is increasing," Jimmy said through the microphone. "We don't have much more time. A 50 knot wind will take us down at this altitude."

"Okay," Charlie responded. He looked to the west and saw the second storm front on the horizon, already covering the most distant peaks in a gray shroud. "Let's look near the tree line."

Jimmy dropped in altitude to 100 feet above the tree tops and turned west to circle around the mountain counterclockwise. Charlie began a visual sweep of areas downslope, looking for cabins or smoke. There was nothing. They circled the peak and were coming around the east side of the mountain heading north when Charlie said, "Jimmy, I see something in the snow near the tree line at eleven o'clock. Let's have a closer look."

Jimmy turned the helicopter westward. As they flew along the tree line, Jimmy dropped in altitude and reduced air speed.

"It looks like a green arrow," Jimmy said.

"Can you land?" Charlie asked.

Jimmy hovered above the arrow Jen had left in the snow and searched the area for a safe landing site. "I see a place about three hundred feet upslope."

"Fine," Charlie answered.

Jimmy moved the helicopter upslope and approached his intended landing site. Although less than ideal, the site was fairly flat and free of obstruction or hazard to the helicopter. He set the skids down in the snow.

Charlie unfastened his harness and seat belt and removed his headphones. He climbed over the seat into the passenger area of the helicopter and reached for his snow shoes. The area was small and cramped, barely large enough for him to attach the snow shoes to his boots. Jimmy handed him a portable two-way radio, which he slipped inside his jumpsuit. Charlie pulled on the attached hood and tightened it with the drawstring, placing the strap of his goggles over his head and adjusting them to his face. Quickly, he pulled on his gloves.

Charlie opened the passenger door and slid out into the snow. Visibility was poor around the helicopter as the rotors disturbed the powder and set the snow flying upward into the air. He sunk down several inches into the snow, lowered his head and ran awkwardly in large, bounding steps downslope until he was free of the rotor blades and could see more clearly. Jimmy lifted up from the snow to a safer altitude and hovered nearby.

Charlie continued downslope until he found the arrow that Jen had made. Snow was beginning to drift over the evergreen branches. Soon the arrow would be gone, covered by snow. Calling out, Charlie shouted for Jen and Allison. He paused, hearing only the beat of the rotors. If they were alive, they would hear the helicopter, he thought. *Why am I calling for them?*

Charlie walked along the shaft of the arrow to the point, where he saw footprints leading into the tree line. Following the footprints, he continued to call for Jen and Allison. The prints led him to a Colorado blue spruce where he saw that the snow on the downslope side had been trampled.

"Jen? Allison?" Charlie called.

He heard a faint response, that sounded like "In here," and rustling beneath the branches of the spruce. Stooping down, he noticed a passage in the snow leading underneath the boughs. He lifted his goggles for better light and, reaching below the boughs, felt movement. Grasping tightly and pulling slowly, he dragged a heavy object toward the packed snow entrance. A gray hiking boot appeared. Charlie spoke softly and quietly, knowing that people found after prolonged exposure sometimes relax and stop struggling, dying in the arms of their rescuers. He didn't want that to happen to Jen and Allison.

"Jen, it's Charlie. Jimmy, my pilot, and I found you. Don't give up. Hang on. Keep going. It'll be just a little longer now, so keep struggling. You'll be fine. Don't stop trying. I want you to think of your daughter."

Charlie had hold of both of Jen's feet and carefully pulled her out from under the tree anxiously wondering what her condition would be. He saw her move and knew that she would survive. Once she was free of the tree, she sat up in the snow, as Charlie continued to encourage her. Except for her eyes, Jen's face was covered with her sweater vest. She looked at Charlie, not recognizing him.

"Jen, can you walk?" Charlie asked.

"I don't know," she answered, her voice thick and slow. "How do you know my name?"

"It's me, Charlie," he said. "I look different because I'm wearing a hood," Charlie explained as he pulled the two-way radio out of his jumpsuit.

"Oh," Jen said. "Allison's inside, too, but she's cold." Jen sounded dazed.

"I'll take care of her next," Charlie said reassuringly.

"Jimmy, this is Charlie, do you read me? Over," Charlie said into the radio.

Jimmy's voice sounded clear in the cold air. "I read you. Over."

"I've found them. Jen is alert, but I'm not sure that Allison is conscious. I'll bring Jen to the 'copter first and return for Allison. Meet me at the drop-off point. Over."

"Roger."

Charlie returned the radio to the inside of his jumpsuit and attempted to lift Jen to her feet. As he supported her, he realized that she wouldn't be able to walk through the snow.

"I'm going to carry you," he said as he bent to lift Jen up onto his broad shoulders in a fireman's carry. She seemed light to him as he started upslope toward the helicopter. Charlie followed his own snow shoe prints back toward the helicopter, but noticed that he sunk in deeper with the extra weight.

When he reached the helicopter, he freed one hand and opened the passenger door. He rotated his shoulder so that he could set Jen down inside on the helicopter floor. She struggled weakly to reach the seat. Charlie loosened his snow shoes and left them in the snow. He climbed in next to her and lifted her onto the seat. Charlie slipped his gloves off and tucked them inside his jumpsuit. He gently removed the sweater vest from Jen's head. Charlie stroked her hair and briefly cupped her pale, bluish face in his warm hands. He searched for white patches of skin, telltale signs of frostbite, seeing instead the bruise on her face resulting from the blow struck by Ski Mask. Anger swept over him.

"Who did this?" he asked quietly.

"Tony Delano and a man in a black ski mask. The helicopter pilot."

Charlie reached into his kit bag and pulled out two wool blankets, placing one behind her back and draping it over her head and shoulders. He wrapped the second blanket around her legs, hips, and torso. She began to shiver violently as the warmth inside the helicopter reached her. Charlie strapped on her harness and seat belt.

Charlie put on his gloves, slipped out of the helicopter, closed the door, and picked up his snow shoes. He lowered his head and moved downslope until he was free of the helicopter. He attached his snow shoes to his boots again and moved downslope toward the blue spruce. The wind had picked up and he saw the first wisps of clouds moving in from the west. He needed to move quickly before the wind from the second storm increased.

As he approached the tree, he heard Allison calling out faintly for Jen. "It's Charlie," he said. "I'm here to take you home." He spoke to her encouragingly as he had to Jen. He reached beneath the branches of the tree until he found her foot. Charlie pulled Allison from beneath the tree. Her skirt scooted up to her hips as he dragged her out and he saw the blue tinge to her skin. He lifted her to his shoulders and carried her upslope to the waiting helicopter.

Once inside, he lifted her onto the seat, unwrapped the slip from her head, looked for frostbite, and bundled her into blankets, as he had for Jen. He pulled his thermoses from the bag and dropped them under the co-pilot's seat, slid out of the passenger door, and closed it. Charlie picked up his snow shoes and climbed into the co-pilot's seat.

Jimmy didn't wait for Charlie to fasten his harness or seat belt before he lifted off. The wind had picked up and was blowing in dangerous gusts. Jimmy flew away from the mountain and eastward toward Jefferson County. Charlie removed his goggles and loosened his hood, pulling it down away from his face.

Putting on his headphones, Charlie heard Jimmy as he talked first to the airport and then to Front Range Hospital, explaining that he had a medical emergency with victims suffering from severe frostbite and hypothermia. His plan was to proceed directly to the hospital and land on the helipad there.

Charlie looked over his shoulder and was relieved to see that Jen appeared more alert but was still shivering some. Allison was semi-conscious. Jen seemed surprised to see Charlie and he smiled shyly at her.

"Can you drink something?" he shouted to Jen over the noise of the rotors.

She nodded dumbly. Charlie opened the thermos containing hot chocolate and poured a small amount into the cap, passing it back to Jen. She reached forward, took the cap with both hands, and held the cup to her lips, taking small sips.

Charlie couldn't see Allison as clearly, but saw her eyes flutter open, although her head lolled on the back of the seat. She rolled her head to the left and looked at Jen. Jen saw her move and turned toward her holding the hot chocolate for her to taste.

Charlie sat back in his seat, suddenly feeling exhausted. He stared out the window as they flew eastward, passing over the mountains of the Roosevelt National Forest, the cabins, and small towns.

He reached for the radio and contacted the sheriff's department. Pete was off duty and another deputy answered.

"This is Charlie. I'm airborne eastbound from Bear Mountain with pilot Jimmy Best and two kidnapping victims," he told the deputy. "Our destination is Front Range Hospital. Jimmy and I have Jen Slater and Allison Henry on board. They were kidnapped last night by Tony Delano and an unidentified accomplice wearing a black ski mask. They were flown by helicopter to Bear Mountain and abandoned above the tree line. I have no other details at this point. We need an arrest warrant for Tony Delano on the charges of kidnapping and attempted murder."

"Acknowledged," the deputy responded. "I'll notify Sheriff Beamer and the FBI regarding the kidnapping. When will you report?"

"As soon as I can settle the victims at the hospital, I'll drive back to Dawson. Don't wait for me. Arrest that bastard now!"

Charlie signed off the radio.

The helicopter flew over Dawson on the return trip. Charlie looked down at the Golden Nugget Casino and saw the west-facing windows of the top floor, where Tony had his private quarters and office. Charlie saw the figure of a man dressed in black and wearing a white shirt peering out of a window at the east-bound helicopter.

❊ ❊ ❊

The sun was shining and the sky was blue, as Jimmy landed the helicopter at the Front Range Hospital and shut off the rotors. A hospital crew met them and transferred Jen and Allison from the helicopter into the emergency room.

Once Jen and Allison were under the care of the emergency room staff, Charlie headed for the telephone and called the sheriff's department. Sheriff Beamer answered the telephone.

"Sheriff, did you hear what happened?" Charlie asked.

"I have a sketchy report. Can you fill me in?"

Charlie quickly recounted for the sheriff what had happened during the last 12 hours.

"I just checked the victims into the emergency room at Front Range Hospital. I have a statement from Jennifer Slater identifying her kidnappers as Tony Delano and an unidentified helicopter pilot wearing a black ski mask."

"Arrest and search warrants are with the judge now. As soon as he signs them, I'll take one of the deputies to the casino with me for the arrest and search. We should have Tony Delano in custody shortly. The FBI has been notified. How are the victims?" the sheriff asked.

"Not bad, considering I found them sheltering beneath a spruce tree in the trough formed by a snow ring. They'll recover, although both suffered frostbite and hypothermia."

"Did you notify next of kin?"

"Not yet. I have a number where I can reach Jen's daughter and nanny. Can you notify Allison's next of kin?"

"We'll take care of it from here."

When he had finished his official business, Charlie found the telephone number given to him by Kaari. He dialed the number and a woman answered.

"This is Deputy Charlie Manydeeds calling from Front Range Hospital in Golden. We brought Jen Slater into the hospital about 20 minutes ago."

"Oh, no," the woman exclaimed. "I'm her friend, Norma Myerhoff. Will she be all right?" she asked anxiously. "What happened?"

"Jen'll be fine and she'll make a full recovery, but will require hospitalization for a day or so for observation. Jen and her friend Allison Henry were kidnapped and abandoned above the tree line before the snow storm hit the area. They found shelter and we rescued them before the second storm front moved in."

"Should I drive up? When can we see her? Can I bring her daughter?"

"You might want to wait until the second storm has cleared the area before you try to drive up to Golden. I think you can see her anytime and you can talk to her now at the hospital. She's conscious and will be giving a full statement sometime soon. The incident has already attracted media attention. I'm sure Jen would love to see Sarah, although you should ask Jen's doctor first."

"Oh, thank you so much," Aunt Norma said. "I'm relieved that she's safe. Thank you for finding her."

"Just doing my job," Charlie answered, wondering to himself if there was really more to it.

Charlie hung up the phone and looked at his watch. It was nearly 1:00 in the afternoon. As he walked back to the helipad, he felt the gusts of wind preceding the second storm front blowing against his clothes and face. It'll be snowing in Golden again soon, he thought. Charlie looked west from the helipad and, seeing the clouds over the hogbacks, knew that the storm was right on time. He wondered absently how the weather forecaster at Jefferson County Airport had managed to accurately foretell Colorado's weather. *Must be a miracle.*

Charlie found Jimmy. They climbed back into the helicopter and flew to Jefferson County Airport. When they arrived, Charlie thanked Jimmy, gathered his equipment, and headed for his jeep.

Charlie felt tired as he drove westward toward Dawson. Clouds from the second storm front covered the sky as he entered Darkhorse Canyon and strong winds buffeted his jeep whipping the snow from the first storm into blizzard conditions in the canyon. Before he reached the town of Darkhorse, snow from the second storm was falling heavily, reducing visibility. Charlie drove slowly up Darkhorse Canyon's snow-packed and icy road.

As Charlie approached Dawson, he saw flashing lights and a barrier across the roadway. He opened his window and one of the deputies approached the jeep.

"Hey, Charlie," the deputy said in greeting.

"What's up?"

"Sheriff went to arrest Tony Delano and he was gone. Think he took off during the lull between storms. We set up road blocks, just in case we could catch him, but I think he's long gone."

Charlie nodded once, feeling frustrated that Tony had slipped through and thinking of the figure he had seen standing at the casino window. He saw us, Charlie thought, and got away.

"Sheriff says for you to come directly to the Golden Nugget and help them with the search."

"Thanks," Charlie said as he closed his window and drove through the blockade.

It was nearly 3:30 p.m. on Saturday afternoon when Charlie reached the Golden Nugget. He parked on the street and entered the main lobby where another of the deputies was taking notes. He directed Charlie to Tony's private quarters where Sheriff Beamer was expecting him.

Charlie took the public elevator to the top floor where the squeaky security door was opened for him by another deputy.

"Charlie. In here. The sheriff wants you," she said.

Charlie stepped through the doorway and looked to the right where the door to Tony's office stood open. To the left was the door to the private quarters. Charlie entered and was greeted by Sheriff Beamer.

"We didn't get here in time to arrest Tony Delano," Sheriff Beamer said. "Looks like he flew the coop."

"He may have seen the rescue helicopter fly overhead on our return through Dawson," Charlie said.

Charlie looked down and saw the bear skin on the floor. He squatted and examined the fur, stroking it with his hands, feeling the silver-tipped guard hairs of the gigantic bear slip through his fingers. *So, here was the bear that provided a tuft of fur for Steve's cabin.*

"We've conducted a search of the private quarters and office and found a smashed cellular telephone," the sheriff said, handing Charlie a plastic bag with the remains of Jen's cell phone as he stood up. "Allison Henry's truck is parked in Tony Delano's private parking area. A second vehicle was parked along side the truck and has been recently moved. I think it might have been Jen Slater's Bronco. Tony Delano might have used it as a getaway vehicle."

"We can add car theft to the list of charges," Charlie said dryly.

"He got out ahead of our road blocks. We have the state highway patrol on the look-out for the Bronco," Sheriff Beamer said. "We notified the FBI regarding the kidnapping, but they haven't arrived here yet. I think their plan was to interview Jen and Allison first and then come on up to Dawson. We were trying to get an ID on the helicopter from the Jefferson County Airport; but since the FBI wants to follow that one up, we'll let 'em. We have plenty to do here.

"We found two women's jackets. One has 'Slater' labeled in the back and probably belongs to Jennifer Slater. The other is a buckskin jacket. See if you recognize it."

Charlie picked up the fringed buckskin jacket and said, "Rick Ansel at the tavern will know if this is Allison's jacket."

"Run it over there and see if you can get a positive ID."

"Sure."

Charlie took the public elevator to the main floor and left the casino through the west door. Snow was falling heavily and the sky was darker. He walked across the street and into the front door of the tavern.

Rick was behind the bar, waiting on a few customers.

"Rick, got a minute?" Charlie asked.

"Sure."

"How 'bout the office?"

Rick and Charlie walked down the hallway into Allison's office and switched on the light.

"Have you heard any of the news?" Charlie asked.

Rick shook his head. "No. What's going on at the casino? A drug bust?"

"No. You know that helicopter you heard last night?"

Rick nodded.

"Tony Delano and an unidentified pilot used the helicopter to transport Jen and Allison to Bear Mountain, where they were abandoned above the tree line."

Rick looked concerned. "Well, are they all right?" he asked.

"Yeah. You know that conversation we had? It helped me to piece together a scenario. Jimmy Best and I rescued them by helicopter this morning. They're at the Front Range Hospital in Golden undergoing treatment for frostbite and hypothermia. They'll be fine."

Rick looked relieved. "So, what are you doing with Allison's buckskin?" he asked.

"Sheriff wants a positive ID on the owner. We also found Allison's truck in Tony Delano's private underground parking area at the casino. We didn't find Jen's Bronco, though."

Rick's eyes opened wide. "I saw the Bronco when I was coming into the tavern before noon. Tony Delano was driving it. I wondered why he was driving Jen's Bronco. That sorry bastard almost hit me at the intersection of Fourth and Grand. Then he took off west, up Grand Street, and drove straight out of town and into the forest. Was he trying to get away?"

"Yeah. Sheriff Beamer set up road blocks, but Tony was already gone. West, you say?" Charlie said, thinking that seemed foolish in this weather.

"Better get back to my customers," Rick said after a short pause. Charlie nodded once and walked to the window in Allison's office. He looked out into the snowy parking lot where the accumulation was nearly three feet. Where did Tony go?

He won't get far in an old Bronco in this weather. Maybe he won't have to go far. Steve's cabin. Of course. He's been there before. He'll try to call his helicopter for a rescue. I can't follow him up there in this snow. After the snow lets up, Jimmy can fly me up to Master's Creek.

Charlie left the tavern and walked back into the casino lobby. Sheriff Beamer had completed his search and was preparing to leave for his office to begin the paperwork.

"Get an ID on the jacket?" he asked Charlie.

"Yes. It's Allison's. Rick said he saw Tony west-bound along Grand Street in Jen's old white Bronco before noon today. Tony drove into the national forest."

"In this weather?" the sheriff asked.

"Apparently so. My guess is that he headed for Steve Myerhoff's cabin to hide out until his helicopter could rescue him after the storm."

"Okay. Get your favorite pilot and have a look as soon as the storm clears. No heroics," he admonished Charlie. Charlie nodded once. "The FBI might want to tag along, too, if they can get here in time," the sheriff added.

"Here's something else that the FBI needs to look into," Charlie said, unzipping his jumpsuit and reaching for his wallet. "Rick found this note taped to the mirror above the cash register about 11:00 p.m. on Friday night."

Sheriff Beamer read the note saying that Jen and Allison were spending the weekend at Steve's cabin and signed by "Jen." The sheriff nodded as Charlie showed him another sample of writing.

"This is Jen's real handwriting for comparison," Charlie said.

The sheriff compared the writing. "Any idea who wrote this note?" he asked holding up the photocopy paper with the flowing script.

"My guess is Barbara Knowles."

"I'll tell the FBI—they'll know how to handle this."

Charlie nodded.

Sheriff Beamer looked at Charlie. "Son. You look beat. Go on over to the lockup and get some rest."

Charlie nodded and headed outside for his jeep. He brushed the accumulated snow off the windshield and drove over to the sheriff's department, parking in the rear. Inside, he used the telephone to called Jimmy Best.

"Jimmy? Charlie again," he said when Jimmy answered the telephone. "Our kidnapper got away in a stolen vehicle and headed into the

Roosevelt National Forest before the second storm hit. I think I know where he went and I'd like to have a look from the air as soon as the storm subsides."

"Sure," said Jimmy. "When and where?"

"As soon as you can get out on Sunday, fly the chopper to the Golden Nugget Casino and land at the helipad. I'll meet you there and we can head out."

"Where abouts?"

"To a cabin owned by Steve Myerhoff up on Master's Creek. It's about a 45 minute drive from Dawson under good conditions."

"I'll be there," Jimmy promised, and they hung up.

Charlie looked for the phone number for the Front Range Hospital, dialed, and asked for Jen Slater's room.

Chapter Sixteen

I could have died of exposure, Jen thought as she smoothed the covers over her rounded thighs and tucked them under her hips. She was comfortable in her hospital bed with her head and knees raised, although her frostbitten toes and fingers were still tender. She had had difficulty picking up the steaming coffee cup served with her dinner, but the hot meal had tasted good.

Jen had spoken with Aunt Norma soon after she arrived in the emergency room and had reassured tearful Sarah that she was fine. Jen longed to hold her daughter close, especially after the terrifying dreams she had had when dozing in the shelter before she and Allison had been rescued.

Alone in her private hospital room without the distraction of television or the conversation of others, Jen reflected on the experience of having been left to die by a total stranger. Greg had left her too, although the circumstances had been different and he hadn't intended for her to die physically. Abandonment by Tony had resulted in a physical ordeal, from which she was making a rapid recovery. Abandonment by Greg had been emotionally devastating, and her recovery had been slow, taking years of her life already.

Have I overcome my loss of Greg? She wasn't sure. *Would my life have been better with Steve?* She would never know. *Why hadn't I realized Steve's love for me?* She felt badly about learning of Steve's feelings for her. Maybe a different choice on her part years ago would have made them both happy, but she had been committed to Greg. Right or wrong, that had been her choice. Jen decided that she still had choices and was ready to move on, finally ending this long and painful chapter in her life.

What about Charlie? What role did he have in her life? She felt that she needed to give some thought to what she wanted. A companion? A lover? Someone she and Sarah could live with in harmony? A spouse?

Jen's thoughts were interrupted when the bedside telephone rang. She answered and was pleased to hear Charlie's voice asking her how she was feeling.

"Not bad. I'm thawed out now, but tender in spots," Jen said, thinking of her fingers as she brushed her hair behind her ear. "I'm still amazed that you found us, and I'm so grateful that you saved our lives. How did you figure out where we were?"

"I pieced together the evidence I had, made a few wild guesses, and ended up at Bear Mountain. The telling evidence, though, was your handwriting."

Jen was puzzled. "My handwriting? It's barely legible."

"Good thing, too. It saved your life," Charlie said.

"How do you mean?"

"A decoy note, signed by 'Jen,' was left at the tavern for Rick saying that you and Allison had gone to Steve's cabin for the weekend. The handwriting wasn't yours."

"Oh, you mean you could *read* it," Jen said with humor.

"Right. Since Rick hadn't seen your handwriting before, he didn't know the difference, but I had a sample."

"My phone numbers and address, of course. Who wrote the decoy note, then?"

"I suspect Barbara Knowles," Charlie said.

"I sort of thought she was involved. She called me to come up to the Court House on Friday night to look at the missing historical maps. I think it was a lure to get me to Dawson. While I was inside looking at the maps, Ski Mask hid in my Bronco and forced me to drive into the underground parking area at the casino."

"We searched Tony's quarters and office at the casino and found your parka and broken cell phone. Allison's truck was parked in the underground parking area."

"My Bronco was parked underground, too. Was it gone?"

"Your Bronco was used by Tony as a getaway vehicle. Rick saw Tony driving the Bronco west out of Dawson in the lull between storm fronts."

"Why would he take my old Bronco?" Jen asked, bewildered.

"Maybe because it's white and harder to spot from the air when there's snow on the ground," Charlie said.

"Or maybe he was afraid to take Allison's truck, because she had told him earlier that it was acting up," Jen said, recalling her earlier conversation with Allison. She was quiet for a moment, hoping that Wild Bill was safe and that she would get her vehicle back.

"How did you know to come looking for us in the national forest?" Jen asked.

"Rick mentioned that on Friday night he had heard a helicopter leave from the casino and fly west, returning 40 minutes later. I figured you were on it and decided to look during a lull between storm fronts. I should have guessed Bear Mountain right away."

"I suppose you saw that gigantic bear rug in Tony's private quarters? Tony told us all about it. He bragged on and on about what a tough guy he was because he shot and killed the bear with a single bullet."

"In my experience, the only single shot that'll kill a thousand-pound bear is one fired from artillery."

Jen was amused with Charlie's dry sense of humor, saying, "You don't believe his story either?"

"It's suspicious…" he said.

"I want to thank you for calling Aunt Norma," Jen said.

"She called me right after you spoke with her. I talked with Sarah for a few minutes, too."

"When are they letting you out?" Charlie asked.

"Tomorrow morning."

"Is your family coming for you?" he asked.

"Yes, probably on Monday, after the roads are improved."

"Do you have a place to stay Sunday night?" Charlie asked with concern.

"Well, no," she answered. "I'll probably check into a hotel near the hospital."

"I have an idea," Charlie said. "On Sunday, as soon as the weather clears, Jimmy is flying the helicopter to Dawson. We're conducting a preliminary air search for Tony and the Bronco. Jimmy can land at the hospital helipad first, pick you up, and bring you to Dawson. There should be plenty of places to stay in Dawson. I can take you back to Morrison on Monday morning and Norma can bring Sarah and the nanny home. The roads should be in good condition by Monday."

"I like that idea," Jen said. "Can I come with you on the air search?"

"Generally, as a civilian, I'd say 'no way.' But, I think you have a vested interest in the culprit, and as a reporter, I'm sure you could use your observations in a story."

"Great," Jen said with enthusiasm, thinking of the story she would write once she was back in Denver.

"I'll arrange with Jimmy to pick you up and I'll have him call you with the details."

"One problem," Jen said, "I don't have a coat anymore."

"I'll ask Jimmy to find one for you," Charlie said. "I'll bring snow shoes for you, too."

❋   ❋   ❋

Late Sunday morning, after Jen was examined by her doctor and released from the hospital, she found Allison's room and sat on the edge of her bed exchanging stories of mutual aches and pains. Jen told her about how Charlie had found them and of the plan to search for the missing Bronco.

"Wish I could go, too," Allison said. "I'd like to see that good-looking helicopter pilot who helped Charlie rescue us."

Allison has an interest in the pilot. Good for her.

"He stayed with me in the emergency room for a while and was all concerned about my frost bite," Allison said smiling. Jen smiled, too, thinking of her growing interest in Charlie but reluctant to mention it, although she wasn't sure why, considering the personal information they'd shared in their shelter.

Allison brought up the subject herself. "What about that Charlie. He's so clever, figuring out where we where," Allison said, shaking her head in admiration. "I think he's sweet on you, Jen."

Jen felt herself begin to blush. "Oh, not me," she said with a depreciating wave of her hand. "Why would he be interested in me?"

"Well, let's see," Allison said, counting the points on her fingers. "First, you're a mature, intelligent, and attractive lady. Second, you successfully conducted an investigation into a suspicious death. Third, you have wonderful survival skills—without your knowledge, we'd be frozen carcasses."

Jen looked down at her hands folded on her lap. Allison reached over and lightly patted Jen's hands as Jen looked up into her large gray eyes.

Allison said with sincerity, "You have many fine qualities that would attract a great guy like Charlie. Don't you forget it."

Jen felt both embarrassed and grateful to Allison for her support. She rose from the bed and kissed Allison's cheek.

"Maybe you're right," Jen said.

"Of course I'm right," Allison said with a smile. "You'd better go—the helicopter'll be here soon."

"When are you out of here?" Jen asked.

"Probably tomorrow," Allison answered. They said their good-byes and Jen headed for the coffee shop.

❊ ❊ ❊

Jen sat at a coffee shop table overlooking the helipad. Much to her distaste, she was still dressed in the same clothes she had worn since leaving home on Friday. Oh well, she decided, at least I'm alive to wear them.

Jen gingerly picked up her coffee cup, wincing slightly from the heat on her tender fingers, and sipped coffee. The sensation, however, wasn't nearly as uncomfortable as submersion in the warm bath provided by the hospital staff upon her arrival in the emergency room. The warm bath felt like scalding water on her face, hands, and feet. Funny, she thought, how your fingers and toes can be frozen, yet when they warm up they feel like they're on fire.

Jen now knew from her experience that a warm bath is the best method for raising body core temperature in hypothermia victims. She was lucky—her core temperature had fallen to 92 degrees, making her a border-line hypothermia case. Jen had overheard the staff saying that Allison's condition was worse, with an internal temperature of 90 degrees. Allison had been too thin to retain her heat, and she smoked, too, restricting her circulation. It's that old famine guard, Jen realized, providing superior insulation. Without it, she knew that she would still be hospitalized. *Thank goodness for those few extra pounds.*

Jen picked up a copy of the Sunday edition of *The Front Range Journal*. She was not entirely surprised to see her publicity photograph on the front page, with a title saying, "*Journal* Reporter Survives Kidnapping." A smaller photo of Charlie, taken from his driver's license, was shown with a subtitle reading, "Daring Rescue Engineered by Monarch County Deputy." After all, she had called her boss and reported the details as soon as the doctor would let her make a telephone call.

About 11:45, Jen heard the sound of a helicopter approaching. She cleaned up her table and hurried to the door leading to the helipad. Soon, Jimmy was landing and motioning for Jen. The snow had been shoveled from the helipad and Jen moved quickly through the cold, dry air to the helicopter, instinctively lowering her head as she moved under the rotors to open the rear passenger door.

Inside the helicopter, Jen found gloves and a bright orange hooded parka trimmed with rabbit fur. She struggled into the coat in the confined space and slipped the gloves on. Jimmy handed her a set of headphones, which she put on. She adjusted the microphone and thanked Jimmy for the coat as she fumbled with the harness and seat belt.

When she was ready, Jimmy lifted off from the helipad and flew west up Darkhorse Canyon to Dawson, arriving at the Golden Nugget helipad before 12:30. The weather was cold but calm and the sky overcast with high, thin clouds. An occasional snow flurry fluttered onto the helipad, which had been dutifully shoveled by the casino crew. The sun will be out later this afternoon, Jen thought.

Charlie was waiting for them with his gear, including topographic maps, two pairs of snow shoes, and a 12-gauge shotgun. Seeing the shotgun made Jen wonder if Charlie expected trouble. He was still dressed in his jumpsuit and Jen wondered if he'd had a change of clothes yet himself.

Once Charlie was inside and ready for departure, he put on the headphones and greeted Jen and Jimmy.

"You think you know where this guy, Tony Delano, went?" Jimmy asked, adding, "What a fool to travel west under such conditions." Charlie showed Jimmy the map of the Master's Creek area and the location of Steve's cabin.

"He doesn't have too much backwoods savvy," Charlie commented as they lifted off from the helipad and turned to the west, flying up Darkhorse Canyon.

"You look tired, buddy," Jimmy said to Charlie.

"Yeah. I didn't get much sleep. I stayed overnight in the lockup because I didn't want to drive back to the cabin with three feet of snow on the ground."

"The lockup is an odd place for a cop to sleep. Did you get to keep the key?" Jimmy asked with a touch of humor.

"It wasn't just the sleeping conditions. I had a busy night, too. I started the paperwork on the case at the office when I got a call from the FBI. Because the roads were bad, the agent couldn't drive up to Dawson for a personal interview, so I spent two hours on the phone with him instead. He gave me permission to conduct this preliminary air search for the missing vehicle."

"You'd have gone anyway," Jimmy said.

"True. Also, Jen," Charlie said, "you'll be pleased to know that the agent requested that we hold Barbara Knowles for questioning regarding her role in your kidnapping."

"Good," Jen said. "Now that I've met her, I concur with general opinion regarding her popularity in Dawson."

"The media was intensely interested in the kidnapping. Jen, did you have anything to do with that?" Charlie asked.

Jen thought he might be teasing her gently, but she couldn't tell. "Well, yes," she confessed. "I did call the newspaper as soon as I could," adding, "It's part of my job." She hoped she didn't sound defensive.

"That explains why the *Journal* has the best story," Jimmy commented.

"And the best photos," Charlie said.

"Each of the three nightly news stations called," Charlie said, "but the weather conditions were too poor for them to send crews."

"They contacted me, too," Jen said, "but I only gave brief statements. I was still trying to thaw out."

"Jen, there aren't any vacant hotel rooms in Dawson for tonight, because they're full of stranded tourists," Charlie said apologetically, "but you're welcome to stay at my place."

"Yeah, that should beat the lockup," Jimmy joked.

Jen knew that she was blushing with the thought of staying at Charlie's cabin for the night and was glad that neither of them could see her face.

"That would be fine," she said, hoping she sounded natural.

As they flew westward, the clouds began to clear and the sun shone through. It'll be a beautiful morning, Jen thought. In 15 minutes they were in the Master's Creek watershed and heading toward Steve's cabin.

They studied the area. Charlie said, "I don't see any signs of passage on the roads or evidence that the Bronco followed this route. If he was here, I'd expect smoke from the chimney."

Jimmy circled the cabin, but they saw no signs of activity.

"He's not here," Charlie said. "Let's see if we can trace his tracks out from Dawson. Two feet of snow fell since he left Dawson. I don't expect to see much."

"Let's look anyway," Jen said.

They flew back toward Dawson along Darkhorse Canyon Road, checking each side road and jeep trail. On the unpaved road to Ghost Mountain Pass, Charlie spotted something.

"I see a hint of tracks where the road's been protected from drifting snow. Let's follow the road up to Ghost Mountain Pass," Charlie said.

Jimmy flew south, following the winding road as it twisted up the mountain. They crossed the pass and flew down the mountain toward the eastward-flowing Roaring Creek that drained the south side of Ghost

Mountain. On this side of the mountain, Jen saw the sky was overcast with clouds covering the sun.

As the stream ford between Roaring Creek and the road came into view, Jen spotted the white Bronco stalled in mid-stream.

"There's my Bronco," Jen said with excitement. "It looks like the driver's side door is open."

"I don't see Tony," Charlie said.

"Amazing that he made it over Ghost Mountain Pass in the snow," Jimmy said.

"No kidding," Charlie said, "especially in Jen's old Bronco. If he was headed for Steve's cabin, he was completely lost. The cabin is to the north of Darkhorse Canyon Road and here's the Bronco miles to the south. Set me down somewhere."

Jimmy flew eastward along the winding stream course looking for a suitable landing site.

"I want to come, too," Jen said. "It's my Bronco and he won't be expecting me."

Jen saw that Charlie wasn't going to answer right away.

He's thinking about it. Maybe he thinks it'll be too dangerous for me and he's worried about my safety.

Charlie placed a hand-held radio inside his jumpsuit and zipped it closed. Before he removed his headphones, he told Jen she could come with him.

About half a mile downstream from the Bronco, the flood plain broadened and a snow-covered gravel bar hugged the inside bank on the north side of the stream. The area was large enough to land the helicopter.

The rotors kicked up great white clouds of powder as they landed, reducing Jen and Charlie's visibility as they removed the snow shoes and shotgun from the helicopter. Jimmy turned off the engine and Jen and Charlie, ducking under the rotors, shuffled through the deep snow covering the gravel bar.

Charlie slung the shotgun over his back and they struggled to put on the snow shoes. Charlie helped Jen with the straps because her fingers were still tender. Jen followed Charlie as they moved carefully along the edge of the stream, searching for evidence of Tony's passage.

Charlie turned to Jen and said quietly, "If Tony's in the area, he'd have heard the helicopter. He might be aggressive. Do exactly as I tell you, okay?" Jen nodded.

They walked westward and around a bend in the stream. On the south side, Jen saw that the snow had been disturbed as though something large had waded through earlier. The sharp outlines of the trail were visible, indicating that the track had been made after the snowfall had ended. Jen and Charlie stopped to study the track, which they were able to trace down to the stream and up the north bank in front of them.

"It looks like something moved from one bank to the other, crossing the stream," Jen said.

"Let's have a closer look," Charlie said as they moved closer to the track on the north bank.

As they neared the track, Charlie said, "It's too wide to have been made by a man wading through the snow."

"Maybe it was made by someone on horse back," Jen said.

Jen and Charlie reached the edge of the track and stooped down for a closer look.

"It's neither a horse nor an elk," Charlie said. "Look at the edges of the track—they're brushed, as though soft fur had smoothed the sides." He continued his examination.

"Look at the floor of the track," he said.

"It looks like some kind of paw prints," Jen said.

"Yes," Charlie said, "it's a bear."

A chill went up Jen's spine, causing a shudder. She couldn't help herself and hoped that Charlie wouldn't notice. He looked at her and asked, "Are you okay?"

"Why does it have to be a bear?" Jen asked, adding to herself, *I hope it isn't hungry.*

"Must be on his own for the first time—a youngster that hasn't gone to den yet. It looks like a black bear, maybe 200 or 250 pounds. The prints are no larger than my hand. The bear was moving south. We'll follow its trail north into the trees and look for signs of Tony." Jen nodded in agreement.

They walked parallel to the bear track, approaching the trees growing along the stream. Charlie continued to look cautiously around. Jen, fascinated with the track, studied the paw prints. Suddenly she said, "Why are these paw prints pink? Look, it getting pinker as we get closer to the trees. Is the bear injured?"

Charlie turned his attention to the track. "No. If the bear had an injury, pink snow would be evident along the length of the track."

"Well, it looks pinker in this direction," Jen said pointing up the track where the pink snow increased.

"We'll follow the track into the pine trees," Charlie said as he unslung his shotgun. "We don't know what's up ahead. We need to be careful." Charlie pulled shotgun shells from his jumpsuit pocket and loaded the gun.

"The bear's gone, isn't it?" Jen asked.

"Yes, it moved south to the other side of the creek."

They walked along the track and into the shelter of the pine trees where the snow wasn't as deep. Jen looked along the bear track where it ended against a large disturbed area of packed snow surrounding a mound constructed of snow and brushy debris. Jen and Charlie stopped to study the area carefully before approaching.

"What is it?" Jen asked.

"It's the bear's cache—something's hidden for safe-keeping," Charlie answered. "Since the bear's gone, we can examine the cache safely."

As they drew closer, Jen saw streaks of blood in the snow and evidence of something heavy having been dragged there from the stream by the bear. Near the mound, Jen saw shreds of bloody cloth in the snow. Charlie bent down and slowly began to remove the snow and brush from the mound. As he dug down, Jen could see that they'd found a human body.

Jen looked over Charlie's shoulder, as he exposed the head, revealing Tony's upturned face. Charlie said, "You might want to turn away." Jen was bound by both fascination and horror to watch, although she felt her breath grow shallow and sweat form on her forehead.

Charlie removed the snow from Tony's trunk and legs, and Jen saw where the bear had ripped away the clothing and consumed flesh from Tony's chest, exposing his ribs, and from his thighs, stripping the muscle down to the bone. Now she did turn away, fighting nausea.

"You okay?" Charlie asked as he rose and stepped toward her, putting his arm around her shoulders as she heaved. When she recovered, Charlie wiped her face and mouth with a handkerchief. Jen felt tears in her eyes.

"This is a new experience for me, too," Charlie said. "I saw a lot of injuries in the Marines as a paramedic, but nothing like this."

Jen nodded, saying, "I'm all right. It was just a shock. He wanted bears to eat us. He told us sickening stories about bears before he took us to the mountains. He told us how they eat you and how they like nice, rotten

carcasses in the spring. We were supposed to be the bear food, not him."
She paused, and added, "Well, at least we can get his fingerprints now."

Jen looked up at Charlie and saw a quizzical look in his eyes. "I'm being macabre," she said with embarrassment.

Charlie gave her shoulders a squeeze and said, "Jen, you are the most practical woman I know." Despite the horror of the situation, Jen sensed that Charlie was teasing her ever so gently and she relaxed some.

"I want to examine the body more carefully. You can wait by the stream if you want."

"No, I'm okay now. I want to help."

Charlie nodded once and released her shoulders, saying, "You look better now. There's more color in your face. Do you feel faint?" Jen shook her head.

They moved back toward the body and Charlie began his examination, commenting to Jen on his observations.

"See these puncture wounds around the head and shoulders? This is where the bear gripped Tony to drag him into the cache. Notice that the punctures aren't filled with blood? That suggests that Tony was already dead when the bear found the body." Charlie examined Tony's arms and hands. "Look at his arms. There are no signs of struggle with the bear, such as wounds on the hands and forearms."

"Plus, his face is placid," Jen observed. "I think that if the bear had killed him, he would look terrified." Charlie nodded in agreement.

"Bears are opportunistic feeders. A little fresh meat before denning could mean the difference between life and death for a young bear," Charlie said.

"If the bear didn't kill him, how did he die?" Jen asked.

"The coroner has the final say on that, but we can take a look." Charlie rolled the body on its side and examined the back of Tony's head. "See where the base of the skull is crushed in?" Charlie asked.

"Maybe the bear hit him on the back of the head with a paw."

"It looks more like a blow from a blunt object rather than the broader damage a bear paw would cause. Let's walk up to the Bronco and look for clues." Charlie rolled the body back to its original position and stood up. He pulled the radio from inside his jumpsuit and contacted Jimmy, telling him what they'd found.

Jen and Charlie continued upstream and found the Bronco around a bend. They stood so that they could see the front of the Bronco and the partially opened driver's side door. Although the Bronco was covered with snow, Jen saw that the hood was unlatched, which she mentioned to Charlie.

"Maybe he stalled out and tried to open the hood," she said. "Look how icy the cobbles are along the edge of the stream bed. Maybe he slipped on an icy rock and hit his head. Then he washed downstream where the bear found him and pulled him out."

Charlie nodded. "It seems like a plausible scenario," he agreed.

"That's what killed Steve, you know. I think a stream-rounded cobble was used to crush the back of his skull...I guess it's fair, after a fashion," Jen said thoughtfully.

After a pause, Charlie said, "I have some bad news for you, Jen. I think your Bronco is snowed in until the spring. I think your insurance company will consider it a total loss after the spring runoff is through with it."

Jen was disappointed and looked sadly at her old friend, Wild Bill. "It was a good car," she sighed, adding, "Oh, well, I needed a new one anyway."

"Your Bronco did an impressive job," Charlie said. "After all, it made it over Ghost Mountain Pass in two or three feet of snow, even if it did stall in mid-stream. Anything you want out of your Bronco before we head back?"

"Maybe the insurance papers and registration," Jen said as she stooped to loosen her snow shoes.

"I'll wade out there for you," Charlie said.

"Oh, no, you don't have to. I can do it myself," Jen said, wondering if she sounded like her five-year-old daughter.

"I don't think the cold water will be good for your toes. You need to protect those frostbitten feet for a while so they can recover."

"Well, that's true," she conceded. Charlie already had his snow shoes off and was stepping into the frigid, calf-deep water of the stream. He approached the passenger side of the Bronco. He removed the papers from the glove box and waded back to the bank, nearly slipping on the icy rocks exposed above the water line as he climbed out of the stream.

"It's cold, all right," he said as he replaced his show shoes.

"And icy, too, I see."

Charlie nodded, saying, "I almost lost my balance."

He pulled the radio from his jumpsuit and contacted Jimmy, telling him that they were ready to return. Jen and Charlie walked through the snow to the gravel bar and boarded the helicopter.

As they flew back to Dawson, Jen felt exhausted and cold. Her head hurt and her fingers and toes ached where they had been frostbitten. Her stomach felt tight but no longer nauseated.

Through her headphones, she heard Charlie talking with Sheriff Beamer and giving him a description of what they had seen.

Beamer said, "The media will have fun with this."

"We'll need a team to recover the remains," Charlie said.

"I'll arrange a team for tomorrow and have someone notify Tony Delano's next of kin. The FBI just arrived. They'll be here waiting to see you. What about the getaway vehicle?" the sheriff asked.

"It's snowed in for the winter," Charlie said.

"And the bear?"

"I guess that we should notify the state wildlife folks to come out and take care of the offending bear. Can't have a man-eater roaming the forest—it's bad for tourism."

Chapter Seventeen

Jen and Charlie sat together on the sofa in front of the fireplace at Charlie's cabin absorbing the warmth from the blaze. Jen, dressed in Charlie's best sweat clothes and wrapped in a warm blanket, sipped mulled cider. The hot bath had felt good once her toes and fingers had adjusted, and she was glad the cabin had plenty of hot water because Charlie had soaked, too, once she had finished. He was wearing his other set of slightly more tattered sweats and told her he was relieved to have a change of clothes.

After Jimmy had dropped Jen and Charlie off at the Golden Nugget helipad, they had spent hours completing reports, talking with the FBI and the media, and arranging for a team to recover the remains. One of the other deputies had brought them sandwiches and coffee. Jen had called Aunt Norma asking her to bring Sarah and Kaari home on Monday afternoon. It was after dark before Jen and Charlie left for his cabin. Now it was nearly 11:00 p.m.

Despite the horrors of the weekend, she felt warm and relaxed. Banshee had taken a shine to Jen and lay with her head on Jen's lap.

"She likes you," Charlie said. Banshee knew when she was the topic of conversation and thumped her tail on the sofa. Charlie reached across Jen and stroked the dog's ears.

"At least she's mellow," Jen said. "After this weekend, I'm not sure that I'll ever feel the same about bears again."

"Bears are powerful animals. To many Native Americans, the spiritual power of the bear is exceeded only by that of the wolverine. The Pawnee believe that the reason the bear is hard to kill is because of the psychic quality of ever-renewing life within the animal. Bears derive their power from the sun and are often used as a sun symbol."

"I don't really know very much about Native American beliefs. I guess I'm a typical white American in that respect," Jen said.

"There're plenty of Native Americans who aren't that well informed either. Me, for instance," Charlie said.

"You seem informed to me."

"My knowledge is scattered. When I joined the Marines at 18, I tried to forget what I knew. I have a renewed interest now, though. Maybe it comes with age. I see how my heritage enriches me in many ways I refused to see when I was younger," Charlie said.

"Why did you want to leave your heritage behind?"

Charlie was thoughtful and paused before answering. "My mother died when I was eight. My father drank heavily and rarely worked at a steady job. My older sister, Eva, and I took care of the household. At 16, Eva became pregnant and began drinking. Her son, John, was born with fetal alcohol syndrome. When Eva was 19, she slit her wrists. John was moved to an institution on the reservation."

"What a sad story," Jen said, reaching for Charlie's hand. He responded by gently cupping his large hands around her small one.

"Unfortunately, it's a fairly typical scenario. I couldn't see myself living like my father for the rest of my life. I had to leave."

"What about John?"

"He's still on the reservation, living in a half-way house and working at a hardware store. He's 19 now. I try to see him at least once a year."

"Does he know you?" Jen asked.

"Yeah. He's always delighted to see Banshee and me. He seems fairly well adjusted, considering his limitations."

"I can understand how your sister might have felt. Having a baby with problems can be devastating, especially if the mother thinks the problems were caused by something she did," Jen said.

"I hope you don't blame yourself for Sarah's condition," Charlie said. "That's not your fault."

"I don't know. Spina bifida might be genetic or result from low vitamin B intake during pregnancy, or it could just come from plain bad luck. I had lots of support, though, probably better than your sister. I managed, but was treated for depression."

"Did Sarah's father help you?" Charlie asked.

Jen paused before answering. Because he'd shared his painful experience with her, she decided to tell Charlie her story. "No. Not Sarah's father." Jen told Charlie about Greg and Steve, revealing what Allison had told her about Steve's love for her, saying, "Now I feel guilty and dumb, like I made a bad choice." She felt tears forming in her eyes and knew that more were on the way.

"You made the best choice for yourself at the time. You didn't have a crystal ball to see into your future with Greg; and, for whatever reason, Steve never expressed his feelings for you. If he had, your decision might have been different. It's not something you can blame yourself for now." Charlie reached for a tissue box as Jen began to sob.

Jen hated to cry in front of other people and this was the second time she was sobbing before Charlie. She rested her elbows on her knees and hid her face in her hands. Charlie placed his broad hand on her back and let her cry.

When she was calmer, Charlie said, "You're exhausted. Everything seems out of proportion right now. You'll feel better when you're rested. Come on, I'll show you to the bedroom."

Jen nodded, and followed as Charlie led her by the hand to his bedroom. He switched on the bedside lamp and turned to face Jen. He put his arms around her, held her close for a moment, kissed the top of her head, and said good night. Charlie quietly closed the door as he left the room.

Jen sat on the bed, wondering why she felt such a tangle of emotions. *I'm just tired.* She let the blanket drop from her shoulders and spread it across the bed. Jen slipped out of the large sweat clothes and crawled under the covers before turning out the light. She dried her eyes, yawned, and soon felt herself drifting into a deep sleep.

❊   ❊   ❊

The morning light reflecting from the snow filtered into the bedroom through the north-facing window, brightening the room. Jen was slow to awaken as she lay on her right side in Charlie's double brass bed, warm beneath the comforter. As she roused from a deep sleep, she slowly became aware of a warm body tucked up against her back. Half asleep, she whispered, "Charlie…" Then, suddenly more alert and experiencing simultaneously a surge of panic and excitement, she said, "Charlie?" She raised her head and looked expectantly over her shoulder, into the smiling face of Banshee, her tail thumping on the bed.

Jen, feeling both relieved and disappointed, reached from under the covers and rubbed the dog's ears. Banshee stood up and delivered an unexpected wet kiss to Jen's cheek. "Oh no," Jen said with a smile, gently pushing Banshee's nose away from her face. "You silly girl."

Although reluctant to move from the warm bed, Jen decided she was hungry enough to dress and visit the kitchen. As she pulled on her borrowed sweats, she wondered if Charlie was awake. The bedroom door was opened where Banshee had nosed her way in. *I must have been really tired,* she thought, *because I didn't even feel the dog jump up on the bed.*

Jen peeked out of the bedroom door, but all was quiet in the cabin. She walked through the living-dining room and into the kitchen with Banshee following behind her. A handwritten note from Charlie was taped to the cupboard over the old gas range saying to make herself at home and that he would be home by noon, less than two hours away.

Jen found some instant coffee, jam, and bread for toast. She sat at the cluttered dinette table and browsed through old newspapers as she ate her breakfast. When she was finished, she ran hot soapy water in the kitchen sink, and began a quest for the cups and mugs she'd seen sitting around the cabin. On Charlie's dining room table, she found three cups and noticed that one cup was acting as a paper weight for her earlier *Journal* article on the history of AMAC mining operations. She was pleased that he had clipped the article, now months old.

After the cups were washed, Jen moved to the sofa and tidied up the blankets and pillows Charlie had used during the night. She walked to the south-facing front windows of the cabin and looked out onto a spectacular scene of trees, mountains, sunny blue sky, and brilliant snow. Way down the mountain, Jen saw the smoke rising from the chimneys of Charlie's nearest human neighbors.

Jen crossed her arms over her chest as she felt the cold air seep in around the old window and saw her breath frost the window pane. She inhaled deeply, noticing the scent of the pine paneling, dusty curtains, and cold ashes from the fireplace—just like an old cabin should smell, she thought.

As she stood at the window, she heard the faint sounds of a vehicle and soon saw Charlie's black jeep pull into the drive, heading for the garage. Jen felt her heart rate quicken and was surprised at her reaction. As she moved into the kitchen, Jen heard Banshee dash out through the doggy door. Leaning against the chipped kitchen counter, Jen heard Charlie talking to Banshee as he walked past the north-facing window on his way to the kitchen door.

Charlie stomped the snow from his boots before opening the door. As soon as the door was opened, Banshee rushed inside, shook the snow from her body, and assumed her begging spot in front of the refrigerator.

Jen and Charlie smiled at each other as he stepped into the kitchen and pulled off his boots.

"Banshee wants her treats. They're on top of the fridge, if you'd like to feed her," Charlie said.

Jen said, "Sure," and turned to find the treats. She fed Banshee as

Charlie unzipped his leather jacket and dropped it over the dinette chair. When she looked up from Banshee, she saw Charlie standing with a long-stem red rose held gently in his hands.

Jen felt herself blushing. "For me?" she asked, feeling pleased. Charlie nodded.

"Oh, thank you," she said as he handed her the rose. "Where did you find a rose in Dawson?" she asked.

Charlie's smiled with his eyes. "I have my sources," he said as he moved to the cupboard and rummaged for a tall glass. He found one and filled it with water. Jen placed the rose inside the glass, realizing how moved she was to receive a rose, and contrasting her experience with that of Allison receiving roses from Tony.

They sat together at the dinette table with the rose between them, balanced on a stack of old newspapers.

"I have more information on Tony's identity," Charlie said. "I received the fingerprint report this morning for the prints I took from Steve's cabin and Tony's beer glass. The FBI ran the prints and tuned up a criminal record on Tony, which incidentally, isn't his real name."

"Who is he?"

"He's a Mafia operator from Chicago named Alfonzo Scarlotti. He has an extensive criminal record."

"Hmm," Jen said thoughtfully, "I think I detect an investigative story here. The state division of gaming doesn't issue licenses to anyone with either a criminal record or with ties to organized crime. Yet the state had issued licenses to Tony to run the casino. I'll have to see Fred Gray again at the division of gaming. He was responsible for the Golden Nugget and conducted the background investigation when Tony applied for his licenses."

"You might want to check to see if Fred has secret numbered accounts anywhere," Charlie suggested and Jen nodded in agreement.

"Any news on Ski Mask?" Jen asked.

"The FBI reported this morning that they apprehended Alec Jenson in Santa Fe. He was waiting out the storm before returning to Las Vegas with his helicopter."

"One thing that Tony said before loading us onto the helicopter was that this Alec Jenson was loaned to him by an 'Uncle Mario' who runs the Desert Dunes in Vegas. It could be an important lead for the FBI," Jen said. "There was something else he said about Jenson—that he gave him a hand with our 'geologist buddy.' I think he meant that Jenson helped him murder Steve. Do you think that the sheriff would reopen the case into Steve's death if we can provide new evidence?"

"He's required to consider new evidence; however, you have no direct knowledge of Jenson's involvement. All you have is hearsay from a man who's now dead. It would be your word against Jenson's."

"Jenson was brutal—he struck my face. I can just imagine him helping Tony murder Steve," Jen said.

"You'll be in court to testify against him later, on kidnapping and attempted murder charges," Charlie said.

Charlie continued, "The FBI questioned Barbara Knowles and found that her handwriting was a match with that of the decoy note."

"I guess I'll be testifying against her, too," Jen said and Charlie nodded.

"Two teams went out this morning—one to recover the remains and another from the state division of wildlife to track down and kill the bear," Charlie said.

"That poor bear has probably already experienced indigestion. Too bad the bear has to suffer further because of Tony," Jen said.

"The bear isn't the only one to suffer because of Tony," Charlie said, "You did."

"At least they don't have to track me down and shoot me," Jen joked.

Jen looked at her watch. "Oh, it's getting late. We should head for Morrison soon," she said, rising from her seat. She brushed her fingers along the edge of the sweatshirt and looked at Charlie, asking, "Would you mind it I wore these home? I can't imagine wearing my same clothes again."

Charlie smiled and said, "Be my guest. Would you like some fresh socks to wear with your boots?" Jen nodded.

They spent the next 20 minutes gathering Jen's belongings and preparing for the trip to Morrison. After loading the jeep and saying goodbye to Banshee, Jen and Charlie started down the mountain toward Dawson. They drove in silence for a while as Charlie concentrated on driving the snow-packed roads.

Outside of Dawson on Darkhorse Canyon Road, conditions were better and Jen relaxed some as they made better time. *What an adventure I've had. One is enough. I hope I don't have another.*

She thought of Sarah and wondered if her daughter would ever feel comfortable around snakes again. The experience with the rattler in the mailbox was truly frightening for her and Jen was afraid she would become obsessive about snakes. Sarah seemed to handle the situation fairly well after the incident and they talked about it together.

She hadn't seen Sarah in days and longed to hold her in her arms.

"Are you thinking of your daughter?" Charlie asked quietly.

"Yes," Jen said. "It's been days since I've seen her and I don't know if Norma told her about my ordeal. She'll be anxious, in any case."

"I'm looking forward to seeing Sarah again," Charlie said. "She's a likable young lady."

"She is," Jen said with pride.

"I'd like to see you again, too," Charlie said, reaching for Jen's hand, gently enfolding her fingers.

Jen knew she was blushing. "I'd like that," she said, "but I'd prefer less arduous circumstances."

Jen and Charlie smiled at each other. He released her hand and concentrated on his driving.

"We'll see what we can arrange," he said.

They were close to Morrison and Jen felt her anticipation rise as she gave Charlie directions to her home.

Norma's four-wheel-drive wagon was parked in Jen's driveway and Charlie pulled the jeep along side the snow-covered curb. The snow plows hadn't made it into the neighborhood yet to thrust up walls of snow on the passenger's side. Jen stepped out into the snow and reached for her things in the back.

"Why don't you go on in," Charlie said, "and I'll bring your stuff."

"Okay," Jen said, "Thank you."

As she made her way across the yard to the front step she saw Sarah at the window, smiling and waving. Kaari opened the front door for Jen as she entered.

Jen hugged her daughter tightly, feeling tears forming again. They crowded around the door, hugging each other and talking at once. Jen didn't noticed that Charlie stood on the front step holding her things. She carried Sarah to the sofa. Seeing how happy Sarah was to be with her again, Jen felt her tears of happiness overflowing.

"Mama, why are you crying?" Sarah asked with concern in her voice.

"Because I'm so happy to see you, sweetie. I thought I might never see you again and, now, here we are." She hugged the child. "You are more precious to me than all the gold in the world. I love you."

"I love you, too, Mama, more than anything. I was afraid you wouldn't come back. I was afraid that we wouldn't live in our own house again."

Moppet joined Sarah and Jen on the sofa and rubbed against Jen, passing back and forth across their laps and purring.

Jen heard Charlie chatting with Norma and Kaari in the kitchen and smelled the aroma of fresh coffee and hot chocolate. Charlie walked in and asked if Jen would like coffee.

"Oh, Charlie," Jen said with embarrassment, "I just left you standing outside. I'm so sorry."

Charlie smiled. "It's okay. Aunt Norma found me and let me in. I put your things in the family room. And how's Sarah?" Charlie asked, squatting on his heels in front of the child so they were at eye level.

Sarah looked gravely into Charlie's face and said, "I'm fine and I'm happy Mama is home safe. Did you save her?" she asked. Charlie nodded. "Are you a policeman?" she asked, and Charlie nodded again, reaching into his pocket and removing a small replica of a sheriff's badge. He handed it to Sarah and she accepted it with a smile. "Thank you," she said with excitement.

Charlie and Jen smiled at each other as he rose to his feet. "Thank you for thinking of her," Jen said. "She loves presents."

Sarah looked up from her examination of the badge and smiled sweetly at Charlie. "I do," she said with pleasure, "I do love presents!" Jen and Charlie both laughed.

"How about some hot chocolate to go with your badge?" Charlie asked and Sarah nodded. Charlie went into the kitchen as Jen let Sarah show her the badge, returning a moment later with two mugs.

"Won't you have some, too?" Jen asked, looking disappointed.

"I need to leave now," he said gently.

Norma and Kaari entered the front room and detained Charlie with their thanks, gratitude, and admiration. Charlie chatted with them, telling again how he had determined Jen's location and found her and Allison sheltered under a spruce tree.

Jen could see that Charlie was ready to leave and rose from the sofa to rescue him from her friends.

"I'll walk you to the door," she said, asking Norma to take Sarah into the kitchen where it was warmer.

Jen opened the door for Charlie, reluctant to let him leave but also hesitant to detain him further.

Jen stood inside the door and Charlie on the front step.

"Oh," she said suddenly, "I'm still wearing your sweats."

Charlie looked at her in amusement. "They look a lot better on you than on me. Why don't you keep them?" he suggested.

To her chagrin, Jen felt heat rising in her cheeks as she thought of keeping something so personal as Charlie's old sweat clothes. To cover her impending blush, Jen laughed and said, "A red rose and old sweats—something to remember you by."

Charlie took Jen's hand, squeezing her fingers gently, and looked into her eyes. "There'll be more to remember me by, I promise," he said and she knew his promise would be kept.

About The Author

A previously published author and co-author, Roberta Lonsdale makes her fiction debut in stunning elegance and style. She presently resides in Colorado

Check Out All The Great Fiction From SterlingHouse Publisher

To Order: 1-800-898-7886 0r Check out one of
our four Websits for rightups and info:
http://www.olworld.com/olworld/sterlinghouse
http://www.1stworldwidemall.com/sterlinghouse
http://www.1stinternetmall.com/sterlinghouse
http://www.1stworldmall.com/sterlinghouse

Contemporary Woman's & Romance Literature

Title	Price	
Colorado Gold	$6.95	❏
The Woman Who Cried	$6.95	❏
Continuum	$6.95	❏
Hidden Past	$6.95	❏

Murder Mystery/Suspense

Title	Price	
Why Johnny Died	$6.95	❏
March Madness	$6.95	❏
The Innocent Corpse	$6.95	❏
Crossings	$6.95	❏
The Deadly Practice	$6.95	❏
The Farewell Principle	$6.95	❏
Succubus	$6.95	❏
In The Fall	$6.95	❏
Desert Duel	$6.95	❏

Sci-Fi/Horror

Title	Price	
VAP'R	$6.95	❏
Curse Of The Shadow Beast	$6.95	❏
Bubble Man	$6.95	❏
Chasing The Cosmic Wind	$6.95	❏

Quality Fiction

Title	Price	
Drive Time	$6.95	❏
Letters To Jacob	$6.95	❏
Flora Springs	$6.95	❏
The High Priest Of Hallelujah	$6.95	❏
Twisted Roots	$6.95	❏
Justinian	$6.95	❏
The Race Is Not Given	$6.95	❏
Mahakan	$6.95	❏
Sentimental Journey	$6.95	❏